THE PROMISE

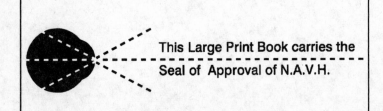

This Large Print Book carries the
Seal of Approval of N.A.V.H.

THE RESTORATION SERIES

THE PROMISE

DAN WALSH
AND GARY SMALLEY

THORNDIKE PRESS
A part of Gale, Cengage Learning

GALE
CENGAGE Learning·

Detroit • New York • San Francisco • New Haven, Conn • Waterville, Maine • London

GALE
CENGAGE Learning·

LIBRARY OF CONGRESS CATALOGING-IN-PUBLICATION DATA

Walsh, Dan, 1957–
    The promise / by Dan Walsh and Gary Smalley. — Large print edition.
        pages ; cm. — (Thorndike Press large print Christian fiction) (The restoration series ; #2)
    ISBN-13: 978-1-4104-6121-6 (hardcover)
    ISBN-10: 1-4104-6121-1 (hardcover)
    1. Married people—Fiction. 2. Large type books. I. Smalley, Gary. II. Title.
PS3623.A446P76 2013b
813'.6—dc23   2013033752

Published in 2014 by arrangement with Revell Books, a division of Baker Publishing Group

Printed in the United States of America
1 2 3 4 5 6 7 18 17 16 15 14

To my youngest son, Michael,
and daughter-in-law, Amy,
whom God used to, literally,
save my life and my marriage.

Gary

To my daughter and son,
Rebekah and Isaac —
the friendship we have
now that you are both grown
and on your own
is one of my greatest treasures.

Dan

When Esau heard his father's words, he let out a loud and bitter cry. "Oh my father, what about me? Bless me, too!" he begged.

— Gen. 27:34 (NLT)

"But everyone who hears these words of mine and does not put them into practice is like a foolish man who built his house on sand. The rain came down, the streams rose, and the winds blew and beat against that house, and it fell with a great crash."

— Matt. 7:26–27 (NIV)

1

Tom Anderson would point to the events of this day as the time his master plan began to unravel. Like many of his flawed schemes, this one, too, seemed like a good idea at the time. Tom wasn't quite twenty-seven years old but felt as if he'd already made enough bad decisions to last a lifetime. He was glad his folks were on their second honeymoon in Italy; he didn't want his father to ever hear about the mess he'd made of things.

It all started to fall apart when the glass door of the Coffee Shoppe flew open and a young man in a black hoodie came in.

Tom was sitting pretty close to the front doors. He always did; it was his table. It had an outlet nearby for his laptop. Normally, he didn't pay attention to people coming through the door, but he couldn't help but notice this guy. The hoodie caught his eye. It was the end of April in central Florida, already hot enough to make you wonder if they'd be skipping spring this year and jumping right into summer.

Everyone else in the café wore short sleeves, including Tom. Most wore sandals and flip-flops too. He glanced over his shoulder at the kid, now standing in line. An elderly man was at the counter in front of him, placing his order. The kid's head swiveled on his shoulders, his eyes scanning the room. Taking in the customers first, then the exit, then the cashier. Back to the exit, then another look at the customers. On this second pass, he looked right at Tom for a moment.

Tom knew then something bad was about to happen.

It wasn't the hoodie so much, but the look on the kid's face. Dead serious, with fierce eyes. He wore baggie jean shorts, the bottoms hung down way past his knees, blue boxers sticking out. That's when Tom saw it. Poking out of his waistband. Something black.

A gun handle.

The Coffee Shoppe was set up so that most of the customers couldn't easily see the counter area because it was blocked by the coffee station. Tom's angle by the front door allowed him to see both sides of the store.

The young man stepped up to the counter. Tom looked at the teenage girl in uniform behind the cash register. Her eyes showed she felt something was wrong, but she gave the programmed spiel. Big smile. "Welcome to the Coffee Shoppe. We're glad you're here. Can I take your order today?"

The kid pulled out the gun and shoved it in her face. He didn't yell, but Tom was close enough to hear what he said. "Give me your money. All of it, or you're dead."

"What?"

"Don't ask me what. You heard me."

"I'm not allowed to open the drawer unless someone buys something."

"Are you kidding me? Open that drawer now or I start shooting."

Tears filled the girl's eyes. "Okay, I will," she said quietly.

"Quick." The kid kept the gun pointed in her face but turned around. So far, none of the other customers seemed to know what was going on. Tom pretended to stay busy on his laptop. When the kid faced the girl again, Tom looked at him then at the girl. She looked terrified.

"That's right," the kid said. "Put it all in that bag." The two employees at the other end of the counter saw what was happening, their faces in shock.

11

One of them, a blond-haired guy named Tim, took a few steps toward the girl. "Don't hurt her, man. She's doing what you want."

The kid pointed the gun at him. "Shut up and stay there or you die."

Tim held up his hands. "I'm not going anywhere. Staying right here."

The kid in the hoodie stuck the gun back in the cashier's face. "Hurry up."

"I'm almost done."

This exchange was a little louder. Some of the customers nearby started paying attention. This thing could get out of hand in a hurry. Tom had studied martial arts all the way through middle school and high school. He hadn't done a thing with it since then. He was totally out of shape and squishy around the middle. But a handful of moves played in slow motion through his head. He could stop this kid, take away his gun.

He knew he could. But he had to act now.

Lord help me, he prayed, wondering if God was even listening to him these days. Slipping out of his loafers, he snuck up directly behind the robber. In a deep voice, he said "Yo" behind the kid's left ear.

"Huh?" The thief turned toward the sound.

Tom quickly shifted to his right side and

struck him in the neck, just below the ear. The boy yelled in pain. Tom kicked the back of his left knee, then spun around, sweeping both legs out from under him. The boy flew backward, slamming his head against the tile floor. The gun fired as it fell out of his hand. It was pointing away from the crowd, but people screamed. Tom bent to one knee and punched the kid full-force at his chest. The kid winced in pain and a panicked look came over his face. Tom jumped over the thief and kicked the gun across the floor.

He looked back at the kid, who somehow managed to jump to his feet. Before Tom could deliver another blow, the thief ran out the door, limping down the sidewalk. He still moved faster than Tom had run in years.

"Somebody call 911," Tim yelled.

"I just did," the manager yelled back as he stepped out from the back office. "I called as soon as I heard the shot. The police are on their way."

The manager ran past Tom out the front door, looked down the sidewalk. He stuck his head back inside. "The guy's gone," he said. "Somebody tell me what just happened."

As relief swept over the crowd, someone started clapping. Soon everyone joined in. Tom walked back to his table to put on his shoes. They all pointed at him, telling the manager what he'd just done.

He was the hero.

People came up, shook his hand, patted him on the back, saying they'd never been so scared in all their lives. The older gentleman, the one who'd been at the counter just ahead of the robber, told the manager it was like something out of a Jackie Chan movie. "Never saw anything like it."

"Anyone get a video on their phones?" Tim asked.

Thankfully, no one had. The manager walked up and shook Tom's hand. "I don't know how to thank you."

"That's okay," Tom said, realizing what came next. "I'm late for something. I've got to go." He closed his laptop lid, unplugged the cord, and put both in his brief bag.

"But the police are on their way," the manager said. "I'm sure they'll want to talk with you."

"You're a hero," one of the customers, a college-age kid, said. "I just called the local news. They're on their way."

"Thanks, everyone," Tom said, not looking anyone in the eye. "Sorry. Gotta go." He hurried toward the door. Just as he opened it, he looked back. The college kid was lifting his cell phone in Tom's direction.

He was taking a video! Tom covered his face with his right hand as he ran down the sidewalk. When he got in his car, he put it in reverse and stayed in reverse until he was two stores away, so no one could take down his license plate.

When he'd passed two traffic lights down the road, he saw a police car with its siren blaring headed in the opposite direction toward the café. As he sat at a red light, a second police car came flying through the intersection right behind the first.

That was close, he thought. Too close. He was shaking all over. Calm down, he told himself. Breathe slowly. You're okay.

He flicked his turn signal on, deciding then to head south toward the nearest Books-A-Million, one town over from Lake Mary where he lived. He'd get there an hour earlier than his normal routine today, but what choice did he have?

Tom split most of his time each day between two coffee shops and a bookstore. Of the three places, he liked the Coffee Shoppe the best. But now he'd have to find another place that offered free wifi to spend the first block of each day. No way he could show his face back there now. Not for a few weeks anyway, maybe a month.

He couldn't afford to be anybody's hero.

He was just grateful the whole incident had happened so fast and that no one caught it on camera. The last thing he needed was his face showing up on YouTube. And there was no way he'd have stuck around to be interviewed by the local news. For one thing, the kid in the hoodie might see it and seek him out, looking for some payback.

But the thing that worried him most was that his wife, Jean, might see it.

Then she'd know.

Tom wasn't where he was supposed to be right now, where she assumed he would be and should be this time of day.

If Jean heard that, she'd soon find out the whole thing. She'd start asking him direct questions, and he couldn't lie then. The only reason he was pulling this off so far was that he'd been playing on her assumptions. His own version of "don't ask, don't tell."

If Jean found out, soon his whole family would find out, including his dad.

There was no way he could let that happen.

2

Tom looked at the digital clock on his dashboard as he pulled in to his third stop of the day. Another local coffee place that competed with Starbucks, called the Java Stop. Compared to his other haunts, this one was nice and quiet. Great for guys like him, not so great for the owners. He wasn't sure how long this place would make it.

Hopefully long enough for him to find a new job. "Any day now" had been his mantra, repeated daily to ward off the unrelenting doubts. When he found another job, all his problems would go away. That was the idea.

But that's not what had happened. He could hardly believe it, but five months had already passed since he'd lost his job, two months after Michele and Allan's wedding.

As he got out of his car, he tried to stop thinking about it. The whole thing still made him mad. Or was he just hurt because of the way it happened? A vicious betrayal. It was difficult to sort through the jumble of emotions stirring inside. Add to that the confusion and guilt he felt from the stock-pile of lies he'd created trying to keep this masquerade intact.

Then there was the struggle with his father. He wasn't sure which of the two things bothered him more. Tom was happy for his dad, really. And for his mom. The two of them were back together and doing so well. He looked at the digital clock again. They should be arriving in Italy any time now to start their romantic second honey-moon.

Good for them. No, really. He was glad.

He just wished there was more of his father to go around. His dad had been so completely focused on winning back his mom that he'd completely ignored his promise to Tom to change what was broken in *their* relationship. They were supposed to start having regular heart-to-heart talks right after Michele's wedding; real conversa-tions, man to man.

But they'd only had one. Just one. A few weeks before the wedding.

After that big dance at the reception, his parents had reconciled. His dad moved back into the house. They started going to a new church together. Got some counseling. Joined a couples' small group. Made some new friends. He was happy for them. Really.

But Tom got dropped.

He had to walk through this whole job loss thing by himself. As with every other big juncture in his life, he had no father to talk to. In that first couple of weeks, he'd tried at least a dozen times to connect with his dad; it never worked out. But then, what if they had gotten together, what would Tom have said? He wasn't even sure he'd have been able to tell his dad everything that happened. Not the way it happened, nor how sick he'd felt inside about it, nor his plan to keep the news from Jean until he'd found another job. He and his dad just didn't have that kind of relationship.

Tom knew he couldn't have borne the weight of his dad's disappointment. It wasn't just the words his father would have said (and he'd have said plenty); he had this way of looking at you that instantly made you feel so small and unworthy. Like you were almost disgusting. Like you'd ruined what little hope he'd ever had for your success.

Tom was almost certain that if his dad heard the whole story, he'd put all the blame on Tom for the mess he was in. How could he have let this happen? Why hadn't he fought harder to keep his job or find a way to turn the situation around? Better yet, if Tom had followed his father's advice and gotten that IT certification right after he'd graduated from college, he wouldn't have lost his job in the first place.

Tom had spent his entire childhood, his teen years, and now the first phase of his adult life trying to win the approval and affections of a man who somehow managed to remain continually just out of reach.

Tom had never measured up to Jim Anderson's expectations, and he knew he never would.

As he walked through the glass doors of the Java Stop, he felt like he was climbing out of a deep and slippery hole. It helped to be greeted by pleasant music, soothing colors on the walls, and the fragrant aroma of fresh-brewed coffee. Glancing to the far west corner, he managed a smile. His table was vacant. But he tensed when he saw Fred Messing sitting nearby, his laptop plugged into the same outlet Tom always used.

Fred was okay, he just talked too much. Tom came here to get things done, not to yak. And Fred was in the same boat he was, another out-of-work IT guy. So they were essentially competing for the same job. Fred had started coming in about a week ago and seemed to think it was perfectly okay to compare notes and share each other's leads. "May the best man win," Fred had said yesterday, big smile on his face.

The problem was, since Tom had been job hunting for almost five months, he'd already sent resumes to all of Fred's "new" leads. Fred wanted Tom to share all his old leads and the handful of new spots Tom found. Tom got nothing useful from Fred in return. Fred acted like the two of them should become good friends, maybe get their wives and kids to meet. "Let's do a cookout sometime."

That wasn't going to happen.

The most obvious reason was that Jean had no idea Tom had lost his job. The other reason? After being betrayed by someone he thought was a good friend at work — the guy responsible for Tom losing his job — Tom wasn't too up on the idea of making new "friends."

"Tom," Fred said, "there you are, buddy." Fred was also a Christian. And thoroughly optimistic that both of them would get great jobs any minute.

"I'm believing they'll be better than the jobs we had before," he'd said. Tom remembered being like that. He'd spent the first five or six weeks like that.

But it was hard to stay irritated at a guy with a smile like Fred's. Tom knew he was just being cynical. "Hey, Fred, how are you?" Tom set his laptop bag on the seat. "Let me go up to the counter and pay my daily rent. You watch this for me?"

"Sure thing," Fred said.

Daily rent, he thought. A Fred expression for the coffee they bought each day. It paid for the privilege of sitting in the A/C and mooching the free wifi. Fred, a big man, at least around the middle, always paid a little more rent than Tom. Tom never saw Fred come away from the counter without a pastry or at least an oatmeal cookie. The first time Fred noticed Tom noticing this, Fred had said, "Fortunately, I'm not as fat as I look." Fred didn't explain what he meant, and Tom didn't ask.

When Tom came back to the table, carrying his latte, Fred said, "Hey, did you hear about all the excitement over at the Coffee Shoppe this morning?"

"What? No." Tom feigned disinterest as he sat and took out his laptop and charger.

"The girls at the counter were talking about it when I came in. Somebody posted it on Facebook or something. They got robbed. Well, almost. Apparently, some masked avenger swooped in and almost knocked the guy out."

"Masked avenger?"

"Well, not really. But a customer really did jump in and stop the guy, sent him packing. Took away his gun, and the robber ran out without a dime. When I went up to refill my coffee, I overheard the manager here talking on the phone, guess he called the owners over there to find out more about it."

"What'd he say?"

"Didn't hear everything, but the owner at the Coffee Shoppe said they felt sure they'd catch the guy pretty fast. The stupid kid wasn't wearing any gloves, so they got some great fingerprints off the gun and the doors."

Tom was relieved to hear that.

"Everyone's buzzing about this mystery guy who broke up the robbery. Looks like he left in a hurry before the police arrived. That's what superheroes do, you know."

"Anyone know who he was?"

"Nope. Apparently, he goes there all the time, but the guy's real quiet, keeps to himself. Sounds like the newspeople showed up and did a bunch of interviews with the customers and staff. Should be on TV later this evening. I've been checking their websites but haven't seen anything about it yet. Wonder what this guy's story is."

"So would you have stayed around if that was you?"

"You kidding? Sure I would. Well, to be honest, I'm not sure I'd have the guts to confront a robber like that. But if I did, you bet I'd have hung around. I'd let it slip out when those reporters questioned me that I'm an out-of-work IT guy, just doing my civic duty. You can't buy publicity like that. People love hero stories. It's going to be all over the news. Some hiring manager might see the interview, and there you go — my job hunt would be over."

There you go, Tom thought.

He sighed thinking about it. Most likely if he had stayed, he'd get so uptight he'd forget to mention he was out of work. He'd still be out of work after his fifteen minutes of fame came and went. Only his situation would be much worse. Life as he knew it would cease, because Jean would find out he had been lying to her all these months, pretending to head off to work every day.

That thought stirred fear inside him. There'd be no way to contain the firestorm it would create. Things could get so bad, his parents might even cut short their Italy trip. He had to slam the door on these

24

thoughts . . . now.

Behind them lay a dark hallway full of more doors. Each one leading to a room that was darker still.

3

Marilyn Anderson was beside herself. She couldn't believe it. She was really here. *They* were here. In Rome, the Eternal City. It was like a fairy tale. When Jim had told her two months ago that they were going to Italy, it didn't seem real. Even when he'd shown her the airline e-ticket and the travel materials started coming in the mail, it was hard to imagine it would actually happen.

But now, standing out here on their hotel balcony, watching the sunset over a skyline that included the Roman Colosseum on one side and the dome of St. Peter's on the other, it was starting to sink in. She heard footsteps and turned to see Jim coming out to join her.

He walked up behind her, put his arms around her, and rested his head against hers. "Isn't this amazing, hon? Have you ever seen anything like it?" He squeezed her gently.

"It's so much better than the pictures. I even loved the drive through town from the airport."

"I know. All those narrow roads," he said. "The way the cab whipped through traffic felt like a scene from a James Bond movie."

She laughed. It kind of did. "The cars are all so little and boxy compared to the US."

Jim came around beside her and put his hands on the cast-iron rail. "I've heard they're like that throughout most of Europe. And so many scooters."

"Hundreds of them," she said, "darting in and out. I'm surprised no one collided. I'm so glad you're not driving." The tour Jim had signed them with used a luxurious air-conditioned bus with large picture windows. They were scheduled to meet with everyone tomorrow morning in the lobby at 9:00 a.m.

"I don't know," he said. "It's not like England. They drive on the same side of the road as we do, and the steering wheel's on the same side of the car. It wouldn't take any getting used to. And there's something else I found out. Something you'd be very interested in too."

"What?"

"It was something Dr. Franklin said. You know, the guy who bought that office space from us. He and his wife have been to Italy

27

a dozen times."

"What did he say?"

"You can drive a hundred miles an hour on the highway."

"No way."

"Yes. He said people do it all the time, and no one gets a ticket. You just have to make sure you stay in the far left lane."

"I can't imagine these little boxy cars even going over fifty."

"Not these little things here in town. I'm talking about a real car, something like a Beemer or a Mercedes." He gave her a mischievous grin. "How would you like to drive a hundred miles an hour in something like that?"

"Don't tease me." Marilyn absolutely loved driving fast. And she loved fast cars. It was a silly thing, and she knew it. But she'd been that way since she was a teenager. Of course, as a wife and mother she had to suppress most of these urges, but from time to time she still felt them. The odd thing was, Jim was the one bringing all this up. The old Jim used to hate that about her. He would scold her driving habits and her occasional "lead foot."

"I'm not teasing you." He leaned his face close to hers, as though on the verge of giving her a kiss. "I'm dead serious. How

28

would you like to drive a hundred miles an hour in a high-performance European car on the Italian Autostrada?"

"Really?"

"Really."

"But how? We're riding on a tour bus the entire trip."

"Not the entire trip," he said. "When the doc told me about this, it gave me an idea. In seven days, the tour through Italy winds up back here in Rome. We're going to stay one more day. I've already booked the hotel for another night. We'll rent a car and drive to Florence. He also told me about a few out-of-the-way places between here and there we just have to see. Some nice little medieval towns. We'll see them along the way, eat dinner in Florence, then you can drive all the way back to Rome on the Autostrada, driving as fast as you want."

Marilyn didn't wait for Jim to kiss her. She inched forward and kissed him. That kiss led to another, then another.

"If we don't stop," he said, "we'll miss our dinner reservation." He gently pulled back. "Why don't you finish getting ready? You brought that red dress, right?"

"I did," she said, still holding him close.

"Well, you put that on and my favorite perfume, and I promise . . . this first night

29

on our second honeymoon will make you forget all about our wedding night."

He said it so romantically, she could hardly bring up what she wanted to say. But she just had to. "You're kidding, right?"

"What?"

"That's the standard you're setting for tonight? Our wedding night? Are you forgetting what happened?"

Jim sighed. "No, but I was hoping you did. Or at least that the memory might have improved in your mind over the years."

She shook her head, smiling.

"Guess not," he said.

"Jim, you didn't even make reservations for a hotel. We wound up spending our first night in that old roadside dive with short sheets and a plastic mattress cover that I kept sticking to."

"I was nineteen. I was a kid. What did I know? My father should have helped me."

"Remember, we found out that during the day certain people rented it by the hour?" She laughed.

Then he laughed and drew her close. "Okay, forget about our first night. Just think about tonight." He turned them both till they were facing the gorgeous skyline again, his arm now around her shoulder. "Tonight I'm going to wine and dine you at an exquisite Italian restaurant. Real Italian food . . . in Rome. I'll be wearing my new clothes, which you picked out, and your favorite cologne. And you in that incredible red dress. We'll take our time, not talk about any of our problems —"

"Or our kids' problems," she interjected.

"Or our kids' problems," he said. "We'll eat our gourmet Italian food and drink our drinks slow and easy at a candlelit table. Pleasant music will play in the background."

"Like the theme song from *The Godfather*?" She heard it now in her head.

"Okay, music from *The Godfather* playing in the background. A waiter with an authentic Italian accent will wait on us hand and foot. We'll finish up the meal with some fine Italian pastry and sip our cappuccinos. Then we'll come back here to our room —"

"And fall asleep from an overdose of carbs," she said.

"No." He looked at her. "Don't spoil it. There's no way I'm falling asleep early tonight. And neither are you."

"But if I eat all that food, I'll —"

He put his finger across her lips to gently shush her. "You'll be fine. I talked with the concierge. He said the streets between here and the restaurant are perfectly safe at night. There'll be a nice breeze outside. So, we'll walk. Burn off all the carbs. Then when we get back to the room, I have another surprise."

"What is it?"

"Well," he said, holding both of her hands, "if I tell you, it won't be a surprise."

4

After a brief wait, the maître d' sat them at a cozy table not far from the outside wall. The courtyard area just beyond was full, but Marilyn could still see and hear the trickling water flowing down from the fountain. They'd walked around it once before they sat down. Goldfish and little turtles swam over the fountain's floor, which was covered with shiny coins.

The restaurant was only two streets away from the hotel. Walking there through the dazzling city lights and sounds, crossing intersections as they dodged small European cars, made her feel like she was walking through a movie scene. Over the past few months, she and Jim had watched a number of old films shot in Italy to help get a sense of what to expect. It had been so much fun.

But nothing compared to actually being here.

"So what do you think?" Jim said, reaching for her hand across the table.

"Jim, it's wonderful. I still can't believe we're here. I've wanted to visit Italy for so many years."

"I know," he said. "I'm sorry it's taken so long."

"Don't be. Some people never get to experience something like this."

"But we could have. We should have come here on our twenty-fifth anniversary. If I hadn't been such an idiot back then."

"The cruise was very nice."

He took a sip of water. "You're just being kind. It was a beautiful ship and we saw some interesting places, but I blew a great opportunity. Spent most of my spare time reading that stupid business book."

Jim was still so hard on himself, even seven months after their marriage crisis had resolved. Marilyn had completely forgiven him and could see his heart had changed in some foundational ways. He wasn't perfect by any means, but as the weeks and months had passed, she had felt genuine joy and a growing excitement about their future, even before he'd surprised her with this trip.

She squeezed his hand as they gazed into each other's eyes. "There's no fruit in regret, remember? You've got to stop looking back and condemning yourself like this.

God forgave you, and so did I. What did they say in that small group discussion last month about repentance? That genuine repentance is more than saying you're sorry. It's about changing direction, asking God to help you go a brand-new way. Well, you've done that, in so many ways these past seven months. Here we are, in Rome, on an amazing trip together. The old Jim would have never taken part of that property sale and wasted it on something like this."

"It's not a waste," he said. "You're the most important thing in my life."

She loved hearing him talk this way. "See? The old Jim wouldn't have thought something like that, and he sure wouldn't have said it out loud."

The waiter came up. "You are Americans?" he asked with a strong accent.

"Yes," Jim said. "Our first time in Rome."

"So glad you are here. I speak pretty good English."

"You speak it very well," Marilyn said.

"Grazie. I mean, thank you. Have you had time to look over the menus?"

"Actually, no," Jim said. "We've just been talking. But we'll look at them now."

"Of course. Take your time. We are in no hurry. May I ask what you would like to drink? Signora, starting with you?"

"I'll have a Diet Coke."

"And you, Signore?"

"I'll have the same, thanks."

He wrote it down. "Very good. You look at the menus, and I'll be back shortly."

"I love the way the Italians talk," Marilyn said after the waiter was gone. "You hear the way he said that? Seen-*yor*-ay."

"You have to roll the *r*'s," Jim said.

Marilyn tried it again. "Seen-*yor*-ray."

"That's it."

"And I love the rhythm in their sentences, the way the words go up and down. It has almost a lyrical quality to it."

"Well, Seen-*yor*-ruh, we better open these menus."

Marilyn began to read. She was relieved to find English explanations under the Italian dishes. But she had no idea how much things cost. "Jim, do you understand these prices? I don't want to pick out something too pricey for our budget."

"Budgeets?" he said with an accent. "We don't need no steenking budgeets."

Marilyn laughed. "I think the movie quote is *badges*," she said. "And you sound more like a Mexican."

"The point is, don't worry about the price. Pick out anything you want. We haven't splurged on a dinner out in ages."

"Are you sure?"

"I'm sure," Jim said. "Tonight, we celebrate."

Marilyn smiled and began to read through the menu items. Before she made it halfway down the first page, Jim said, "I love you, by the way."

"I love you too." He said it all the time now, and she never grew tired of hearing it.

After a few more minutes, Marilyn selected a dish of homemade ravioli filled with crab in a lemon butter sauce. Jim picked out swordfish agnoletti with red pepper sauce. The waiter returned with their drinks and took their orders. Jim ordered for them. She got a kick out of the way he talked, butchering the Italian accent.

"Very good choices, Signore," the waiter said.

Jim noticed her laughing. "Hey, at least I'm trying. You wait, by the time this trip is over, I'll have this thing nailed."

"I'm sure you will." As the waiter walked away, she looked at all the paintings, the thick beams in the ceiling, and the ancient stone fireplace on the far wall. "This is a lovely place."

"Isn't it?" Jim said. "It kind of reminds me of something you'd see at Disney or Epcot. Except there, you're just seeing replicas of places like this. This is the real deal. I'll bet this building is hundreds of years old."

Marilyn thought about the last time they had visited the Magic Kingdom. They were all there together as a family. Michele and Allan weren't even a couple then. Tom and Jean had joined them; little Tommy was just a toddler. "Remember the last time we were there?"

"At Disney? That was a couple years ago, wasn't it?"

"I think so," she said. "That was so much fun."

"Tom and Jean really had their hands full with little Tommy. Remember?"

She did. The terrible twos. Tommy had spent at least half the time whining and crying. "He screamed bloody murder whenever any of the Disney characters came within ten feet of him. Remember what Jean said?"

"I don't remember seeing this on the brochures." Jim tried to imitate Jean's voice.

They both laughed. "It was still a great trip," Marilyn said.

"It really was," Jim said. "I just wish Tom hadn't been so uptight the whole time. Guess he thought Tommy was ruining everything for the rest of us."

Marilyn remembered that too. "Speaking of Tom . . . I've been meaning to talk to you about something. I've been having some concerns about him. About them, as a couple." Jim got a look on his face. "What's wrong?"

"We weren't going to do that tonight, remember?"

"Do what?"

"Talk about our problems . . . or our kids' problems."

"I'm sorry. You're right. I forgot."

"New subject then," Jim said. "Have I told you how incredibly beautiful you look tonight?"

After a delicious dinner, topped off with a tasty torta di ricotta and coffee, they walked slowly back to their hotel on Via Nazionale. Once they passed through the lobby and up the elevators, Marilyn said, "Do I get my surprise now?"

"Yes, you do," Jim said as he led her by the hand down the hall and into their room. Inside, he walked her straight out to the balcony until they were leaning against the rail.

"Look at the city lights," she said.

"It's amazing. But that's not the surprise. Turn around. Tell me what you see."

She did. They were facing the double set of doors that led back into their room, bordered by a row of brilliantly colored Italian tile. She could see the king-size bed centered in the room, but given the occasion, that hardly seemed like something he'd consider a surprise.

"Look down," he said gently.

"Okay, I see a balcony."

"A big, wide balcony," Jim said. "I asked the front desk clerk for the room with the biggest balcony, and it just so happened to also have the best view of Rome."

It was a great room. And it did have a wide balcony with a splendid view. But Jim had just said that wasn't the surprise.

"When I talked to the tour people about the trip," Jim continued, "I found out there really wouldn't be any opportunities to dance together the whole time. I thought, I'm going on my second honeymoon with my beautiful wife in Italy, and we're not even going to dance?"

"So what did you do?"

He led her to the center of the balcony. "We're going to dance, my love. Just the two of us."

"Out here?"

"Right out here. We'll leave the doors open. I put together a short playlist of our favorite songs. The music will be playing softly in there, so it won't disturb anyone else in the hotel. We'll step out here, with the moon and the stars and the night lights of Rome behind us, and dance off all our carbs. Just you and me. See?" he said, spinning around. "With just the two of us, there's plenty of room."

"For slow dancing, you mean."

"Nice and slow," he said. "Starting with one song we have never danced to, but one I've been wanting to dance to with you for the last seven months."

"What is it?"

"It's the reason why I wanted you to wear that dress." He walked past her into the room, tapped on his iPad, which earlier he'd set on some speakers. He rushed back out and took her in his arms. A moment later, a familiar song filled the room and flowed out onto the balcony.

Chris DeBurgh's "Lady in Red."

He swung her out, then pulled her back and whispered in her ear. "That's who you are. *My* lady in red."

5

Jean heard the crashing sound over the roaring vacuum cleaner. She looked at Carly sitting in her playpen. She'd heard it too. Jean shut off the vacuum. "Tommy?" she yelled. He wasn't in the living room. "Are you okay?" He didn't answer. "Tommy?"

She ran around the family room couch toward the hallway. As soon as she reached it, she felt instant relief. Tommy was standing halfway between her and the front door, his little hands covering his mouth, eyes popped wide open. He looked at her, then at the framed portrait lying on the hardwood floor by his feet, then back at her. Her broom lay next to the portrait.

She figured out what had happened. He'd knocked over the broom, which knocked the portrait off the wall. The look on his little face made the situation almost comical. He lowered his hands and said, "Mommy, I bwoke it. Not me. The bwoom did it. It fell on the pitcher and bwoke it."

How could she be mad at that face? It was really her fault anyway. She should have known better than to leave the broom leaning against the wall like that. She bent down. "Come here. Are you okay? Did you get hurt?"

He walked over and held out his arms. "No, but it scared me."

"I'll bet it did," she said. "That was pretty loud. You go into the family room and watch Carly a few minutes while I clean this up. Can you do that?"

He nodded then looked back at the portrait on the floor. "But it's bwoke, see? The glass cwacked."

Jean looked. It was cracked, diagonally from the top left to the bottom right corner, like a lightning bolt running right through the three people in the photo. The wooden frame around it was slightly bent. But as far as she could tell, the portrait looked just the way it always had, hanging up there on the wall. "That crack was already there, Tommy. You didn't make it any worse." She hugged him. "It's okay. Now go keep an eye on Carly."

He ran off.

She picked up the frame to examine it more closely. It was a sturdy thing, to take a hit from that height and not break any further. Ugly . . . but sturdy. By the sound it made she'd expected to find something smashed to pieces. She stood and turned, intending to hang it back on its hook. That's when she saw the hole.

The stupid thing was so heavy. When Tom hung it up a few years ago, he had to drill a big hole in the plaster and insert a plastic anchor. When the picture fell, it yanked the anchor right out of the wall. She looked around on the floor till she found it. The anchor had slid all the way down the hall onto the welcome mat by the front door.

She set the picture down and picked up the anchor. It was all bent and twisted. There was no way it would go back in that hole. And the plaster around the hole had split, making the hole too big, even if she could find another anchor somewhere in the garage.

She dreaded the thought, but she'd have to tell Tom about this when he got home from work.

Tom loved this portrait almost as much as she hated it. It wasn't the picture inside so much as the whole look of it that she disliked. They'd had an argument over it the first week they moved into the house five years ago.

Before they'd moved in, Tom had promised she would be in charge of decorating the house. He'd take care of the landscaping and everything in the garage, she'd get to make all the calls inside. Things had gone smoothly until she proudly showed him the family picture wall she'd created in the hallway.

Her family always had one growing up. Tom's did too. Family photos of all different shapes and sizes, people and places arranged just so on the hallway walls next to the stairs. On one side, the family pictures from the past — a few of Tom and her as kids, their parents, some pics of their siblings, aunts, uncles, and grandparents.

The opposite wall was mostly empty . . . for now. Just a few 8-by-10s from their wedding day. The idea was to fill this wall with pictures of *their* family in the years to come. To Jean, it was perfect. Just the way it was.

Tom had taken one look at the family picture wall and said, "Where is it?" He wasn't smiling.

Somehow she knew which picture he meant but pretended not to. "What do you mean?"

"You know what I'm talking about. Where is it?"

"There's no room for it, Tom. You can see

that. The whole wall is filled up."

"Then we need to make some room. I want that portrait on this wall. Where is it?"

It was time to take a stand. "Whatever happened to 'I'm in charge of the outside, and you get to be in charge of the inside'?"

"You are in charge of the inside," he said. "But this isn't a decorating decision. You get to decide where it goes on the wall, not whether it goes up there at all." He sighed, the way he did when he was trying to tone down the edge in his voice. "Jean, that portrait is important to me. You know that. I can't believe you thought you could leave it out. It's the only picture of my grandfather, my dad, and me together. The only one."

She did know that. She knew it then and she knew it now, standing there in the hallway alone.

She looked at the picture again. Tom was only four years old at the time, maybe six months older than Tommy was now. He was sitting on his grandfather's knee; his own father, Jim, stood behind them, his hands resting on his father's shoulders. Although the crack ran right through the faces of the three Anderson men, she could still see the resemblance between Tom and their sweet little son, especially the way he smiled.

Part of the reason she didn't like the portrait was that Tom was the only one in the picture who was smiling. Jim, her father-in-law, and Tom's grandfather both stared straight ahead with stern looks on their faces, like people did back in the 1800s. Jean had heard that the two older Anderson men barely got along. Maybe that had something to do with it. But why couldn't they set their differences aside and smile for a family portrait?

She'd asked Tom about it several times, but he didn't know the answer and he kept forgetting to ask his father about it. She might have been able to look past the serious looks on their faces, if Tom would have let her replace the broken glass and get a decent frame for it. But he wouldn't hear of it. "That's the original glass and frame," he'd said. "The same one my grandfather put the photograph in when my dad gave it to him. I don't ever want to change it. Why do you care how it looks anyway? It's not like we're trying to impress anyone. None of the other picture frames match."

Holding the portrait up again, she looked it over. Not only was the glass broken and the frame bent, but it was also all scratched up. Not in a way that made it look old and collectible, but in a cheap and crappy way.

47

She wasn't even sure if it was real wood.

She looked at Jim's unsmiling face again as he stood there behind his father. She was struck, by contrast, how much Jim smiled these days . . . and how little Tom did. Tom's typical expression now looked more like Jim's stern image in the portrait. They were probably close to the same age.

Tom and Jim had always been so much alike; everyone thought so. That was, until seven months ago, before Tom's sister Michele got married. Just before that, Jim and Marilyn had gone through a major marriage crisis. It was hard to believe that just a few months ago, Marilyn had moved out of their big house in River Oaks. Tom was afraid she'd left for good. But God seemed to do a remarkable work in Jim's heart that turned everything around. Jean smiled as she remembered that amazing scene at Michele's wedding when the two of them danced for the first time. That beaming smile on Jim's face.

Jim was smiling almost every time she saw him these days. He was probably smiling right now. She looked down at Tom's face in the portrait. *Why don't you smile anymore, my love?*

Carly started crying. "Mom!" Tommy yelled. "Carly won't give back my truck."

"I'll be right there. Don't you grab it from her." She lifted the broom off the floor and put it in the hall closet for now, then carried the bent anchor and portrait into the family room. She'd leave them on the kitchen counter for now, out of the kids' reach until Tom got home.

Hopefully, he'd come home in a better mood than the one he'd been in the last several weeks. No, more like the last several months. He said it was just some things going on at work but that he didn't want to talk about it.

She needed him to be in a better mood soon. She had something more important to talk with him about than this portrait falling in the hallway. For the last several mornings she'd been fighting off waves of nausea. She was pretty sure she knew why.

6

Tom pulled up in the driveway of his three-bedroom/two-bath home, in an older but nicely kept subdivision in Lake Mary, Florida. Just like he had every weekday and some Saturdays for the last five years. Occasionally, before losing his job, he'd have to work late or else come home late because he'd get stuck in bumper-to-bumper traffic on I-4. Most of the time he got home right at 5:30, so that's what he did today.

It had been quite a day. Off and on, he'd checked the local online news websites to see if anyone had run the story about the botched robbery attempt at the Coffee Shoppe. No one had. He grabbed the leather strap of his brief bag and looked up. The sight through his windshield generated a completely opposite reaction from the pronounced joy and excitement he'd felt when he first pulled up in this driveway five years ago.

Back then, he was a king coming home to his castle. Just one year out of college, he had a great job, a promising future, a lovely wife, and a new baby boy on the way, Tommy Junior. His father hadn't bought his first house until he was thirty. Tom had him beat by seven years.

As it turned out, he was actually the proud owner of a house inflated to twice its actual value. A fact he would not discover until a year later. Tom and Jean had spent all they had to get into this place. They wound up furnishing and decorating it with credit cards. His father would've pitched a fit had he known. Jean was uncomfortable about it, but Tom knew better. He had eased her fears with a barrage of well-thought-out rationalizations. Look, he had a fairly high-paying, cutting-edge IT job with a regional banking firm, and he was certain to get a number of promotions very soon. They'd pay off the credit cards then.

That was the plan.

Gazing at the house once more, he sighed then got out of the car. The sight sickened him. He walked up the driveway toward the front door, wondering how much time he had before he lost both the house and the car to the vultures. Pulling out his keys, he opened the front door and yelled, "Jean,

I'm home."

From the kitchen, Jean heard the front door open and close, and Tom call out her name. He was going to wake up Carly; she'd gone down for a late nap. Oh well, Carly needed to get up anyway. "I'm in here," she yelled. "In the kitchen."

Normally, she'd greet him in person, but she was shredding cheese in a bowl. She still had to spread it over the casserole and get it back in the oven for ten minutes.

"Daddy!"

Good, Tommy would greet him.

"You came home."

Tommy always said that, every night, as if it was some great surprise.

"I did. I came home," she heard Tom reply. It sounded like he picked Tommy up. "Where's your sister?"

"Sleeping."

Jean heard a sweet little voice saying "Daddy home" through the monitor.

"I don't think she's asleep anymore," Tom said. "Let's go see."

"Okay."

"I'm going to have to put you down. I can't carry both of you."

"I know."

"Hey, wait a minute," Tom said. "What

the . . . Jean? Where's that portrait? The one with my dad and me and my grandfather?"

"It's right in here," she said. "On the kitchen counter."

"I bwoke it, Daddy."

"You what?" His voice had a sharp edge.

"Not me, it was the bwoom that did it."

"How did a broom break the portrait, Tommy?"

Jean shook the cheese off her fingers and wiped her hands on a dish towel. She'd better get in there. She picked up the portrait and headed toward the hallway. "It's not really broken. It's fine. See?" She held it out as she rounded the corner. Carly yelled out "Daddy" again, a little louder. Tommy stood next to his father, his face on the verge of tears.

Tom all but grabbed it out of her hand. "Let me see."

Did he have another bad day at work or was his love of this portrait bordering on obsession? Either way, this was a ridiculous overreaction. She bent down to pick up Tommy. "It's okay, Tommy."

"Daddy's mad." His bottom lip began to pout. "Daddy's mad at me."

"I'm not mad at you," Tom said, not even looking up from the portrait. His voice had the same edge. "It looks the same. I don't

53

see any new damage."

Carly began to cry, loudly enough to hear downstairs. "I told you, it's fine." Jean walked toward the steps, still carrying Tommy.

"I'll get her," Tom said. "I told you I would." He came down the hall, still holding the picture. "You go finish up in the kitchen."

She set Tommy down. "You want to give me that?" Pointing at the portrait with her eyes. Tom handed it back to her. "Come on, Tommy. You come with me."

"Is Daddy going to spank me?"

"No, he's not."

"I'm not even mad at you, Tommy," Tom said.

Jean took Tommy's hand, and they walked toward the kitchen. Tom disappeared up the stairway. When she got to the kitchen, she turned the oven on, put the casserole inside, and set the timer for ten minutes. When she turned around, she almost knocked Tommy over he was standing so close. "Tommy," she gasped.

"Why is Daddy mad again?" he said softly. "I don't like Daddy to be mad."

"I don't know, Tommy." She bent down and looked him in the eyes. "Maybe he's just had a bad day at work. But it's not your fault."

"Are you sure, Mommy?"

"Come here." She hugged him. "It's not your fault. Do you believe me?" She felt his little head nodding on her shoulder. "You go on and play for a few minutes, until I call you for dinner." Tommy smiled and ran off.

She heard Tom's heavy footsteps coming downstairs. In a moment, he appeared carrying Carly in his arms. The air-conditioning kicked on. Tom looked up at the nearest vent. Then he got this look. He turned around, back into the hallway. *What is he doing now?*

"Jean? Could you come here a minute?"

She did. Tom was standing in front of the thermostat, still holding Carly.

"You have this set on 75?"

"Yeah, I guess."

"I thought we agreed to leave it set on 78."

"I don't remember that."

"Well, I do. We talked about it last week, or maybe the week before."

"What's the difference? It's only a few degrees."

"A few degrees? A few degrees affects the electric bill . . . a lot. Air conditioners are the biggest item on the bill."

Why was he making a big deal of this? "What's a lot? Like twenty or thirty dollars? A hundred dollars?"

"I don't know. I'll have to check. Can't you just keep it on 78 from now on?"

"I suppose. But it's starting to get pretty warm in the afternoons, especially when I have the oven on."

"Don't we have a fan?"

"Just the one in Carly's room. But I need that upstairs. The noise helps her sleep longer when she's taking a nap."

"Well, I don't know what to tell you. But we need to keep this on 78. From now on."

"Okay, I get it," she said. But she didn't. She was about to argue the point further. She doubted they kept the A/C on 78 down at the bank. Probably more like 72. But why keep this going? It would only get him more upset. As he reset the thermostat, she noticed something. "What happened to your hand?"

"What?" He quickly pulled his hand down by his side.

"Let me see. What did you do to it?" She held her hand out. He finally put his hand in hers. She turned the palm over. "Your knuckles, they're all red."

"They're fine."

"Is this some kind of rash? Did you bang

it somehow?"

"I don't know."

She rubbed it gently. He winced in pain and pulled back. "It hurts that much?" Carly started fussing in his arms. The timer went off in the kitchen. As Carly squirmed, an unmistakable odor filled the hallway. "I'll go take care of dinner," she said. "You go take care of that." She pointed at Carly's bum.

"Sorry," he said. "I should've checked that before bringing her down. Not the kind of thing you want to smell at the dinner table."

"No, it's not." She started walking down the hall toward the kitchen, then stopped. She turned around. He was just about to go upstairs. "And while you're up there, could you change something else?"

"What?"

"Your attitude. I'd like to have a pleasant atmosphere during dinner. If that's not too much to ask."

He put on a smile, then ascended the stairs.

7

Tom came through the front door again. After changing Carly's diaper a few minutes ago, he realized he'd forgotten to check the mail. Getting the mail every day was a critical part of his plan.

Fortunately, they had one of those group mailboxes located three doors down, shared with eight other houses on the street. Jean had her hands full with two small children. He'd told her not to ever worry about picking up the mail. He'd get it every day. Every single day. She even occasionally thanked him. It always bothered him when she did, though he'd say you're welcome anyway.

He set the mail down on his dresser, along with his keys and spare change. Mostly bills and junk mail. He lifted the one envelope that had caught his eye when he'd pulled the stack from the mailbox; something from the Social Security office. He had no idea what it was and no energy to open it now, so he slid it to the bottom. The main thing was that Jean didn't see it.

"Dinner's ready!" Jean's voice rose through the stairwell.

"Dinna's weddy!" Tommy's little echo followed right after.

"I'll be right down." He walked into the bathroom to wash his hands. His knuckles weren't only red, they were sore. Must have injured them with that solar-plexus punch at the Coffee Shoppe this morning. What a crazy thing that was. If he wasn't so tense and guilt-ridden about almost getting caught, he might even feel a sense of pride.

He really had saved the day. The moves were still there, and they'd all come back at just the right moment. The odd thing was, all those years of martial arts training in his youth, and he'd never once called on them in a fight.

The one and only fight he'd been in at school, he had lost to a bully two years older and twenty pounds heavier. He came home in sixth grade with a fat lip and a black eye. His father had dragged him down to the studio the very next Saturday and signed him up for lessons. Tom had gone back to that studio almost every Saturday for the next six years, filled his bedroom wall with trophies and ribbons from various martial arts matches. His father never attended. But that never stopped Tom from looking for his face in the crowd every time he came out of the locker room.

"Tom? Are you coming?"

"Sorry. I'll be right there." He turned out the bathroom light and headed toward the stairs. All the while, scolding himself for losing his composure with Tommy. Jean too, for that matter. They didn't deserve his "bad attitude," as she called it. As he came around the hallway corner and walked into the dining room, he saw Jean grab the remote to turn off the TV. Tommy and Carly were already at the table.

Instead of turning off the TV, Jean stood there for a few moments, captivated by something on the screen. "Oh my."

"What is it?" Tom got up to look. "Tommy, you stay put." There was that same edge in his voice. "I'll be right back," he added gently. As he came closer, his heart almost skipped a beat.

"Are you hearing this?" She was watching the local news station. "Some kid with a gun tried to rob the Coffee Shoppe this morning. In broad daylight. The poor cashier said he stuck the gun right in her face."

What should he say? What could he say? "Did they catch him?"

"Not yet. But some customer almost knocked him out. The thief ran out of the store, leaving the gun behind."

They stood there a moment as the on-scene reporter finished the story. The reporter was standing right outside the front door of the coffee shop. "The police have some strong leads and believe they will apprehend the suspect in the next day or so. One of the customers got a partial video, not of the robbery itself, but of the back of the customer who bravely stepped in, as he's leaving the store. Witnesses claim this customer fled the scene before police arrived, even covering his face with his hand to avoid being photographed. The video already has over ten thousand hits on You-Tube."

The reporter's eyebrows raised and she began to smile. "Speculation is rampant about who this man is and why he wouldn't stay to receive the credit he's due. Some have said they think he might be a CIA operative or part of the Witness Protection Program. While everyone is calling this mystery customer a genuine hero, the police do not encourage citizens to take matters into their own hands when a store is being robbed. The police chief mentioned they believe this is the same suspect who shot and seriously wounded a cashier at a convenience store in a similar incident last week."

"I hope we don't start seeing that kind of thing around here," Jean said. "This town's always felt so safe before. Can you imagine being there when it happened? That's the little coffee shop you and I have gone into before, isn't it?"

"I think so. I think we went there after a movie a few months ago." It was at least five months ago, Tom thought. There was no way he'd have brought her back there after he'd lost his job. He couldn't take a chance one of the kids behind the counter might say something. He had started to tense up hearing that news reporter talk about the YouTube video. But it sounded like he was in the clear, that the video didn't catch his face.

"Mommy . . . Daddy . . . I think Carly wants to eat."

Jean turned the TV off. "Okay, we're coming."

Tom watched her as she headed toward the dining room, then followed behind. He didn't know how much more of this he could take. But at least there was a glimmer of hope. He'd gotten an email just before he'd headed home for the day from the IT manager at a large retail restaurant chain.

Tomorrow he had an interview with an actual human being.

He'd been disappointed so many times that such things no longer excited him. But hey, he thought as he walked into the dining room, one could always hope.

8

"Did he say why they call these the Spanish Steps?" Marilyn whispered.

Jim turned. "I don't think so. Want me to ask him?" He turned back to face their tour guide, who continued to explain why this fascinating landmark was so famous. His Italian accent was thick but mostly understandable. The stairs were fairly crowded with tourists stopping to take pictures at various levels along the way.

"This is considered to be the widest staircase in all of Europe, not just Rome," he said. "The 138 stone steps rise from the Piazza di Spagna, or the Spanish Square, to the upper piazza named after the magnificent church you see at the top. Poets and painters have been captivated by the architectural beauty of these steps for over two centuries."

"See? He just explained why," Jim said.

"No, he didn't," she said quietly. "He just

said it begins at this piazza, called the Spanish Square. But why do they call it the Spanish Square? This is Italy." She looked at the large pots full of beautiful purple azaleas and the attractive old buildings that rose up on either side.

Jim laughed. Obviously he didn't know the answer to her questions and wasn't too concerned, but he still raised his hand on her behalf.

"Yes, Signore. A question?"

"Could you explain why they call this the Spanish Square and the steps the Spanish Steps?"

"Certainly, a very good question. The steps were named for the nearby Spanish Embassy to the Vatican, which was established in the seventeenth century. The embassy is still here to this day. Are there any more questions?"

Jim looked over at Marilyn. "There you go."

"Thank you," she said and squeezed his arm affectionately.

No one asked any more questions. The tour guide looked at his watch and said, "We'll wait here for about twenty minutes in case anyone would like to climb the steps and take pictures. There's a beautiful view of the Piazza di Spagna from there. For those lacking the energy to make such a climb, you might enjoy taking pictures right over there by the fountain."

With that, the tour group began to break up.

"Are you up for climbing the steps?" Jim asked.

Marilyn looked to the top. She wanted to, but they had already been walking for hours, touring the Colosseum and the Roman Forum before lunch. After this they were supposed to tour St. Peter's Basilica. Clearly, her four weeks of training on the treadmill were not nearly enough. "Remember that episode of *Everybody Loves Raymond,* the one where they took the Italy trip?"

Jim thought a moment, nodded his head, and smiled. "You mean the one when Raymond was standing at this very spot and asked, 'Where is the Spanish Elevator?' "

She nodded. "Do you mind? I can wait here if you'd like to go up."

"I'm sure the view is great, but I didn't come here for the view. I came here to spend time with you." He led her to one corner of the steps and positioned her in front of a beautiful azalea bush. "I'll stand back here so I can get an angle with the steps over your left shoulder. Then maybe

66

we'll get a few pics by the fountain."

"After that, do you mind if we sit on the steps for a little bit?"

"Not at all, I could use the break too."

Marilyn still wasn't used to how flexible Jim had become. She loved it, but it was so unlike the man she'd married and lived with for so many years. Jim would have insisted they go up the steps and take in the view. "We've come all this way," he'd have said. "Let's just push it." Or at the very least, he would've run up there on his own and left her here at the bottom.

Another couple in their thirties watched Jim taking her picture by the azaleas and volunteered to take one of them as a couple, which was great. Jim stood behind Marilyn, put his arms around her, and drew her close. After, Jim offered to take the couple's picture, an offer they happily accepted. "Do you mind after this," he said, "if we do the same thing over there by the fountain?"

"That would be great," the husband said. "That's one of the problems of going on these trips. Most of the pictures have just one of us in it."

"Well, how about we fix that?" Jim said. "We can do this throughout the rest of the trip if you'd like, as long as we're near each other. That way we'll have plenty of pics to take home with us as couples." They shook hands and introduced themselves to each other. The younger couple's names were Brian and Amanda. Brian gave Jim his camera, then he and his wife struck a pose in front of the azalea bush.

Marilyn's cell phone rang. "Jim, it's Michele." She and Michele had been missing each other on the phone ever since they'd left Florida.

"Well, you can go ahead and take it. I'll be here for a couple of minutes. Then I'll take the pictures of them over by the fountain."

Marilyn answered the phone as she walked a few steps away to a quieter spot. "Michele, good to hear your voice."

"Good to hear you too, Mom. Can't believe how far away you are."

"Is everything okay?"

"Everything's fine."

"How is Doug doing? Have you been able to check in with him?"

"Allan and I had him over for dinner last night. He seemed just like Doug. You know how he is, it's like pulling teeth to get him to open up. But he seems fine. We're going to have him over every other night until you guys get home."

"Thanks so much for doing that. How are

you and Allan doing?" Marilyn asked.

"That's why I called. I have some exciting news."

She's pregnant, Marilyn thought. What else could it be? Michele and Allan had only been married seven months, but she knew Michele wanted to be a mom in the worst way. She looked over at Jim, now at the fountain taking pictures of that young couple. "Okay, I'm ready."

"Well, after Doug left, Allan and I got to talking. I'm not even sure how we got into it. Maybe I was talking about the little kids in my kindergarten class." Michele had graduated back in December with a degree in elementary education, but so far she'd only been able to get work as a substitute teacher. "Oh I know," Michele continued. "I just mentioned another teacher at my school is moving away at the end of this month. I told Allan I was thinking about talking to the principal to see if she might hire me full time to take her place."

Hearing this, Marilyn quickly adjusted her expectations. It certainly didn't sound like Michele was building up to the kind of news she hoped to hear. "So, did she offer you the job?"

"No, I haven't even asked her yet. But now I'm not sure I'm even going to."

"Why not?"

"Because," Michele said, "Allan asked me how badly did I want to have children. And I said, like you really have to ask me that. So he said, how about we get started right away. Isn't that exciting?"

Marilyn had thought they were already trying, so this wasn't exactly earthshaking news. "That's wonderful, Michele. So you guys can definitely live on what Allan makes?"

"It will be tight, but that's how he wanted to set things up from the start. And we've been sticking to it. What little I've been making as a substitute teacher has all gone into the bank. So we're going to start trying to have a baby as soon as possible. Isn't that amazing? Maybe in a couple of months I'll be calling you with some more exciting news!"

"That's great, hon. I'm so happy for you. But did Allan say he *didn't* want you to check on that full-time teaching job?"

"Not exactly."

"Well, I wouldn't close the door on that just yet. You know it could take a few months to get pregnant, right? And these days doctors say you can work almost until you're ready to give birth. You guys can save a lot of money between now and then.

Maybe enough to set up the nursery."

"I guess. But it will be a little hard to get excited about teaching. I love these kids, but I really just want to be a mom."

"Marilyn? Are you almost ready?" She turned to find Jim standing by the fountain with that couple.

"I'm sorry. Looks like I've got to go already. Maybe we'll get to talk again soon. I'm so thrilled with your news. Give Allan my love."

"I will. Can't wait till you get home and we can start planning the nursery together."

"That will be so much fun," Marilyn said. "Gotta go. Love you." As she walked toward Jim and the others by the fountain, she tensed up a little. Jim wouldn't be nearly as excited by this news.

9

An hour later, the tour group and guide had been dropped off at the entrance of St. Peter's Square, which Marilyn found odd, since it was clearly oval-shaped. She decided not to have Jim ask that question. The area was massive, so much bigger and wider than she'd imagined, with that tall stone tower, called an obelisk, rising from the center. It kind of reminded her of a smaller, fancier version of the Washington Monument. The tour guide had just finished pointing to it and said Emperor Caligula brought it to Rome for his circus in 37 BC. It was present during the martyrdom of the apostle Peter and many other Christians. Some pope had moved it to its current position in the 1500s.

The guide had said the exact year and the pope's name, but she was only half-listening now, holding Jim's hand. They walked around the large space to the right of the Obelisk. The tour guide said something about how many columns encircled the square and how many statues were situated around the top. Now he was saying something about the two large fountains on either side.

But Marilyn was watching Jim's face, specifically, his eyes.

She knew this look. It was something she'd come to recognize these past seven months since their reconciliation. The look said he was thinking about something he wasn't ready to talk about. She should be grateful, and she was, mostly. In the old days, Jim never wore this look. He would rotate through a variety of angry faces, and he'd never sit on anything that bothered him very long. Those angry expressions would quickly be followed by even harsher words.

But that was then.

Now Jim didn't react harshly or hastily when something upset him. Instead, he'd hold it in temporarily, try to process it calmly. He'd pray about it, think about it, and consider what to say, or if he should say anything at all. She had to admit, this was better. But it was also unnerving at the same time, and often left her totally distracted.

What is he thinking about?

She knew it didn't help if she needled and

prodded him. That had come out in one of their counseling sessions with their small group leader. Men can't just shut their emotions down like throwing a switch. He needed time to downshift and get his feelings under control. And she needed to be willing to give him that time.

It had been working pretty well at home. Jim would often get over whatever was eating him in an hour or two, and they would calmly talk it out. For the last several months, and for the first time in twenty-seven years, they were actually talking through their problems and learning to listen to each other at a heart level.

The problem was, they were walking around this incredible place full of beauty and history and wonder, and Jim was stuck in his head, totally distracted. She had been enjoying his undivided attention since the moment they had boarded the plane, and she didn't like the familiar feeling of being together but still alone.

The tour guide moved the group back to the center, toward the steps of the Basilica itself. He was now pointing out the statues of St. Peter and St. Paul on either side, talking about who sculpted them and when. Jim's head faced the right direction, his eyes were on the man speaking, and they blinked at appropriate times. But she knew he really wasn't there at all. And she didn't want to wait for him to work this through on his own as she walked through this magnificent architectural masterpiece holding Jim's hand.

"Can we talk about what's bothering you?" she whispered in his ear.

"What? No, I'm okay."

"Really? Okay, how many steps do you have to climb to get to the dome of St. Peter's?"

"What? I don't know."

"He just said it — 330. There are 330 steps. Come here, Jim." Taking a firmer grip of his hand, she led him toward the back of the group. "I know I'm supposed to give you a little space when you're struggling."

"I'm not struggling. Well, maybe I am a little. But I'll be okay. Really."

"Is it me? Something I said?"

"No, it's not you. I'm mostly feeling bad that this thing is bothering me at all. I know it shouldn't. I'm mad at myself, that I can't just let it go and enjoy our time right now."

"Can you tell me what it is at least? Does it have something to do with Michele's phone call?"

Jim sighed, then nodded. The tour guide began directing the group toward the stairs leading up to the main entrance. They walked a little slower, allowing a small gap to form.

"Is it about the idea of her and Allan trying to have kids right away?"

"Resistance is futile," he said. Then seeing her confusion, he added, "An old Star Trek saying. You always seem to know what I'm thinking. Most of the time, I miss what you're going through completely."

"You do, but see, at least now you're trying. Are you struggling about the money? About all the money you spent sending her to college?"

He laughed. "You're a scary woman sometimes. That's pretty much it." He looked up at the group now beginning to climb the steps of the Basilica. "We better not lose them."

"We won't. You know he's going to pause once they're inside and talk for a few more minutes. If you're okay with it, I'd like to talk this out a little, so I have you *really* with me once we go inside."

"It's just, I can't believe how much money I spent on her education. Tens of thousands of dollars. She hasn't even started teaching full-time yet. If she has a baby right away, you know what's gonna happen. She's gonna want to stay home, just like you did."

"Is that such a horrible thing?"

"No, you know I don't think that. I'm glad you were able to stay home with the kids."

"Then what's the problem?"

"There isn't a problem. You're right. I should be fine with it."

"But you aren't."

"It's just . . . I wish she had figured out that all she wanted to be was a stay-at-home mom before I spent all that money."

Marilyn looked up and saw that the tour group had all moved inside the church. The pause also helped her to gain control of her anger. She couldn't believe Jim had just said that. Had he really forgotten the fiery arguments they'd all gotten into about this very thing after Michele graduated from high school? She looked into his eyes. It was clear that he had. And she reminded herself, he really felt bad that he was struggling with this in the first place. *Lord,* she prayed, *help me to help him.*

"Maybe we should finish this at the top of the steps," Jim said. "So we can at least keep our eyes on the group."

"Good idea." As they walked, Marilyn considered how to put this. "Jim, you do remember, don't you, that Michele didn't want to go to college at all, right? You remember all those fights the two of you got in about this, toward the end of her senior year in high school and just after she graduated?"

"I guess I don't. I believe you, but I don't remember."

"I remember, because I was the referee. You were insisting she had to go to college, and she kept insisting that all she wanted to do was be a mom, like me. She wanted to stay at home and, when the time came, homeschool her kids. You were telling her that she needed to think of her future, that women today couldn't depend on finding husbands that would provide for them the way you did for us. Those days were dead and gone. Do you remember any of this?"

"It's starting to ring some distant bells." A disgusted look came over his face.

If Marilyn guessed right, it was self-loathing. "I'm the one who suggested Michele become a schoolteacher," she said, "as a compromise. Because it would help her when the time came to homeschool her kids and, at the same time, satisfy your requirement for her to get a practical education. In case that man in her life she was hoping and praying for never came."

Jim shook his head. "I remember now. I was such a jerk. And look, the man she was hoping and praying for did come." His eyes got watery. He blinked the tears away. Looking in her eyes, he said, "You did a great job back then mediating between me and the kids. And you always had such great ideas."

"Had?" she said.

"Still have. Now I've got one. Let's get in there and join the group before we get lost." He leaned forward and kissed her, then they turned and headed into the building.

As she walked through the magnificent doorway and beheld the grandeur of this place, she could almost imagine if God did have a house on earth, it might look something like this. But she knew what the Bible said, that the God of heaven chose to live within human hearts.

And she had experienced, firsthand, the power of God working in Jim's heart just now. She could tell by the look in his eyes.

He was back.

10

Tom was in the handicapped stall in a public library restroom putting on a dress shirt and tie. For him, it was just a few minutes before 10:00 a.m. He remembered the six-hour time gap for his parents in Rome. It was odd to think it was already late afternoon for them.

Here he was, just getting ready to start his day. At his old job, the dress code was "business casual." That's how Jean would expect to see him as he left their house in the morning, so that's how he looked.

But this morning, Tom had an interview. The first solid bite in over a week. He wanted to look his best. It sickened him to do this, but last night when he'd brought the trash out to the curb, he'd snuck out the suit coat, shirt, and tie to the car.

He put the coat on, looked in the mirror, and straightened his tie. After folding up his casual clothes, he laid them carefully in his brief bag. One more look in the mirror, one release of a deep, pent-up sigh, and Tom zipped up the bag and headed out the bathroom door.

He smiled and nodded to one of the librarians behind the counter as he walked by, a middle-aged woman he saw almost every day. She shot him a curious look but said nothing. He was certain she was puzzling over the change in his appearance. He opened the glass front door and held it for an elderly couple walking through. Behind them a couple of college students. He loved the look on all four of their faces as they passed him. It was funny how people treated a man in a nice suit with a greater sense of respect. He liked the feeling but, at the same time, was glad he didn't have to dress like this every day.

When he got in the car, he checked the address and directions to Wilson Foods. It was the main office headquarters for a regional chain of upscale steak houses located throughout central Florida. The position was for a network administrator for a small IT team that took care of all the restaurant chain's computers and information systems. The position had just gone online a few days ago. As far as Tom knew, Fred hadn't seen it yet. Of course, he was certain dozens of other people had.

Twenty minutes later, he pulled into a crowded parking lot of a business complex, a full fifteen minutes early. Grateful to find a spot under a shady tree, he rolled down the windows to allow a nice breeze to blow through the car. He pulled the sheet highlighting the job requirements out of his brief bag and read it over one more time, mumbling aloud.

"Maintain secure networks using a variety of network equipment, software, and protocols . . . Recommend appropriate equipment and work with vendors to obtain quotes . . . Assist with backup and restore requests as needed . . . Assist end users with laptop and desktop installs and configuration . . . Monitor systems availability and handle emergencies as they arise."

He looked down at the bottom half, under the qualifications heading. Especially the last line in the paragraph, which provided a serious glimmer of hope. "Great problem solving abilities and a team player with a great attitude a must. Microsoft MCSE certification a definite plus."

"It says a definite plus, not a requirement," he muttered aloud. He had everything else they were asking for, including a bachelor's degree. They mentioned "computer science or network engineering" and then added "or equivalent." His degree was in business management, but he minored in computer science. And they were asking for three years of experience; Tom had five.

He could do this job. He was perfect for it. This thing described to a T what he'd done for the bank over the last five years before they let him go.

Let me go. Yeah, that's one way of putting it. No, don't go there. Keep a positive attitude. Look him in the eye. Smile a lot. Give short answers. Sit up straight. Don't crack your knuckles. Stay confident. Act like you're perfect for the job, because you are. But don't get cocky. Nobody likes a know-it-all.

He took a deep breath and stepped out of the car.

Tom couldn't help it. He was nervous. There was so much at stake. The starting pay for this job wasn't quite as much as he'd made in his last one, but it was a decent salary with solid benefits. If he got it, his financial problems would be over. They hadn't lost the house, not yet. Foreclosure proceedings hadn't even begun; he'd only missed four payments so far. From what he'd read, he could string this thing out for over a year.

He didn't want to, of course. And he certainly didn't think he could keep up this charade for that long, but if he could start making mortgage payments again, he might still have a chance to restore his credit, maybe get a bank to work with him on some kind of loan modification.

Of course, the tricky thing here was not what to do about the house, or the car loan (which was two months overdue), or the credit cards.

It was how to tell all this to Jean.

No, don't think about that now. Keep a positive attitude. That's what they're looking for.

He looked around the waiting room, which he shared with two other out-of-work IT guys. They didn't talk much, other than to confirm they were there for the job interview. After that, they read magazines or checked for messages on their phones. Tom was the best dressed of the lot. One of the guys wore jeans and a pullover shirt. Was he kidding? Tom thought. What a moron.

Tom was next.

The door opened. A tall, thin, balding fellow with little John Lennon eyeglasses walked out. Midthirties, dark mustache. He was smiling like he had the job but then stopped when he noticed the other guys looking at him. Insecure, Tom thought. Not a leader. *Not so fast, Bub, they haven't interviewed me yet.*

That's right, stay confident.

"Mr. Anderson?" The receptionist called out his name. "You may go in. Mr. Hampton will see you now. The first door on your left."

Tom took a deep breath and got out of his chair. "Thanks," he said as he nodded. He walked through the same door the other guy had come out of, then tapped gently on the first door in the hallway. It was closed but not shut all the way. He walked in before being asked. *Be assertive. They're looking for a team leader.*

"There you are, Mr. . . ." The man looked down at his resume. "Anderson. Have a seat." Mr. Hampton had a pleasant face. He was about his dad's age and — Tom was happy to see — he wore a suit. "You're here about the network administrator job, correct?"

Tom sat in the office chair. "That's right, sir."

"Please, call me Sid," he said. "I see here you have five years' experience. That's good. Were you the team leader the entire time?"

"For the last three years I was, sir. I mean . . . Sid." *He's got to be wondering, if you were such a good leader, why'd they get rid of you? No, stop.*

"So, tell me a little bit about your old job. What were your day-to-day responsibilities?"

Tom spent the next five minutes running through his checklist, trying to touch on everything he'd read in their online job description. Sid then asked him some specific follow-up questions on several items, which Tom had great answers for (at least it felt that way). Sid smiled and nodded as he listened, wrote a few notes in the margin of Tom's resume.

Then he sat back in his chair, and his pleasant expression became more serious. "I wonder if you could share, from your perspective, why you think you were let go when that big Canadian bank took over your regional bank? Off the record, I mean."

Off the record? Tom thought. Did he want to know the *real* reason Tom had been laid off? What should he say? That a young man Tom had befriended and mentored, had treated like a brother, had taught all the ins and outs of their system — a guy whose mistakes and blunders he'd covered on numerous occasions, sometimes even taking hits the guy deserved — had stabbed Tom in the back, had painted himself as an IT genius and Tom as an unqualified fool? That this guy had actually told lies about him in the interviews, blaming Tom for everything that was wrong with their system and giving himself credit for everything that had been done right?

"Well," Tom said, "they told me it was because I hadn't gotten my Microsoft certification yet. I'm working on it now, by the way. And I was actually doing the job effectively without it — not that I think it's unimportant — I'm just saying, it hadn't hindered me from learning and doing everything I needed to do, day to day. But they said when they merged the two companies that they had an excess of IT guys and decided to use the certification issue as the make-or-break criteria."

"I take it you don't agree with their decision," Sid said.

"No, I don't. But there were some other factors. And one of the key guys I had trained had his certification, so they decided to go with him."

Sid looked down at the resume again. Tom waited a few moments, unsure how that sounded. He'd tried to hide all the bitterness and hurt he'd felt from the betrayal in his answer and hoped he had succeeded.

When Sid looked up again, the pleasant expression had returned. He sat forward and said, "Well, clearly, you do meet all the qualifications we're looking for and have more than enough work experience." He stood up and stuck out his hand. The interview was over. "I have a few more candidates to talk to this afternoon, but we'll be in touch, Tom."

Tom shook his hand and said before leaving the room, "Thank you, Sid. I really appreciate the opportunity to talk with you. I know I can do great things for this company, if you give me the chance."

"We'll be in touch," Sid said, smiling.

As Tom walked through the hallway, then through the waiting room past the three remaining guys, he had absolutely no idea whether he should be happy or sad. It had seemed to go well. Sid seemed to like him. What he said there at the end sounded encouraging. But he'd been through the same process now so many times.

Why get your hopes up only to have them come crashing down a few days later? What did that proverb say? Hope deferred makes the heart sick? He didn't need any more heartsickness. So, he was all done with hope.

It was a highly overrated emotion.

11

Jean walked back into the kitchen to pour Michele and herself a second cup of coffee. It was a magic moment; Tommy and Carly were both down for a nap. Michele was Tom's sister, and she'd just popped in for a visit after returning some purchases at a nearby store. "You want another cup, right?"

"Yes, I'd love one," Michele said. "I can only stay for another half hour or so, then I need to get home and start dinner."

"What time does Allan get home from work?"

"It depends whether he ends his day in the office or out in the field. If he's in the office, like today, he'll be home right at 5:30. His office is only about fifteen minutes from our apartment."

"So you're off today?" Jean came back to the dining room table carrying both cups.

"Unfortunately. I'm still a substitute, so I don't get to teach every day. But even on days that I do, I'm usually home at 3:00. So, I usually make dinner."

Jean stirred in enough half-and-half to get the creamy beige look she required, then added one Splenda. "Tom has always worked in an office. What does Allan do when he works in the field?"

"He's an environmental biologist," Michele said, "so asking him 'How'd your day go?' usually ends in me staring at him with this blank look on my face. He's getting better at seeing that and skipping the parts that are seriously boring. He does things like check companies' well water systems, making sure the water is healthy. And he makes sure they're complying with county regulations with their retention ponds and wetlands areas. Things like that. All I know is, he loves doing it, and it pays well enough that I can be a stay-at-home mom someday. Like you."

Jean smiled. Like me, she thought. She was mostly happy that she got to stay home and raise her kids. But some days she had doubts.

"Tell you one thing I'm not overly fond of," Michele continued. "When Allan does work in the field, I have to do tick checks over his whole body before he sits down to the dinner table."

"Tick checks? Is that —"

"It's exactly what you're thinking," Michele said, laughing, then sipped her coffee.

"I'm not even going to let the picture form in my head," Jean said. "Doesn't sound like a very romantic encounter."

"No, it's not. I'd put it in the opposite-of-romance category. But every now and then, I find one, so I know I have to keep doing it. Ticks are disgusting."

"Maybe next time you should try it over a bottle of wine."

Michele laughed. "Anyway . . . I have some exciting news to share with you. That's really the reason I stopped by. I called Mom and Dad yesterday in Italy and told them."

"You're pregnant!"

"No. Not yet. But Allan and I talked about it, and he said we can start trying to have a baby right away. So who knows? Maybe I'll be pregnant in a month or two."

"That's wonderful, Michele. I'm so happy for you. You're going to be a great mom."

"I hope so. That's what I want to be. More than anything else in the world."

Jean heard a noise on the monitor in Carly's room. "Did you hear that?" Please don't wake up, she thought. Not yet.

"Hear what?"

"Listen." Carly made a little singsongy sound through the speaker. "Maybe if we give her a minute, she'll go back to sleep. There's no way she should be up already."

"See?" Michele said. "That's what I want. I want to know my baby so well I can tell little things like that."

"You're okay with not being a schoolteacher anymore?"

"I'm sure some days will be a struggle, but no, I'd much rather be a stay-at-home mom."

Jean hadn't known this about Michele. She'd always wanted the two of them to be closer, but Michele had spent most of the last four years away at school. During the last two, even when she was home, she was always with Allan. Maybe the two of them could finally become friends. "You don't hear too many women with that ambition these days."

"What? Being a stay-at-home mom?"

Jean nodded, then listened for any more noises from Carly. All was quiet.

"I guess," Michele said, "but even economically it's not that great a trade-off if you think about it. We've been living on Allan's salary since the wedding. If I work full time after we have our baby, we'd have to pay hundreds of dollars a month for day-care. And keep two cars running, so that's hundreds more for a car payment and insurance, and a lot more for all the extra gas driving back and forth to work. And you know our food bill would be much higher. Who'd fix dinner if we both come home wiped out from working all day? I feel wiped out now some days, and I only work part time."

As she said these last few lines, Jean noticed a growing edginess in Michele's voice. "So, you think it's wrong for moms to work outside the house once the kids come?"

"No. Do I sound like I think that?"

"A little."

"Well, I don't mean to. I guess I've gotten a little defensive about it. When I tell some women about what I want to do, they make me feel like I'm an idiot for wanting to give up my career."

"You know I don't think that way, right?" Jean took the final sip of her coffee, sad to see it go. She waved her hand. "Obviously, stay-at-home mom, right here."

"I know."

"I'm just careful about how I share my views on motherhood," Jean said. "I know some women at church would love to stay home if they could, but it's not financially possible. And single moms don't even have a choice in the matter."

"You're right," Michele said. "The last thing I want to do is tell other people how to live. But I also don't want to feel like apologizing all the time for wanting to be a stay-at-home mom."

"Speaking of becoming a mom," Jean said, "can you keep a secret?"

"You know I can."

"You can't say a thing. I haven't even told Tom yet."

"What . . . you're pregnant?"

"Maybe," Jean said. "I'm late, and I started getting queasy in the mornings, several days in a row now."

"Have you taken a pregnancy test yet?"

"No, I was going to get one the next time I went to the store."

"Have you and Tom been . . . trying?"

"That's the thing, we haven't."

"A surprise baby. When are you going to tell Tom?"

"I'm not sure," Jean said. "He's been so uptight lately."

"About what?"

"Not sure about that, either. I think he's having problems at work, but he doesn't want to talk about it. I don't know if he's worried about getting laid off or what the problem is. But he's been all tense about money lately too. Last night, he started talking about couponing, if you can believe that. Said he watched a show all about it and thought I should start doing it. You know anything about couponing?"

"I've been too busy for anything like that. But hey, once I become a stay-at-home mom I can look into it. I know you're supposed to be able to save a lot of money once you get a system figured out."

"Well, it's something Tom wants me to learn. If I find any great websites, I'll send you the links."

Michele set her coffee cup down and looked at her watch. "I better get going. I just remembered I have one more stop to make. Hey, do you mind if I ask you something?"

"Sure."

"Has your relationship with my brother always been like that?"

"Like what?"

"Like . . . him possibly having problems at work and not talking to you about it. And you possibly being pregnant and not telling him?"

Jean thought a moment. Had they always been this way? Sadly, the honest answer seemed to be yes. "I suppose it has. I'm guessing you and Allan talk about everything freely?"

"Pretty much," Michele said. "It's just . . . I don't know, Tom has always been so much like my father."

"He's always admired your dad."

"That's not necessarily a good thing," Michele said. "Dad and Mom always kept things from each other, especially when they struggled. Used to, anyway. And look at the kind of trouble they got into." She sighed. "Well, I better go." She walked to the front door, turned, and gave Jean a hug goodbye. "I hope I didn't say anything that upset you."

"I'm a little discouraged," Jean said, "but not at you. Tom really is like his father in some ways. Well, like he used to be before your wedding."

Even as the words left her mouth, Jean wished that wasn't the case. As she closed the door, a tear escaped and she whispered a prayer. What had happened to her marriage? Why couldn't Tom be more like Allan, or even the way his father was now?

12

"Would you look at that?" Jim said, his face all lit up. "Up on that hill, another castle."

Marilyn looked where Jim pointed with his eyes. It was splendid. Yet another medieval castle fortress on an Italian hillside, surrounded by a small village. They had seen several since their tour bus had left Rome an hour ago. This was day three of their journey. She was so excited; they were on their way to Florence now. Jim had insisted she sit by the large picture window, but so far he'd spent the entire time leaning across her lap, his head a few inches from hers.

She didn't mind, and she perfectly understood why. There was so much to see around every curve, beyond every hill. The photos in the travel magazines didn't come close to capturing the visions outside her window. She'd already spied a dozen little places she wished the bus would stop so they could take some pictures.

"I wonder if that's one of those little towns Dr. Franklin was talking about," Jim said. "You know, for our drive after the tour ends." He sat back in his seat and looked at the map.

Seeing him so animated about sightseeing, she found it hard to believe this was the same man who had brought business books on their twenty-fifth anniversary cruise. "I don't think we'll go wrong no matter what little towns we visit," she said. "They're all so charming."

She looked across the aisle through the windows on the other side of the bus. More breathtaking scenery. A narrow winding road, lined with those tall skinny evergreen trees you see in every Italian painting, weaved its way through a smattering of hills, up to a gorgeous Italian villa. The morning mist hadn't fully burned off. It lingered in small pockets here and there as if clinging to the vines, hovering just above a sprawling vineyard that ran along the north side of the property. The vines were so beautiful. Row after perfect row, continuing out toward the horizon.

"Look at that," Jim said, noticing the scene that caught her eye. "Did you ever think you'd see something like this?"

She squeezed his hand. "No, not in person. Thank you for bringing us here." He squeezed back, leaned forward, and kissed her softly. She followed the sight as it drifted from view. "What are those tall skinny trees called again?"

"I think the tour guide said they were Italian cypress," Jim said.

"Too bad our yard is already landscaped. I'd love to plant some of those."

"I don't know," Jim said. "There's that section in the backyard along the left side of the fence. We've got a bunch of little shrubs there. I don't even know what they're called. Wouldn't take much to move them somewhere else and plant some Italian cypress trees in their place. If we spaced them right, we could get four or five in there."

"Could we? I'd love that."

"Then consider it done," Jim said. "It'll be like a living souvenir of this trip. I'll get to work on it as soon as we get home."

Marilyn didn't know why, but hearing this released a wave of emotion inside her. She had never felt so loved, so cherished before. Not even in their dating days. It was as if Jim was totally focused on her happiness now, as if there was nothing in life, big or small, he wouldn't do for her. *Thank you, Lord,* she prayed quietly, *for changing this man so completely.*

She was also happy to discover that all the bitterness and loneliness, all the rejection she'd felt — emotions that had defined her life for so long — were completely gone.

Her thoughts were momentarily interrupted by the tour guide as the bus made a wide sweeping turn and another amazing sight came into view. "If you look outside your right window, you'll see the ancient Etruscan village of Orvieto sitting atop that rocky plateau. At the center you see the twin spires of Orvieto's famous duomo, or cathedral." She continued to talk, but Marilyn stopped listening. She was captivated by the visual splendor.

The scene looked like something out of a medieval fairy tale. An entire walled city resting atop rocky cliffs rising up on every side. Lush green forests encircled the base. If she had traveled back a thousand years in time, she'd expect to see something just like this. "Oh Jim," she said. "Is there any chance we could go there?"

"That sounds familiar. Orvieto, Orvieto," he repeated, scrolling through a document on his phone. "Yes," he said. "That's one of the towns on Dr. Franklin's list. Marta, Bagnoregio, some ruins outside of Viterbo, and Orvieto. We're going to come back here, just the two of us, when our tour is through."

She couldn't wait. She sat back in silence as this ancient city on a hill passed slowly by. Jim snapped a few pictures. Michele would love this place. She'd always loved stories with princes and castles. Thinking of Michele brought Marilyn back to the bon voyage party Michele had organized last week, a few nights before they'd left. Everyone had come, even Doug, their youngest.

Michele had baked a cake in the shape of the Italian boot, with little flags stuck at the approximate locations of the big cities on their tour. Everyone was laughing and getting along the entire night. But still, at several moments, Marilyn couldn't help but notice Jean, Tom's wife. The look on her face. Marilyn thought about it now. She remembered that expression. It was the same look she used to wear at all those parties Jim forced her to host or attend.

There were the eyes that didn't match the forced smile. Laughing just a little late at every joke, because you were supposed to, not because you were enjoying yourself. You did what was expected. All the while fighting off feelings of being alone in a crowd.

Marilyn was convinced something was wrong between Jean and Tom. She didn't know what just yet; it wasn't anything anyone had done or said. But her instincts on these things were rarely off. Jean was unhappy, profoundly unhappy. She was certain of it.

It didn't take a whole lot of thought to imagine why. It was the way Tom treated her. Her and the kids. Not just lately but for years. Tom was the spitting image of Jim . . . the *old* Jim. He'd grown up wanting to be just like his dad. And that was the problem.

Tom had succeeded.

He was like his dad had been for so many years: tense, edgy, irritable, controlling. Totally focused on himself. My way or the highway.

She sighed as one image after another ran through her mind. Example after example of the very real trouble she believed Tom and Jean were in. Still in. Right now.

"What's the matter?"

"Huh?"

"Something's happened," Jim said. "You were radiant a moment ago. Now you look so sad."

How could she tell him what she was thinking? It would totally ruin their day.

13

"It's nothing," Marilyn said. "Well, it's not nothing. But it's certainly something that can wait."

Jim stared at her a moment as if trying to read her. The bus tour guide interrupted them with an update. "We'll be taking a more scenic route to Florence this morning. It will add about thirty minutes to our journey, but I'm sure you'll agree it will be time well spent. We'll be stopping at the historic town of Siena for lunch, just about ninety minutes from now."

"Isn't that the city where they have that fancy horse race called the Palio?"

"Are you sure you're not trying to change the subject?"

"I'm not."

Jim smiled. "Then yes, I think it is."

"Okay, I am," she said. "But we said we weren't going to talk about our kids' problems on this trip."

"That's a relief."

"What is?"

"I thought it was me, something I said. But if it's one of the kids, I'm in the clear."

"It's nothing you said. But really, we don't have to talk about this now." She looked around the bus, hoping their conversation wasn't being overheard. That couple they'd met — their new picture-taking friends — were sitting across from them, one aisle up. Everyone seemed totally preoccupied with the sights out the window.

Jim leaned a little closer toward her. "I don't mind if we talk about them . . . a little, here and there. It was probably unrealistic to think we could avoid talking about them completely. But I'd like to help you work through whatever you're wrestling with, if we can. Like you did for me at St. Peter's. So you can enjoy this beautiful scenery with me."

But this was different, she thought. Then, she was helping him work through an internal struggle he was having. Her struggle was about *him,* a problem involving him. And this was a big conversation, something she'd been thinking about a lot these past several months. Really, every time they had gotten together with Tom and Jean or had spent any time with them. Was this really a good idea? To get into something like this with Jim now? Here? Was it a *safe* time and place? In their small group back home they had been talking a lot about cultivating a safe atmosphere when resolving difficult relational problems.

If Jim didn't respond well to what she was about to say, it could prove to be the opposite of "safe." It could literally ruin their day. "I really think we should postpone this conversation to another time," she said.

"You do. Why?"

"Remember that small group discussion we had about a month ago, about the importance of creating a safe environment for resolving conflicts?"

"Hmmm," he said. "It's that bad, eh?" His face suddenly grew serious.

What was this new look? she thought. See? She shouldn't have brought this up. "We can just talk about it later. Really, it'll keep."

Jim looked around at the people nearby. "I think this is a safe place, hon. We'll be sitting here for over an hour. If we talk quietly, we should be fine. Look around, everyone's pretty distracted. I think the safe idea has more to do with the *way* we talk to each other. Why don't we give it a try? If it starts to get edgy, for either of us, we'll back off. I can tell this thing is bugging you. I'd really like you to be freed up and, to be honest, now you have me concerned. I know I'll just keep trying to figure out what this is all about."

Part of her wanted to risk it. He seemed like he could handle this, if she chose her words carefully. "All right. I'll give it a try. But this won't take an hour. Only a few minutes at the most. And there's really nothing you can even do about it right now. Just something to start thinking and praying about for when we get home."

Jim sat back in his seat and grabbed the armrests with both hands.

"What are you doing?"

"I'm bracing for the hit. Okay . . . I'm ready. Let me have it."

"Jim, this is serious."

He relaxed his grip and sat up. "I'm sorry. I know it is. Go ahead."

She took a deep breath. "It's about Tom and Jean. I think their marriage is in some trouble."

"Really? They seem fine to me. They get along great, from what I can tell. I never see them arguing. Tom seems pretty attentive to the kids. Did she say something to you?"

"Who, Jean?"

"Yeah. Because Tom hasn't said anything to me."

"Would you expect him to? I mean, if he was struggling with something. Would he open up to you?"

Jim thought a moment, then shook his head. "I'm not sure. I'd like to think he would. Before Michele's wedding, we had a good talk."

"What about?"

"Mostly about areas where I've blown it with him. Things in our relationship he'd like to see done differently."

"Really?" This was encouraging to hear. "I never knew that. What kind of things did he say?"

"There was really only one. It was a pretty big thing for him. He got pretty emotional about it."

"What was it?"

"He wanted to have more . . ." Jim stopped talking, like he'd suddenly recalled something awful. He sat back in his seat again.

"What's the matter?"

"I never did it. I can't believe it." He was shaking his head back and forth, and his eyes dropped toward the seat. "I totally dropped the ball."

"What is it? What's the matter?"

Jim sighed. "After that one talk with Tom, things started moving pretty fast. I had those dance lessons with Audrey, trying to

107

get ready for the wedding. Then that hurricane hit, and then there was the wedding itself. Then you and I got back together."

Even though Jim hadn't said what the "big thing" was, Marilyn saw where this was heading. "So . . . Tom wanted to have more heart-to-heart talks with you, like the one you had before the wedding. And that was the last one you guys had."

Jim sighed again and nodded his head in resignation. "So I guess it's fair to say, I have no idea how Tom's really doing. But still, from what I can see, they seem fine. He seems fine. He's got a great job, a nice house, a fairly new car, a loving wife, two healthy kids."

Marilyn tensed up hearing Jim talk this way. Didn't he realize how this sounded? "Jim, every one of those things are just externals. They're not good indicators of whether Tom and Jean are happy, how they're doing on a heart level. You could've run through that same list of things describing your life — our life — just before everything fell apart last summer."

Jim didn't reply at first. But it seemed like what she said hit the mark. "So, has Jean said something to you about what's really going on with them?" he asked.

"No, she hasn't. And I wouldn't expect her to."

"You wouldn't. Why?"

"Because she's a loyal wife. She wouldn't want to say anything or do anything that would embarrass Tom or make him look bad in our eyes. Instead, she'd rather just suffer alone in silence, hiding her hurts and fears, sometimes even from herself, hoping that things between them will get better if she can just hold on a little longer, give things a little more time." Marilyn looked down.

Things got very quiet between them for a few moments.

Jim gently reached his fingers under her chin and lifted her face toward his. Tears had welled up in her eyes. "We're not just talking about Jean anymore, are we?"

Marilyn shook her head. "No, we're not. I know what she's feeling. Tom married a young woman very much like me, and he's been treating her very much like you — the old you — did ever since."

Just then, the tour guide said over the intercom, "Now, if you look out on the left side of the bus, a long section of the ancient Roman aqueducts will soon come into view."

14

Tom sat at his usual table at the Java Stop, the last of three places where he spent the bulk of his days. Fred Messing was already there, sitting at his table just a few feet away. Thankfully, he was working on something that required his undivided attention, giving Tom a break from his constant chatter. It was just after 2:00 p.m.

He raised his laptop lid and opened an Excel program he'd created to help juggle his meager finances. Then he lifted a manila folder filled with bills and threatening collection letters out of his brief bag. The folder felt like it weighed ten pounds. He did a quick check of his bank account to make sure his unemployment check had auto-deposited. It had, but the realization brought no joy.

There wasn't enough in there to cover a fraction of their household expenses. The severance money the bank had given him when they let him go had just run out. And he only had four weeks of eligibility left to continue collecting unemployment funds.

His life was a nightmare, pure and simple.

But he felt a small glimmer of hope flickering inside, put there by that job interview yesterday. Who knows, like Fred always said, today might be the day. He clicked on the keys and moved a bunch of numbers around, trying to figure out what things he could take care of now — *must* take care of now — and what things he could put off a little longer. He moved those things into a column called "Unpaid Debts" he'd been filling these past few months. It grew bigger and bigger by the week, and now totaled in the thousands.

It was silly, really. But somehow moving the money into that column made him feel a little better about his situation. It was just temporary. But it was as if, mentally, he could close that amount behind a door and pretend it wasn't really there. Deep down he knew it was like one of those old-timey slapstick routines, where a guy keeps shoving more and more things into a closet. Then one day somebody else comes along, opens the closet, and this avalanche of junk rains down on his head.

But today was not that day. Today was a

day he just shoved more debt into the closet.

"So how did it go yesterday? Your interview, I mean."

Tom looked up into the smiling face of Fred Messing. "Hard to know for sure, but I think it went really well. You know how these things are. Those interview guys are hard to read."

"Yeah, I know. Especially that guy."

"What guy?" Tom asked.

"That guy at Wilson Foods. I interviewed with him the day before."

Great, Tom thought. How did Fred find out about that opening? Had he been looking at Tom's laptop? A memory flashed through Tom's mind. A few days ago. He had to use the restroom and had asked Fred to watch his stuff. That was the day he'd been filling out the online application for Wilson Foods. Anger began to stir inside him. "You did, huh? How did you find out about that opening?" Tom wasn't going to let him off the hook.

Fred smiled and said, "The Lord just opened the door, I guess."

I'll bet, Tom thought. "Oh? How did he do that?"

"A friend at my church works there. He called me," Fred said. "He's a delivery guy for them, but he saw the job go up on the board in the office. He knew I'm an IT guy and that I'd recently lost my job." Fred's eyes shifted to the stack of bills lying next to Tom's computer. "That's the biggest temptation for me in all this."

"What's that?"

"Juggling the bills, when you know there's not enough coming in to cover what's going out. Trusting that God will come through somehow before it's too late. I know his Word promises that he will. Those are the verses my wife and I read together every morning these days. Some days I'm in the ditch, and she pulls me out. Some days I pull her out. It's just hard trying to keep your mind off the negative, what-if stuff when you don't know God's plan. How are you guys handling that part of it? You been out of work a lot longer than me."

What should Tom say? How should he answer this? "You know what? I never got my coffee." He stood up and grabbed his refill cup. "Gotta pay the rent, right? Can you watch my stuff for a minute?" Obviously, Fred hadn't been stealing his leads.

"Sure, go get some coffee. I'll be here."

As Tom stood there in line, his stomach was churning. He looked back at Fred happily clicking away on his laptop. He didn't seem to have a care in the world. How was that fair? They were both going through the same trial, but clearly Fred was in a totally different place. He tried to convince himself the difference was just the amount of time he'd spent in this ordeal compared to Fred. Give Fred another few months and he'd be in the exact same place as Tom.

But as soon as he thought it, he knew it wasn't true. He got a sense that somehow Fred would be doing better, still managing to find a way to keep his smile. Fred was going through this with his wife's support and encouragement. Tom had thoughts about that lately, especially after spending time with Jean. Wondering if he should have told her all about losing his job from the beginning.

Right now, though, telling her seemed like an impossible option. She'd be worried sick. Tom had always managed their financial affairs. Part of the reason he did was because of how much it used to upset her when things got tight. She just couldn't relax till everything made perfect sense. Of the two of them, Tom had the business mind. Business was his major in college. It just made sense that he should take over their finances, and so he did. Just like his father had done in their home.

Jean's emotional state had completely

improved after that, and Tom's desire to keep her in that happy state had grown stronger year after year, especially after Tommy and Carly were born. That was why he couldn't tell her that he'd lost his job. He had to be strong, for her and the kids. Besides, at the time, he'd been convinced he'd find a new job in a matter of weeks. A month at the most.

Then, of course, there was the issue of his father finding out the mess he'd made of things. And he would have found out, once Jean knew. She would want to get his dad involved, seek out his advice. Tom couldn't face that on top of everything else.

He stepped up to the counter, paid the refill price for his coffee, and dropped two quarters in the tip jar. As he added sugar and cream, he thought about another obstacle to telling Jean the truth. Perhaps the biggest obstacle of all. How could he ever explain why he'd lied to her and kept up this charade for so long? That was a door he never wanted to open but knew someday he must.

But not today.

He walked back and sat down. Fred picked up where he'd left off, repeating the question, "So how do you and your wife handle all the discouragement that comes in a trial like this? Got any tips for me?"

Tips? Gee, fresh out today. He didn't know why, but he decided just to say it. Maybe the shock value would get Fred to back off and give him some space. "To be honest with you, Fred, I don't think I can help you at all. My wife doesn't know I lost my job."

Tom might just as soon have hit Fred in the head with a baseball bat. "Really?" That was all Fred said. For the first time in their odd relationship, Fred was speechless. After a few more awkward moments, he finally added, "Do you think that's a good idea?" Then Fred's phone rang.

Tom watched as Fred's face instantly changed from shock to sheer joy. Whatever he was hearing, it was obviously good news. He said things like, "Really?" and "Seriously?" and then "That sounds perfect" and "I can start whenever you're ready" and "Okay, then. Sounds great. See you Monday."

Fred put down the phone. "You're not gonna believe this," he said. "That was the hiring manager for Wilson Foods. I got the IT job. I start on Monday. Can you believe it? Thank you, Jesus."

Tom couldn't believe it. It was his turn to be hit in the head with a baseball bat. He looked down at his laptop screen, his eyes focused on the column "Unpaid Debts." Tom felt like he was standing in front of that closet door and Fred had just walked up and opened it, and an avalanche of junk rained down on top of him, burying him under its weight.

15

Tom was due home any minute. Jean was so nervous as she put the finishing touches on their dinner. She'd been out shopping and found a nice top sirloin in the marked-down cooler. It was almost half off but had to be either cooked today or frozen.

Today was a good day for a steak dinner, or at least she hoped it would be. They hadn't had a steak in so long. Normally, she'd wait and let Tom grill it. But she decided to do it herself today so that everything would be ready when he got home. The meat had been marinating in his favorite teriyaki sauce for hours.

She'd also found fresh asparagus and some sourdough bread and was just now tossing a fresh garden salad. She wanted everything to be perfect here at home and hoped he'd had a smooth day at work for once, so she could finally tell him the news tonight after dinner, after they put the kids in bed.

That morning, she had taken a home pregnancy test, the same brand she'd used with both Tommy and Carly. It had come out positive. She'd expected it would, but, unlike Tommy and Carly, this baby wasn't planned. She wanted to be excited, and part of her was. They had always said they wanted at least three or four children, although they hadn't talked about starting to try for number three just yet. Carly would be just over two years old when this baby was born. That was pretty good spacing, she thought.

But what would Tom think? That was the question.

She walked out from the kitchen to the family room to check on the kids. Carly was entertaining herself in her playpen, and Tommy's eyes were glued on a Veggie Tales video. "Tommy, you keep an eye on your sister while I go out on the patio and check on the steak."

"Okay, Mommy." He didn't even look up.

She slid the sliding glass door open and was greeted with the most enticing smell. She turned the steak over, and the sizzling aroma grew even stronger. She smiled as she watched the flames kick up momentarily in response to the savory juices spilling through the grate. Tom used to love to grill; the marinade for this teriyaki sauce was his recipe.

She remembered him talking about all the wonderful "Old Testament smells" he created while he grilled. He was convinced that part of the reason God had established burnt offerings and sacrifices in the Old Testament was because God loved the smell of great barbecue. She remembered walking out with a platter as he shared this belief with his little brother Doug the last time they had him over, quoting some passage in Leviticus. "And the priest shall burn all on the altar as a burnt sacrifice, an offering made by fire, a sweet aroma to the Lord."

She poked at the sirloin in a few places and said a quiet prayer that she wouldn't turn it into a burnt sacrifice. Tom liked his steak medium rare. She guessed she had maybe three or four more minutes.

Walking back into the house, she heard the front door open. She listened a few moments but didn't hear him speak. Not a good sign. When he was in a good mood, he normally yelled out a greeting like, "Hey, hon, I'm home!" She waited a few moments more. Nothing.

Then Tommy looked up from the TV, saw

him down the hall, and yelled, "Daddy, you're home!" with that generous enthusiasm he lavished on Tom every day. He got up and ran toward his father. Still, Tom said nothing.

Then after a few seconds, a dreary moan. "Hey, Tommy." As if Eeyore had uttered the words. She heard him sigh but couldn't see him yet from where she was standing in the family room. She wasn't sure she wanted to now.

She walked back into the kitchen instead of toward the hall.

Tom could barely taste his steak. If it had been a different day and he had been in a better mood, the steak might've tasted wonderful. But nothing tastes good when you're depressed.

He couldn't believe they gave that job to Fred. To Fred, of all people. Tom had two more years of IT experience than Fred, and he had leadership experience too. Fred had never led a team. Fred didn't even have a bachelor's degree. The only thing Fred had that Tom didn't was the Microsoft certification. Tom was doing his best to study, taking courses online to prepare himself for the test. But why should that matter? He could do the work; he'd been doing it for the bank for years without the certification.

Every time. Every single time . . . someone else got the job. For five months now. It was almost as if Tom had been blacklisted. Like someone was out there spreading lies about him, trying to make sure he'd never get hired. But that was crazy, wasn't it?

"Tom?"

"Huh?" Jean was talking to him from the other end of the table. What was she saying?

"The steak, is it all right? If it's not pink enough, we can switch because mine is perfect."

"What? No, it's great. You cooked it just right." He sawed off a piece and put it in his mouth. Smile as you chew, he told himself.

"I used your teriyaki recipe," she said. "Did I get it right?"

Tom thought a moment, then swallowed. "I think so." Smile, he reminded himself. Tell her how grateful you are for all the trouble she went through to make this dinner for you. Look at this spread. Grilled asparagus in a lemon butter sauce. Sourdough bread. Homemade chocolate cake for dessert. Say something. Thank her.

But he didn't. All he could think about — the overriding, preoccupying focus that choked out every other thing — was the cost. They didn't have money for something like this. There was at least three dinners' worth of food on this table. What was Jean thinking?

Tom, you idiot. What should she be thinking? She has no idea you're almost broke. Why would she?

But he'd been dropping her hints left and right, almost every night for weeks now. Was she really that dull?

"I'm eating steak, Daddy. Just like you. See?"

"What?" He looked over at Tommy sitting in a booster chair to his right. Carly was at the other end of the table in her high chair, near Jean.

"Mommy cut it up weel small so I wouldn't choke. See?"

"That's great, Tommy. You chew it up real good now."

"I am. Carly's pieces are way smaller than mine. Wight, Mommy?"

"That's right," Jean said. "So . . . guess you had a bad day at work?"

"Not the whole day. Just . . . something crummy happened at the end of the day, that's all." Which wasn't totally a lie. Something crummy had happened, just not at work.

"What?"

"Just something. I really don't want to talk about it." He cut off another piece of steak and ate it.

"Well, I wish you would."

"Would what?"

"Talk about it. I wish you'd talk about it. I wish you'd let me into your life a little. You're so moody and mopey all the time. I don't know why. Because you never want to talk about it. Michele stopped by yesterday. She and Allan talk about everything. Did you know that? They've only been married for seven months, and she probably knows Allan better than I know you."

He looked up at her. They stared at each other a few moments.

"So . . . are you going to tell me what's bugging you?" she said.

Just tell her.

The thought came into his head like an audible voice. *Tell her the truth. For once in your miserable life, tell her the truth. You lost your job. You've been moody and mopey with good reason, because you're out of work and you have absolutely no idea how you guys are gonna make it. You can't make the car payment. You're starting to get threatening letters from a collection agency about it. You've just signed up for food stamps — wouldn't your father love to hear that? You're*

probably gonna lose the house. You're start-
ing to pay half the utility bills on credit cards,
and those cards are just about ready to max
out. For reasons that make absolutely no
sense, on any level, no one will hire you. Oh,
and here's the best part . . . you've been hid-
ing all of this for five months now, lying to her
the entire time.

Go ahead, tell her.

But he couldn't. What he did say was, "So you've been talking about me behind my back with my sister?"

"What?"

"What did you tell Michele about me? About us?"

Jean's face filled with rage. She stood up.

"What's the matter, Mommy?"

She didn't answer their son, she just stood there glaring at Tom.

"Where are you going?" he said.

She threw her napkin on her plate and walked out of the dining room and up the stairs.

16

Jean was exhausted. And a little bit frightened. She was washing the dishes from last night, keeping an ear out for Tommy and Carly, who for the moment were entertaining themselves in the family room.

After crying herself to sleep last night, as quietly as she could, Jean had awakened this morning the same time she always did. She couldn't remember any of her dreams, only that they were disturbing and left her feeling anything but rested.

Tom had eventually apologized before bed for the scene at the dinner table. But his apology was wholly unsatisfying. He volunteered that he was sorry for not thanking her for the fine dinner she had made and for making her feel uncomfortable about talking to Michele. But that was all. He'd said nothing about the question she'd asked him: *So . . . are you going to tell me what's bugging you?*

126

It was obvious after his perfunctory apology that he had no intention of answering that question or talking about anything else that mattered. He'd leaned over, pecked her on the cheek, lain back on his side of the bed, and stuck his face in a book.

Ten minutes later he was sound asleep.

This morning as he'd gotten ready for work, he'd barely said a thing. He just went through his normal routine and left at his normal time. Gave Tommy a hug good-bye, kissed Carly on the forehead as she sat in her high chair, kissed Jean on the cheek. "I should be home at the usual time," he'd said. And then he walked out the door.

Before he'd left, she had tried to read his eyes, since that was all the communication she was going to get. If there was anything different about him, it was only that he seemed more distant and aloof, and possibly a little more depressed.

If he wasn't, she certainly was.

She didn't know what to do or whom to talk to about this. She really didn't have any close friends, which was why she was so happy when Michele had stopped by the other day. She'd hoped that might be the beginning of something meaningful. But Tom's nearly paranoid reaction last night properly nipped that in the bud. And his apology was so flat and lifeless, she didn't get the impression he'd be okay if she tried talking to Michele again.

She wished she could talk to Marilyn, Tom's mother. But she was in Italy on her second honeymoon. Even if she was home, talking to her would likely invite the same angry reaction from Tom. Because anything she'd say to Marilyn would likely be repeated to Jim. For whatever reason, above all things, Tom wanted his father to think well of him.

But Jean knew that Marilyn would understand everything she was going through. It had taken Marilyn tremendous courage to do what she'd done last summer. Leaving Jim like that after twenty-seven years. Even though it might have cost her everything.

Jean certainly wasn't at that place of desperation yet. She'd only been struggling with Tom for a few years, and he wasn't nearly as bad as his father had been. Was he? Even still, she was certain Marilyn could help her learn how to better cope with all this. Maybe help her understand how to chip away at this wall that had grown up between her and Tom.

She heard Carly start to cry from the other room. A moment later, "Mommy!" It was Tommy calling. After turning off the faucet, she dried her hands with a dish towel and walked toward the growing noise.

As she did, she thought of something else. Something she wished for more than being able to talk with Marilyn. What she really wanted was for Jim, her father-in-law, to come home from Italy and give his son a strong dose of whatever medicine he had taken seven months ago.

It was as if he'd become a totally new man. That's what she needed.

A totally new Tom.

It really wasn't such a crazy idea, robbing a bank.

Tom sat back in his chair at the Java Stop, mulling it over. This was normally his third stop of the day, but today he had decided to make it his first. Since his "Masked Avenger" heroics had made the Coffee Shoppe off-limits for a while, he had been starting his days off at the local library. But this morning, kids from a private school had filled the place, working on their science projects.

He had just finished reading an online news story about two out-of-work white-collar criminals that the FBI had arrested in Orlando. From what he could gather, they had devised a brilliant scheme. The problem was, they had gotten greedy. The FBI estimated the pair had robbed over a dozen banks in central Florida in a three-month period. Four in the last two weeks . . . and that's why they had gotten caught.

They weren't taking as much time to plan the jobs anymore. That much was obvious. At the beginning, the robberies had been happening every two or three weeks. Tom decided the time must have been spent working through the details, coming up with a foolproof plan for each one. And it had been working, flawlessly. No one had gotten hurt in any of the heists. In the interview, the FBI special agent in charge said he didn't believe the guns they had used were even loaded.

At the time of their arrest they had made off with well over $130,000 in cash. Tom did the math. That was an average of $10,800 per bank. He didn't know what standard of living these two guys were shooting for, but even splitting the money in half, that came out to just over $21,000 per robber, per month.

No way those guys needed that much money every month. See, he reasoned, that was how greed had sunk them. If they had continued robbing banks at the pace they had started with and been content with that, they'd still have each cleared over $10,000 per month. And they'd still be free, able to live their lives as they pleased.

Now their lives were ruined.

But Tom wouldn't get greedy. And he wouldn't have to split the money with a partner. He'd only need to rob one bank. Not one bank a month, either. Just one bank. And he could take a whole month to plan it out. That was when his unemployment checks would run out, in one month. Then he'd rob the bank. *After* he'd worked out every last detail. If he got even $10,000 for his efforts, with his food stamps kicking in, he and Jean could live on that for three months.

By then he'd be able to finish all these online courses for his IT certification. With that certification in hand, and with his bachelor's degree and his five years of IT experience, there'd be no reason for an employer to turn him down.

It was a perfect plan. Except for the robbing-a-bank part.

Who was he kidding? He could never rob a bank.

But desperate times call for desperate measures, right? That was the saying. These were certainly desperate times. For Tom, as desperate as they could get.

But God would never let him get away with something like this. It was stealing. He'd be breaking one of the Ten Commandments.

But all the money would be insured by the FDIC. It wasn't like the bank customers themselves would be out anything.

"Tom? Your name is Tom, right?"

Tom turned around. He instantly recognized the man standing over his shoulder. It was Alvin, the manager of the Java Stop. Or maybe he was the owner. "Yeah, my name is Tom. How can I help you?"

"I was hoping you'd come in today," Alvin said. "Last night my assistant manager had to quit suddenly. Well, actually, I had to fire him for stealing. I'm kind of in a bind. None of my other workers are assistant manager material. My guess is you're probably overqualified for this. But you've been out of work for a while, haven't you?"

"Yeah," Tom said.

"Would you consider working for me for a month or so? Till I can hire someone on a permanent basis? If you get a job in your field, you can quit right away. No hard feelings. But it would help me close the gap I have right now, and I'm sure I can pay you more than what you're getting on unemployment. So, whatta you say? Can we talk about it?"

"Sure," Tom said. "Pull up a chair."

17

The sun was up, starting to make its presence known. Minutes ago, its rays began to highlight the treetops in Henry Anderson's backyard. Henry lived in an older but well-kept section of cottage homes and bungalows in New Smyrna Beach, between the river and US 1.

The temperature outside was perfect. A slight breeze had found its way over Henry's wooden privacy fence. Sitting in his wicker chair, he could see houses in every direction, but because the neighborhood was so old, most were completely obscured by large, shady trees. Made it feel like he had the place all to himself, like a place out in the country. There weren't any children living in the homes nearby, hadn't been for well over ten years, so it was always real quiet in the morning. Truth was, it was quiet most of the time. He almost never saw any of his neighbors in their backyards . . .

morning, noon, or night.

As Henry closed his Bible, a snowy egret glided across the sky from east to west, on the way to its first tasks of the day. Henry's day wasn't firmed up completely yet. That was part of the reason why he took this time each morning — to get his heart and mind in sync with God, renew the sense that he was the follower and not the one in charge. Beside his wicker chair on a matching wicker table sat a perfectly brewed cup of coffee, compliments of his wife, Myra. She was inside now, preferring to have her quiet time under a floor lamp on her favorite side of the couch.

"Too muggy out there in the morning," she'd said. But it suited Henry just fine. Weather permitting, he always took his quiet time out here. Living in Florida made that possible more months out of the year than in most places.

He closed his eyes and meditated on two Bible passages he'd just read. Psalm 16 in the Old Testament and the story of Martha and Mary in the New, the one in Luke's Gospel. They kind of went together in his mind. David talking about the joy of spending time in God's presence; Mary sitting quietly at Jesus's feet. Then hearing Jesus defend her right to do so by saying she had chosen "the best part."

This really was the best part, he thought. A time to treasure. There was nothing like starting off his day alone with God. He hadn't always thought that way. For years, he'd have been right there nodding his head along with Martha, wondering how it was fair for Mary to be sitting there doing nothing when there was so much work to be done.

But now, he viewed life differently. God had led him through his own version of the "valley of the shadow of death" about six years ago. A number of difficult things had happened to him, both physically and financially. Seemed like that one year, for the better part of the year, it was one thing after another. Those tough times forced him to seek God every morning just to keep his sanity intact, for the strength to make it through the day.

But something wonderful happened through that fiery time. He learned why Jesus said Mary had chosen the best part.

Ever since then, with few exceptions, Henry chose the best part every day. He'd read his Bible awhile and talk to God the way a man talks to a good friend. He'd start off surrendering his day, asking the Holy Spirit to guide him through the day and to help him not focus so much on himself. He'd pray for Myra, their kids and grandkids, and others God brought to mind. Then he'd just pour out whatever was on his heart. Sometimes it was high praises, sometimes cries of desperation, or anything in between. And then he'd just sit there in God's presence — just like he was doing now — and wait for God's peace and rest to come over him and fill his soul.

This morning, Henry waited there an especially long time. His heart became so full and his soul so quiet, he didn't want to move, didn't want to do anything to disturb it. Minutes went by, or was it an hour? He couldn't tell.

Finally, he heard some movement inside the house. Probably Myra finishing up her quiet time, getting things squared away in the kitchen. She hated an untidy kitchen. He opened his eyes and took in a deep breath. Then this strong urge came over him to write down what he was feeling. He reached for his pen and wrote the words "No Greater Place to Be" at the top of a page in his journal.

Then he wrote:

I have no greater place to be, no greater
thing to do,

than to sit at your feet, Lord, gaze at your
beauty,
and listen to your Word.
Your Word speaks peace to me.
With you my soul finds rest.
Fears are stilled; sorrows cease.
Lord, there is no one like you;
no other thing in life that can affect me this
way.
Only you.
Only being with you, spending time alone
with you.
When I am with you this way, in silence
and stillness,
time seems to stand still.
The clock within me slows to your pace.
And it is a lovely pace.
My heart is refreshed, my mind is renewed.
I find I don't ever want to leave this place,
sitting here,
alone with you.
What manner of love is this, that you would
first die for me?
And then, call me your own?
And offer me new mercies every morning.
And invite me to come and draw near to
you, every day.
And I can, every day, without fear
until the day I see you face-to-face.

After a time like this morning, Henry felt a deep longing to meet Jesus face-to-face very soon.

He got up, grabbed his things, and headed into the house. Myra wasn't in the kitchen, though. She was sitting at the computer desk in the family room.

"Whatcha looking at, hon?" he said.

She looked at him then back at the screen. "Some pictures on Facebook. Marilyn must have put them up last night."

"From Italy?"

"Yep. She put up fifteen or twenty of them. They're marvelous. Most are from different places in Rome, but it looks like these last few are from Florence. Guess that's where they're at now."

Henry remembered when he and Myra had gone to Italy a few years ago on their fortieth wedding anniversary. "Let me see." He walked over and massaged her neck, looked at the pictures over her shoulder.

"That was such a wonderful trip," Myra said, touching his hand softly. "Our best one ever."

He thought so too. "I'd go back in a minute if we could afford it." Henry had saved for over five years to pull off that trip. They were doing okay now, living on his modest teacher's pension and Social Security. But it wasn't enough to take trips like that anymore. Neither of them minded, though. Gave them a chance to do something they both loved and could afford more often.

Camping.

Last year, he'd almost finished restoring an old '65 Midas mini motor home they had bought. It was just like the one they'd used to take their boys camping when they were little. Now when they went, it was just him and Myra. Their two boys, Hank and Michael, had families of their own. Both lived out of state.

Myra pointed at the computer screen. "Look at Marilyn's face. I don't think I've ever seen her look so happy."

Henry agreed. It was so wonderful what God had done for them last fall. "I wanted to mention something. When I was praying, I got this burden to pray for Jim and Marilyn's kids. You have any idea why? Heard from any of them lately? You know, since Jim and Marilyn left for Italy?"

"No," she said. "Haven't talked with anyone on the phone for a while. I've been keeping up with things Michele puts on Facebook. But I can't see anything that seems off. 'Course, that doesn't mean anything. Michele's not like some of those

140

foolish girls who air every stray thought that fires off in their head."

Henry thought about it. The impression was still pretty strong. "I'm not thinking it's about Michele and Allan. I'm a little bit concerned about Doug. But mostly about Tom and Jean. Don't know why. Have you seen Jean on Facebook lately?"

"She's got a page, but she hardly ever puts anything up. Occasionally a picture of Tommy or Carly. Maybe she'll write something today. Marilyn posted on her Facebook site she was craving to see her two grandbabies."

"Well, I was thinking. I've still got a few little projects left to finish on our motor home. There's that store over in Altamonte I like to go to for parts. They keep an inventory for the older models. I think I'll head over there today, pick up a part for that gas oven. Maybe I'll stop in on Tom and Jean, see how they're doing."

"Well, you know Tom works during the day, right? He won't be home."

"That's right." He thought a moment. That burden was still right there, as strong as before. "Maybe I'll just stop in on Jean, then, see how she and the kids are doing."

And maybe he'd get some clarity about

why this concern for them had suddenly
become a part of his morning.

18

Henry drove his yellow '68 Chevy Impala south on 17-92, the part for his motor home sitting next to him in a small box. Going through that RV parts store in Altamonte was dangerous. He always saw a thousand little things to buy.

But he and Myra had agreed, they needed to stick to their budget, which meant he could only fix it up a little at a time. The nice thing was, he'd already done enough work so they could take it on road trips. Like this part for the gas oven. Until now, he'd had to cook outside using a gas grill. Once he got this new part installed, they could start cooking inside the motor home again.

He stopped at a busy intersection and sang quietly along with a praise song on the radio. One they sang at church some Sundays. Just then, he felt a familiar rumbling in his stomach. He glanced at his watch. No wonder, it was almost noon.

Tom and Jean's place was in Lake Mary, twenty minutes up the road. Myra had pointed out that Tom would be at work this time of day, but seeing the time, Henry wondered if it still might work out. Henry had met Tom for lunch a handful of times over the past year; Tom always took his lunch break at noon. The main branch was only a five-minute drive from here. The car behind him blared its horn. The light had turned green.

He drove through the intersection and pulled into a gas station on the corner, watched the guy behind him speed by hurling silent profanities into the air. Henry never understood why people got so worked up in traffic. If he and that same man had been at a grocery store, and he'd accidentally blocked the man's shopping cart, the man would have politely said, "Excuse me." And Henry would have just as politely replied, "Oh, I'm sorry," and moved out of the way.

Out here, the same mistake was enough to incite road rage.

Henry pushed the send button on his cell phone and waited through five or six rings. Tom didn't pick up, so he left a short voice mail message. Maybe he should just head on down to Jean's house. But first, he decided to get something to eat. Wouldn't be right to just pop in on her at lunchtime. She'd feel obligated to feed him.

He thought a moment, and just the right place popped into his head. It was right up the road, one of his favorite spots for coffee and sandwiches.

He pulled back into traffic and turned right, headed for the Java Stop.

Tom had only been working at the Java Stop for two days now, but he was starting to get the hang of it. Alvin, the owner, had spent lots of time with him yesterday in moments when little to no customers had been in the store. Unfortunately for Alvin, there had been a lot of those moments. But by the end of the day, Tom had picked it up so well that Alvin decided he'd let him run the show for a few hours today while he ran some errands.

So far, things had been going well. Alvin said he'd be back before lunch, but noon was fast approaching and there was no sign of him. The other two employees knew their jobs, but technically, Tom was supposed to be their supervisor, and he didn't want to feel stupid constantly having to ask them questions once the customer traffic picked up.

At the moment, he was fixing a breve latte, which he'd learned was a latte made with half-and-half instead of milk. Regina, one of the two employees under him, had been busy the last hour doing food prep, partially assembling two or three of each of the Java Stop's most popular sandwiches, getting ready for the lunch hour crowd. Regina divided her time between here and the local community college.

Frank manned the register. He was an odd one. Worked hard, kept a clean appearance, but he was at least in his mid-forties. He seemed like he could be doing a whole lot more with his life than this.

Tom put a lid on the latte, added a cardboard sleeve, and handed it to a smiling blonde woman in her fifties, who thanked him and said, "You just saved my life."

Tom smiled as she walked away. No, he thought, in a way, you just saved mine. Not the woman exactly, but this job. He couldn't believe he'd actually been contemplating the idea of robbing a bank. What was he thinking? Would he really have gone through with it? Probably not, but his level of desperation made him wonder how far down that road he might have traveled.

146

Thankfully, his career as a criminal was over before it had begun. The money here wasn't great. But Tom had done some figuring and decided it might just buy him that three months' time he needed to finish studying for his certification. He still couldn't make their house payments, but he could start making car payments again and the minimum payment on their credit cards. From everything he'd read, it would take the mortgage company over a year to force them out of the house anyway. By then, he was sure he'd be in a high-paying job again.

But he'd done a few more calculations, and he had decided the house was a goner — it was just a matter of time. They would never get out from under the mountain of money they owed on the mortgage. But hey, he was working. Some money was coming in. Real money. Money he was earning with his own two hands, not a government handout, and that felt good.

He was also surprised by how much he enjoyed this kind of work, and he wasn't sure why. He had never done anything like this before. He and Jean had always practiced a conventional marriage. She owned the kitchen, which included cooking all the meals. He took care of the bills and the yard chores. The only break from that was when they grilled something outside. Occasionally, very occasionally, he would make an omelet.

But here he was, making a variety of high-end café drinks and gourmet sandwiches. Alvin had even promised to teach him how to start baking the different kinds of bread they used for sandwiches and pastries. Tom didn't figure he'd be staying on that long, but he still found it all very fascinating.

Besides the low pay, the only setback was the hours. Being the assistant manager involved closing two or three nights a week. On those nights, he wouldn't get home until after nine. Tomorrow would be his first closing shift. Last night, he had to think of something to tell Jean to explain his absence. He had never worked that late at the bank. He'd had to come up with a story — a lie, an outright lie — and he hated doing it.

He knew that was odd — his whole life had been a lie these past five months. But he'd created a system of vague answers, head nods, and ambiguities that made him feel like he was engaged in something that was, at least, less than outright lies.

But he couldn't think of anything ambiguous to tell Jean to explain these late hours, so he simply said the bank was adding a couple of new branches, so for a few months he'd have to work late two or three nights a week to keep up with all the IT work involved. He'd even added another tier to the lie: that he would be getting paid overtime. He didn't know why he'd said it. It was a stupid thing to say. He'd just blurted it out last night over dinner.

Well, that was that, he thought. No sense worrying about it now. He had a job to do.

The little bell above the door rang, signifying more customers. Tom looked up and saw a young couple come in, followed by three college kids, but no one else. He hoped for Alvin's sake that wasn't the extent of the lunch rush. He walked toward the counter to give Frank a hand when he heard the little bell ring again.

He looked up and then instantly froze.

It can't be.

But it was.

Uncle Henry had just walked through the door.

19

It was now dinnertime in Florence, Italy. Jim and Marilyn, along with the entire tour group, were spending their last evening in this magnificent city. Tomorrow the bus would take them to the famous Leaning Tower of Pisa. Marilyn couldn't wait to see it, but she already knew nothing would top her time spent here in Florence.

As much as she loved all the history and architecture in Rome, being in Florence was like living a dream. It was so much more romantic and charming. The colors on all the buildings so much more vibrant and alive than the other cities they'd visited so far. And since Florence was considered the birthplace of the Renaissance, there was so much art to see, not just in the museums but in the streets and squares.

Florence was enchanting.

At the moment, the group was eating dinner in an upscale restaurant right on the banks of the Arno River. Jim and Marilyn sat at a table outside. Marilyn had only to look over Jim's left shoulder to see Ponte Vecchio, the oldest and most famous of Florence's six bridges. They had toured the bridge earlier that afternoon, stopping to take at least a dozen pictures from every angle. Then they'd wandered in and out of all the quaint little shops built right on top of the bridge.

"Can you get a picture of it from here?" Marilyn said. "This is a great angle, all those colorful buildings on either side and the sun setting on the other side. I want to remember this moment just like this."

Jim stood up and walked behind her, near the stone rail.

"Where are you going?"

"I want to remember this moment too," Jim said. "But I want to remember it with you in the picture."

"My hair's a mess."

"It's not a mess. It just looks windblown. You look like a model in a fashion shoot. A photographer would have to pay extra to get that effect on your hair. I'm getting it free."

"You're just being silly."

"You're just being gorgeous. I love that you have no idea how amazing you look right now."

She smiled. A warm feeling came over her. She still wasn't used to how often Jim complimented her. He said things like this all the time now. She never knew what to say when he did.

"Okay, smile."

"You're mostly getting the bridge, right?"

"I've got plenty of the bridge in here."

"But still, take one of just the bridge. I might want to frame it for the house."

"I will. Now smile." He took three shots then returned to his seat. "I got a beautiful shot of the bridge. I think you'll like it."

"It will be a memory I'll cherish forever."

The waiter came up and refilled their drinks. After he walked away, Jim asked, "Is this your favorite part of Florence? Ponte Vecchio?"

"Maybe. It's certainly one of them. I've loved so many of the things we've seen these last two days. It's still hard to believe we're here. So, what's your favorite part of the trip?"

"Mine? All the parts no one will ever see but you and me. It's not one thing, it's all the times we've been alone together. In the hotel rooms, dancing out on that balcony. The times we got to break away from the group for a few hours. I loved walking down those crowded little streets, holding your hand. I love . . . just being with you." He squeezed her hand. "And I didn't realize how much I've missed your smile. I *love* making you smile."

"I am not being ridiculous!"

Jim and Marilyn stopped talking and turned toward the table behind them. It was that young couple, their picture-taking partners, Brian and Amanda Holbart, apparently getting into another spat. Jim and Marilyn hadn't spent a great deal of time with them since the tour began but enough to know they weren't doing very well.

Marilyn had learned they were both Christians who attended church regularly, but as Amanda talked about her church, it seemed to have a lot in common with their old legalistic church, the one in River Oaks they had left months ago. Marilyn recognized the telltale signs of a controlling husband and a wife straining under the weight of his heavy-handed approach.

Amanda had said yesterday they were celebrating their tenth anniversary. And here they were, in this incredibly romantic location, but they couldn't enjoy it.

"You are, Amanda. And keep your voice down. People are beginning to stare."

Jim and Marilyn turned to face each

other. "That's such a shame," Marilyn said quietly. "They've been bickering like that off and on since we met them at the Spanish Steps."

"I know," Jim said. "I wish we could do something to help them."

"Maybe we can." Marilyn glanced back at them over Jim's shoulder. The conversation still appeared tense, but at least they were keeping the volume down.

"How can we? We don't even know them."

"I don't know, but we'll be together several more days. Let's pray God gives us some kind of open door. Maybe we could share a little bit of what we've been through. I think Brian would definitely benefit from hearing your story."

"I was thinking the same thing just before you said it." A worried look came over his face.

"What's wrong?" she said.

"I have absolutely no idea what I'd say. If Brian's at the same place I was a few months ago, and I say the wrong thing or say the right thing the wrong way, he could get pretty upset. Then there'd be all this tension between us for the rest of the trip."

Jim had a point. If this idea backfired, it could ruin their trip as well.

20

Henry walked through the front door of the Java Stop. As he did, he thought he saw something that didn't make any sense: a young man behind the counter who looked very much like his nephew, Tom Anderson, wearing the same garb as the other employees. The young man looked up at him and a startled expression came over his face; he quickly ducked through a doorway and disappeared.

They say people have a twin somewhere in the world, and every now and then Henry would see someone who bore a striking resemblance to someone else he knew. But usually, the person they looked like lived somewhere else, maybe a different state, sometimes even in a different time period. And when you looked at the person more closely, differences would become readily apparent. Henry had only seen this guy for a moment, but he looked *exactly* like Tom.

And he was right here in Lake Mary, where Tom lived. It had to be Tom.

But that made no sense.

Henry walked up to the counter and stood in line. He was greeted by a man named Frank, according to his badge. Frank asked if he was ready to order. Henry had been so distracted, he hadn't even looked up at the menu. He turned around; there was no one behind him. "I'm sorry, I need another minute, if that's okay."

"Sure, take your time."

Henry stepped off to the side and tried to peek through the doorway the man had ducked into, but he didn't see anyone.

Noticing this, Frank said, "Can I help you?"

"I don't mean to be nosy, but I thought I saw someone I know go through that doorway."

"You mean Tom?"

Hearing Tom's name startled Henry. "Uh . . . yes. Tom. Tom Anderson — is that his name?"

Frank nodded. "That's him. He's our new assistant manager. Want me to get him?"

Henry didn't know how to answer that. What was Tom doing here — in a place like this — in the middle of the day? He was supposed to be at the bank. He wouldn't be surprised to learn Tom had taken a second job to help pay the bills, times being what they were. But he'd expect to find him working at night somewhere, not here in the middle of the day. "Yes, that would be nice. Could you get him? And I'll look up there and figure out what I want."

Henry eyed the menu board, trying to get his mind on the task at hand. He saw several things that he had ordered before. One in particular stood out. A Reuben on rye. The thing was, the last time he'd ordered this sandwich was when he'd met Tom here for lunch. Had to be eight or nine months ago.

What was going on?

Frank came back through the doorway and up to the counter. "I'm sorry, Tom stepped outside for a moment. He's on his cell phone. I can send him over to your table when he gets back in."

"That'd be great, thank you."

"Know what you want now?"

"I'll take the Reuben on rye with chips, pickle, and a diet soda."

"You want anything from the café with that?"

"I might get something on the way out."

"You can step on down to the other side of the counter, and we'll have that up for you in a sec."

Henry walked down to where Frank had pointed and joined the others who were now just picking up their food. This was just the craziest thing. He had no idea what to expect from here. But he had a sneaking suspicion that coming to the Java Stop hadn't entirely been his own idea.

Tom put his cell phone back in his pocket. He wasn't talking to anyone. He had just pretended to when the back door had swung open and Frank said, "Hey, Tom, there's a guy at the counter who thinks he knows you." Tom had pointed to his cell phone, and Frank went back inside.

This charade had bought Tom a few extra seconds, at best.

He paced back and forth. His heart raced, his temples pulsated in his head. Uncle Henry, of all people. He had considered the remote possibility that someone he knew might walk through those doors one day. But the Java Stop was a full twenty minutes from where he lived. And there were at least three other coffee shops between here and there.

What should he say? What *could* he say?

He was doomed. The jig was up. That's all there was to it. He'd have to go back in there and face this. If it were someone else

— anyone else — he might be able to come up with a story. But it was Uncle Henry. Uncle Henry wasn't just anyone. Uncle Henry seemed to have a direct line to God. For a moment, Tom even wondered whether God himself had sent him. How else would his uncle have known to come here?

Tom's relationship with God had all but shriveled these past five months. He didn't pray anymore, didn't read his Bible anymore. Of course, he still went to church with Jean and the kids, but he didn't get anything out of it. How could he? He knew God enough to know he wouldn't think too highly of Tom's little scheme.

He looked down at the curb, saw a crunched soda can, and kicked it as far as it would go. Staying out here any longer would just cause more trouble, since he'd have to come up with some kind of lie to tell Frank. He walked back toward the door, opened it, and walked in. Two more people had come up to the counter in his absence. Not much of a lunch hour rush.

"There he is over there," Frank said. "In the corner by the window. Says he's your uncle Henry."

Tom didn't want to look over, but he did. Of course, Uncle Henry was looking right at him. He smiled and waved. Tom saw confusion in his eyes. Tom nodded, forced a smile.

"Regina's almost finished with his order," Frank said. "We're not all that busy right now. Why don't you take it over to him? He was supposed to wait here to pick it up. Guess he doesn't know that."

"I guess I could do that."

"Does he live around here?"

"No, he lives in New Smyrna Beach."

"Did he know you work here?"

"I don't see how he could have," Tom said. But yet, he thought, here he was. Tom walked toward Regina. She was finishing up Uncle Henry's Reuben. "How about I take that off your hands? The guy who ordered it is my uncle. Well, great-uncle."

"Sure," Regina said. "He's right over —"

"I see him."

"Don't forget the pickle."

Tom grabbed a pickle and set it on the plate. He grabbed another one, remembering how much Uncle Henry liked pickles, then headed to his table. He felt like a man walking to the gallows.

"Hey, Tom, how are you?"

Uncle Henry always had such a wonderful smile, such warmth and love shining through his eyes. Tom hated the idea of disappointing him almost as much as the

160

idea of disappointing his father.

Almost, but not quite.

"Hey, Uncle Henry." Tom set the tray down. "Should have guessed you'd pick the Reuben on rye."

"I do love a good Reuben, and they make great ones here."

"Yes, they do." Tom sat across from him. He glanced back at the counter. A few more people had trickled in but nothing Frank and Regina couldn't handle. "Guess you're wondering what I'm doing here."

Uncle Henry smiled. "Well, kind of. I actually called your cell phone a little while ago, assuming you'd be at the bank. I was hoping we could grab lunch together. You know, like we used to whenever I'd come over."

Tom had always enjoyed those visits. "Well, I wish I could eat lunch with you, but as you can see . . . I'm serving it." Uncle Henry didn't reply. Clearly, he was waiting for Tom to explain. "The thing is, I lost my job at the bank. I'm just working here temporarily until I land another IT job." Saying that didn't hurt too badly, Tom thought. But of course, that wasn't the hard part.

"So sorry to hear that. From what I recall, you really liked that job."

"Yeah, I really did." Tom looked down at the table.

"So I guess this layoff came as a surprise?"

Tom looked up, sighed. "Totally. But it wasn't just the fact I got laid off, which was bad enough. Somebody else should have gotten the ax instead of me. A friend — well, someone I thought was a friend — stabbed me in the back, conned the people around me, and stole my job."

"That's too bad," Uncle Henry said. "The world's a dark place sometimes. Cold and dark. When did this happen?"

Should Tom tell him? Did he need to know? He got this feeling that he had better say it straight. This was Uncle Henry. "Five months ago."

Uncle Henry looked shocked. "Five months," he repeated. "Wow. I had no idea. I'm so sorry, Tom. I should've looked in on you sooner."

"No, don't worry about it, Uncle Henry. It's not your fault."

"I know, but getting laid off like that . . . it's a pretty tough thing to go through. If Aunt Myra and I had known, maybe we could have helped you guys out somehow."

"That's kind of you to say."

"That fellow at the counter said you just started working here."

"That's right."

"So . . . what have you been doing before this?"

"Looking for work, mostly. And doing some studying on the internet. I'm trying to get ready for this big test that should help me improve my chances of getting hired."

"Oh. So how's Jean taking it? How are you guys doing emotionally?"

Tom tensed up. Here goes . . .

"She doesn't know."

21

Michele Anderson stared at her cell phone, wrestling with the idea of calling her sister-in-law, Jean. It had been four days since Michele had stopped by Jean's house to give her the news that she and Allan were going to start trying to have a baby right away.

Michele was off today. As a substitute teacher, unfortunately, she didn't get to work every day. She was so grateful for Allan's job, that they could make it on his salary alone. Hopefully, someday soon she'd be a stay-at-home mom like Jean. But her visit with her sister-in-law revealed one area of Jean's life Michele didn't want to imitate: the way she and Tom communicated with each other.

Better said, the way they *didn't* communicate.

It really bothered Michele as she thought about this on her drive home that day. Tom was her big brother, and in some ways he was a fine man. But she didn't like the way he had idolized their father growing up. Tom wanted to be just like him. Sadly, in some areas he had succeeded. Too well.

Their father, on the whole, had been a lousy communicator, proven by the marriage crisis he and Mom had experienced last summer. Mom had been so unhappy for so many years, and her dad had been totally clueless.

Tom was just as clueless as their dad had been. And Jean was walking down that same lonely, unhappy road that Mom had. It was only a matter of time before they ended up in the same place.

Sure, her mother and father had reconciled. It was evident her father had experienced some major changes, in his attitudes and in the way he treated Mom now. They were on their second honeymoon in Italy and seemed to be having a wonderfully romantic time. But she had seen no evidence that her dad had spent any time with Tom trying to undo his bad example.

She looked down at her cell phone again. *Just call her.* She had wanted to get closer to Jean for the last several years and got the feeling on her visit the other day that Jean wanted the same thing. *And that's what friends do, they talk. Good friends move beyond superficial things and talk about things that really matter.*

This really mattered.

She had talked with Allan about all this last night before bed, and he'd agreed with her concerns. His only advice was to take it slow, to remember she was still at the bridge-building stage with Jean. For the last six years they had been more family than friends.

She pressed the send button and waited through four rings.

"Hello?"

"Hi, Jean?"

"Hi, Michele."

"How are you doing?"

"Pretty good. I made it through the morning with most of my sanity intact."

Michele laughed. "What are the kids doing now?"

"They just finished lunch. Tommy is playing with some toys on the family room rug. Carly is still in her high chair, but she looks like one of those bobble head toys you put on the dashboard. I think she's about ready for a nap."

Michele laughed some more. It was nice to hear Jean in a good mood. She hoped this phone call wouldn't spoil it.

"So what are you calling about? You're not

pregnant already."

"No. At least I don't think so." How should she break into this? "But I was thinking about what you said, about you being pregnant, or at least thinking you are."

"Oh, I'm pretty sure I am. Especially after taking that home pregnancy test." Her tone had changed.

Okay, just say it. "How did Tom react when you told him?" Michele waited through a long pause. "You haven't told him yet?"

"No, I haven't." All the joy had left Jean's voice.

"Jean." It came out like a scolding. She had to be careful.

"I wanted to. Believe me."

"I do."

"A few nights ago I was all set. I made a special dinner for him. Grilled steaks, which I never do. Fixed his favorite side dishes and dessert. Then he came home from work in that same lousy mood he always comes home in lately, and it ended in a fight."

"I'm sorry. What was the fight about? No, don't answer that. It's none of my business."

Jean laughed.

"What's funny?"

"The fight was partly about you."

"Me?"

167

"Yeah, Tom got mad that I talked to you about our personal business. He'd be mad now if he knew we were having this conversation. But I don't care anymore."

What Jean said about Tom sounded so much like her dad, or the way her dad used to be.

"Of course," Jean continued, "that's not the only thing we argued about. I told him how you and Allan talk about everything and that I wanted our relationship to be more like that. I wanted him to open up and talk to me about what's eating him up inside about his job. But he refuses to talk about his work with me. Says when he comes home he doesn't want to think about work, let alone talk about it." She paused, released a sigh. "After that, I wasn't in any mood to talk about having babies."

This was so discouraging. Michele felt so bad for her. Men could be such idiots sometimes. Well, some men. "So what are you going to do?"

"Oh, I suppose I'll tell him eventually. If I am pregnant, it's not like there's any big hurry. I thought maybe I'd make an appointment with my doctor, just to be absolutely certain. Then I'll figure out another way to bring it up. But you can be sure it won't include a sirloin steak."

"I'm sorry my brother is being such a moron."

"I'm sorry too. But I have to say, I'm not sorry I'm talking to you. I really appreciate you calling me like this. I don't have any real friends, not any I can really talk to."

"Well, I'm glad I called too. I probably better go, though. But you call me, anytime. I mean it. I'd really like for us to be friends."

"I'd like that very much too," Jean said.

They chatted a few moments more then exchanged good-byes. Michele set her phone down on the end table next to her chair. She had to do something to help Jean and Tom.

She wished she could call her mom. That's who she always called for advice. But her parents were in Italy and Michele didn't want to do anything to spoil it. It wasn't like this was some kind of emergency.

Then she got an idea. Aunt Myra. She could call her. She was only an aunt in a technical sense; she really functioned more like a grandmother. Uncle Henry and Aunt Myra had made it abundantly clear that they really cared about their family and wanted to help them in any way they could.

Day or night, Uncle Henry had said. Call them anytime, day or night.

■ ■ ■ ■

"Hi, Aunt Myra, how are you?"

"Michele, so good to hear from you. It's been too long. But I keep up with you all on Facebook. Sounds like your mom and dad are having a great time in Italy."

"It really does. I'm so happy for them."

"So what's new with you and Allan? How are you enjoying married life?"

"It's been wonderful, Aunt Myra. The honeymoon has definitely not ended yet around here. Except, of course, when I'm at work."

"I'm so glad to hear that. So why are you calling? Is this . . . *that* call? Are you and Allan —"

"No, we're not expecting. Not yet. But we're certainly trying." That sounded a little weird, she thought, for a conversation with your great-aunt. "But someone else you know might be."

"Oh? Really? Who?"

"Well . . . you have to keep it to yourself. You can tell Uncle Henry, but no one else. At least for now."

"Okay, I suppose I could do that. But why all the secrecy?"

"Well, that's part of the problem, part of

the reason why I'm calling you. It's Jean, Tom's wife."

"I'm not sure I get why that's a problem."

"She hasn't told Tom yet, and I've been trying to get her to do that for days."

"Oh, I see. Do you know why she hasn't told him?"

"She says it's because he's been so uptight lately . . . about money, about problems at work."

"I see."

"You do? Because I don't. I can't think of any reason why I wouldn't tell Allan something like that. But Tom and Jean's relationship is so different than ours. It reminds me of what my parents were like before their big crisis last summer."

"Well, your brother is an awful lot like his father. Uncle Henry and I have talked about that before."

"You have? Well, that's really why I called. Could you talk to Uncle Henry, see if he can do something to help Tom? I know Tom really looks up to him, and I think he'd listen to any advice Uncle Henry had to offer. Jean is really hurting. She wants a husband who will just talk to her, share what he's thinking. Tom won't do that. I'd talk to him myself, but I'm his sister. I'd probably just make him mad."

171

"You're not going to believe this, but your uncle drove over there this morning for that very reason. I don't know if he was going to get to talk to Tom, though, because he works during the day, but he was gonna try. He was praying for them this morning, got a strong sense from the Lord that they might need some help."

Michele loved this about her aunt and uncle. Such simple faith. They prayed then obeyed. "Well, they do need help, Aunt Myra. They really do. I hope Uncle Henry can connect with Tom. I'm worried they're heading down the same path my parents were."

But Michele was almost certain Jean wouldn't put up with another twenty-plus years of this like Mom had.

22

Tom waited a few moments to let the words sink in. The shock of what he'd shared was all over Uncle Henry's face. But he'd held his peace, picked up his Reuben, and taken a bite. "I brought you an extra pickle," Tom said.

He could see in Uncle Henry's eyes he was working through all that Tom had said, trying to figure out his next move. He took another bite. Tom glanced over his shoulder; Frank and Regina still had everything well in hand. "I guess you heard me."

Uncle Henry nodded.

"I suppose you're wondering why. Why I haven't told Jean yet, I mean."

"I am. You said five months, right? You've been out of work for five months."

Tom nodded.

"I'm sure you have your reasons, Tom, but do you really think that's wise? I can't think of a single thing I would keep from Aunt

173

Myra for more than a few days. Maybe if she was out of town or wasn't feeling well."

Tom had no idea how to explain this. He held little hope he'd come up with something Uncle Henry would buy. "I never intended for it to take this long. I thought I'd find a new job within a week or two at the most. I mean, I'm an IT guy. It's a cutting-edge line of work. There's this guy, Fred, who used to come in here every day like me, looking on the internet for work. He's an IT guy too. He got a new job within three weeks. I thought it would be like that."

Uncle Henry finished chewing. "But you've been looking for five months?"

Tom nodded. He saw where this was going. "Fred got the job right away because he had this certification I'm working on. I think that's why I keep getting overlooked."

"That could be the reason," Uncle Henry said.

"I'm sure it is. I should've taken care of this certification thing years ago. Dad wanted me to right after I got the bank job, but I kept putting it off. It didn't seem like a big deal at the time. I had just gotten my bachelor's degree and they hired me at the bank without the certification, even promoted me twice. I can do the work either way. This certification thing is really just a formality."

Reaching for a pickle, Uncle Henry said, "And you think that's the only reason you keep getting overlooked in these interviews?"

"I'm sure it is." Tom could tell Uncle Henry thought it might be something else.

"This Fred guy you mentioned, you think he told his wife he'd lost his job?"

There it is, Tom thought. Uncle Henry thinks I'm being punished for hiding this from Jean. "I'm pretty sure he told his wife," Tom said. "In fact, I know he did. But that's not why he got the job. It's this certification thing. He had it, I didn't. End of story."

Uncle Henry chomped on his pickle. His smile said he didn't think so. "So let me get this straight . . . every day you leave the house, and Jean thinks you're heading off to work?"

"Pretty much," Tom said.

"And you're okay with this?"

"I'm not okay with it, Uncle Henry. But for now I'm kind of stuck. What choice do I have?" He instantly regretted saying that.

"I can think of one."

"I can't tell her. Not now. Not after all this time."

"You think it'll get easier if you let more time pass?"

"No, I'm sunk no matter what I do at this point. But I think I'll be less sunk if I have a new job lined up when I finally do tell her."

"But you've got a new job now. Here at the coffee shop. Why not tell her now?"

"This isn't a good job." Tom looked around, realizing how that sounded. Frank and Regina were too far away to hear. Still, he leaned forward and said in a lower voice, "I don't even make enough here to pay our mortgage payment. It's barely enough to cover everything else in our budget." Then he remembered. "Well, not everything. I can't even think about adding health insurance back in yet. My plan is to work here a few months until I get my IT certification. Then I'll get the right kind of job, and then I'll break the news to Jean."

Tom studied Uncle Henry's face. Disappointment was written all over it. But it was something less than disgust, which was what he'd see on his father's face if he were here. "Like I said, I'm sunk with Jean either way. We're probably gonna need to go in for marriage counseling to get through this, once she finds out what I've done."

"Wives do put a lot of stock in that thing we call trust," Uncle Henry said.

Tom turned to see how things were doing

at the counter. A few more people had come in, but it still wasn't bad. But it might give him an excuse to cut this conversation short. "Well, look, I'm real sorry you had to come in here and find out about this, this way. I can tell you're disappointed, and I don't blame you."

"It's not that, Tom."

"You're not disappointed?"

"Well, yes, I guess I am. I'm not saying I can't understand why you thought you needed to keep this from her. I'm guessing it had something to do with trying to protect her, right?"

"That was certainly it at the beginning," Tom said. "But as more and more time passed, I began to realize how upset she'd be with me not being straight with her all along. I can see her being really upset. What am I saying? She's going to totally freak out. After I climb out of the rubble from that earthquake, I just know she'd insist my parents get involved, which means my dad would find out. He'd insist on looking into my finances, which are a total mess right now."

Tom's fingers began to tremble. His heart began to pound. "I can't have that. Do you understand? I can't." He was raising his voice. "You've got to promise me, Uncle

177

Henry. You won't tell my dad."

"Tom, your father's in Italy now, I —"

"Promise me you won't tell my dad!" Tom was almost yelling. "I'll tell him. And Jean," he said. "But not now. Not until I get this situation under control."

Henry felt so bad for his nephew. Tom was so upset, he was shaking. "Okay, Tom, settle down," he said gently. "I won't say anything to your dad for now, or Jean. But I love you too much not to say I think you're making a terrible mistake. The longer you let this thing go on, the worse it'll get. For you, for Jean . . . for everyone involved."

Tom slid his chair back. It seemed he was about to get up. "Maybe I am. No, I'm sure I am. But it's too late now to turn back. I've got a plan, and I've got to see it through. And I need to know you're not gonna do anything to interfere."

That stung. Is that what Tom thought Henry was doing here? Interfering? But he had to set his personal feelings aside. They weren't important. His poor nephew had fallen into a pit. A deep one. That's what mattered. He was lashing out because he imagined Henry might do something to make the hole even deeper. *Lord, give me wisdom.* "I can assure you, Tom, I would never do anything to hurt you or Jean. Your aunt and I love you, Michele, and Doug like you were our own kids." Henry had to get control of his emotions. Wouldn't do for him to start getting weepy right now.

"I know you love me. Really, I do." Tom was talking much more quietly. "But for now, I need you to love me in a different way . . . by letting me do this thing my way. Can you do that for me?" He stood up.

"Tom, I won't talk to anyone else except Aunt Myra without talking to you first." Uncle Henry didn't like it, but he felt he could at least agree to that much.

After all, what choice did he have right now?

23

Henry pulled into the driveway of their little bungalow in New Smyrna Beach. On the way home he'd been totally distracted. The shock of seeing Tom behind a lunch counter at a coffee shop didn't upset him near as much as listening to him explain how and why he had covered up his job loss for the past five months. He had no idea Tom was in such bad shape, not just financially but spiritually.

He'd thought he knew Tom pretty well . . . until now. The Tom he knew would never have thought of doing something like this. It seemed so out of character. Whatever angle he played over in his mind, Henry still couldn't come up with a rationale for Tom's behavior.

It was deception on a massive scale.

Henry had read a newspaper story last year about a young man from a wealthy family who had murdered his wife because she'd discovered he had been living a lie for over a year. He had quit attending a university due to failing grades but couldn't face the shame of his parents learning about this failure. He hadn't just hid this from them but from her also. After his wife found out, she planned to tell his folks, and he decided he had to stop her.

At the time Henry read the story, it had seemed totally outrageous and far-fetched. But now . . . This was their family. Tom was their nephew. What could he be thinking that could possibly justify doing something so outlandish and absurd?

As he sat there in the driveway pondering this, flashes from his past began to surface. The tension and anxiety he used to feel every day living under the iron claw of his own father, Gerald Anderson.

Henry knew Tom's father, Jim, had been hard on his kids growing up. That came out last summer when he and Marilyn went through their marriage crisis. But Jim was a teddy bear compared to Henry's father back in the sixties. Gerald Anderson was a cruel, angry man. He was all about business and making money. Lots of money. "You can never have too much money," Henry had heard him say many times. He'd made his fortune in real estate and insisted his two sons follow in his footsteps.

He had picked out the colleges they would attend, the kind of clothes they would wear. Even the high-society families his sons' wives would come from. Getting a proper wife was all part of cultivating the right image. Henry's older brother, Jim's father, was all too happy to comply. He'd bought into everything their father was selling.

But not Henry.

One memory stood out above the rest. He was sitting in a car in the driveway back then too. He had hand painted all kinds of hippie and anti-war slogans on it. Henry's hair, now almost gone, went halfway down his back. He remembered sitting there, his stomach grinding and churning as he squeezed the steering wheel till his knuckles turned white. Working up the nerve as he rehearsed in his mind what he would say once he walked inside their enormous home.

That weekend, his father had laid down the law. Henry had to cut his hair, trade in that stupid car, switch from an education to a business major, and dump that ridiculous girlfriend, Myra, because she had the misfortune of being raised by a single mom in a trailer park.

If Henry refused, he would be cut off.

Thrown out of the house, left to fend for himself. Henry might have found a way to meet most of his father's demands, even though he'd have hated giving in to a single one. But he loved Myra with all his heart. She was the one, the only one for him. He knew he could never part with her, no matter what privileges his father threatened to take away.

That day, he'd gotten out of his little Bug, stormed into his father's den, and told him "No deal."

"You know I'm serious about cutting you off if you defy me," his father had said. "Dead serious. You walk out that door, there's no turning back."

Henry turned around and headed for the door. All he said on his way out was, "Myra and I will send you an invitation to the wedding." They didn't talk for years after that.

Henry hadn't thought about these things for so long and wondered why they came to mind just now. Then it dawned on him. One of the last things Tom had said in their conversation at the Java Stop, and his reaction to the idea that his father would find out what he had done. He didn't want Jean to know, yes. But Tom hadn't gotten emotional until he started talking about his dad. He got louder and his hands even trembled.

Is that what this was about? That lousy Anderson legacy? Harsh, demanding fathers begetting more harsh, demanding fathers. No one ever being truly happy, or ever measuring up to their father's expectations or experiencing the simple joy of hearing the words "I'm proud of you, son."

Henry had broken free of the Anderson curse, but it had cost him dearly. As he got out of his car and considered the marvelous lady waiting for him just inside and the children they had raised together, he knew it was all worth it. He'd never once regretted his decision to walk away and leave his family fortunes behind.

But he suspected his older brother, Tom's grandfather, had pretty much treated Jim just as badly. And he was pretty sure — especially after everything that had come out last summer — that Jim had followed in his father's infamous footsteps.

Henry walked toward the front door, carrying the white paper bag with his leftover sandwich and the little box containing the RV stove part. *Wonder what Myra will make of all this?*

"What was that for?" Myra asked as their lips parted.

Henry couldn't help himself; he had

walked in the house, spun Myra around in the kitchen, and given her the kiss and hug of a young man in love. "What, can't a man kiss his wife when he has a mind to?"

She left her arms around his neck and said, "You can kiss me like that anytime you want."

After giving her one more peck, he let her return to unloading the dishwasher. He stood by the cabinet and lent a hand. "I just had quite a lunch," he said. "Got a lot to share with you."

"You mean with Jean? Did you stop in and see her and the kids?"

"No, I had lunch with Tom."

"Really? That's wonderful. I got a phone call while you were gone, from Michele. I heard some news from her I want to share with you. Actually, she called hoping I might get you to visit Tom. Did you stop by the bank?"

"No, not the bank. He doesn't work there anymore."

"What? He got laid off?"

Henry nodded. "But you can't tell a soul. Not yet, anyway."

"That's such a shame. I mean about Tom losing his job. But why can't I tell anyone?"

"I'm going to need a few minutes to explain, and you're not gonna believe the story I'm about to tell." He set the white paper bag on the counter beside her. "There's half of a Reuben in there if you want it. Lost my appetite after hearing what Tom had to say. So, what's your news? What did Michele have to say?"

"It wasn't anything she said about her, or Allan. It was about Jean. Jean told her she's pretty sure she's pregnant, that she's known for a little while, but for some reason, she hasn't told Tom yet."

"Oh my."

"Michele was hoping you'd find a way to talk with Tom, get him to start opening up a little with Jean, start sharing his heart more. Sounds like they both need some help in that area."

Henry pointed to the little white bag. "You better eat that Reuben now if you're interested. Pretty good chance you won't want it if you wait to hear what I have to say."

24

Marilyn walked back toward a little souvenir booth the tour group had passed about thirty minutes ago. As she did, she kept looking back over her shoulder, but she wasn't noticing the most obvious thing in view, the Leaning Tower of Pisa. She was looking at Jim standing just below it. Each time she saw him she nudged him with her prayers, asking God to give him the courage to talk with Brian Holbart and give him the wisdom to know what to say.

Today, Jim and Marilyn had woken up at a charming bed-and-breakfast villa just outside the town. As they ate breakfast, they noticed the Holbarts didn't say a word to each other. At one point, Marilyn looked up to find Brian eating alone. Jim had said if God gave him an opportunity today, he would try to talk to Brian.

Well, the opportunity had come.

After breakfast, the group was led on a

one-hour guided tour, where they learned some fascinating facts about the infamous tower — not just details about its history but all the efforts being made now to keep it from leaning over too far. Jim had whispered to her, "Imagine your claim to fame as a city is that 850 years ago some lousy engineers built this bell tower on a puny foundation with unstable soil. If they had built it right, nobody would probably even visit this town."

After the tour had ended, the group was given two hours to walk around on their own. Of course, everyone immediately began taking turns posing for the obligatory picture where you stand just far enough away from the tower and hold out your hand so that it looks like you are keeping it from toppling over altogether. Jim and Marilyn had opted to skip that picture and instead asked Brian and Amanda to snap one of them in a more affectionate pose. Jim stood behind her, wrapped his arms around her, and snuggled his chin on her shoulder. When Jim had offered to take a picture of them, Amanda politely declined.

A few minutes later, Marilyn had noticed Brian standing under the tower by himself. Amanda was nowhere in sight. That's when she whispered to Jim, "Now's your chance."

Jim's eyes bugged out a moment, and he shook his head no.

A few moments later, he changed his mind. "Do you still want to buy those Leaning Tower figurines you were looking at before?" Marilyn nodded. "Maybe you could do that now," he said, "while I talk to Brian?"

"I'll be praying for you," she had replied.

Now she was standing by that booth. She turned to look back once more. Jim was definitely saying something to Brian. Across the field, she couldn't see his mouth moving, but his hands were talking up a storm.

She wanted this to go well for another reason beyond just the obvious desire to help out this young couple. She hoped it would inspire Jim to initiate a similar conversation with his own son when they got home to Florida in a few days.

"But Jim, she's just being ridiculous. Do you know what she said to me this morning? She said, 'I'm not sure you even love me anymore.' Can you believe that? I must have told her I loved her half a dozen times since we got here. I spent thousands of dollars to take her on this 'romantic adventure,' used up half of my vacation time, and she says that to me?" Brian seemed almost at the breaking point.

"Mind if I ask why you took this trip in the first place?"

"To prove to her that I *do* love her, that she means more to me than my business. She's been saying for months that I don't love her the way I used to, that my business and even my friends matter more to me than she does."

"And that's not true?"

"Of course it's not true. We're here, aren't we?"

"I see you here," Jim said. "But where is she? Where's Amanda?"

"Right," Brian said, looking down as he leaned against the railing. "Where is she?"

Jim turned around and leaned next to him. "See, Brian, changing locations — even coming to a romantic place like this — won't fix these kinds of things." That reminded Jim of something he heard in a sermon a few Sundays ago. "My pastor said in a sermon once that changing things on the outside can't fix problems in our hearts. That's like a dog running down the hall trying to get away from its fleas. He doesn't realize the fleas go wherever he goes."

"Our problems certainly followed us here to Italy," Brian said.

"I'm not trying to judge you. You know

that, right? I'm just trying to be a friend. My wife and I almost called it quits last summer, after twenty-seven years of marriage. Well, she almost did. I was so dull, I didn't even see it coming. It turned out, she had been unhappy, seriously unhappy, for years. One day I came home and she was gone."

A startled look came over Brian's face. "Really?"

"Really. We're on this Italy trip for the same reason you guys are. It's like a second honeymoon for us. I spent the money and took off the time from work for the same reasons you did."

Brian sighed. "But it's working for the two of you. Every time I see you, you're both smiling. Always holding hands, always touching. Amanda's even talked about it. She points at you two and says, 'That's what it looks like when a couple is in love.' She said it, implying, not like us."

Jim almost got choked up hearing this. "Brian, just last summer I thought I had lost Marilyn for good. I had so destroyed our relationship, she didn't even want to be with me, wouldn't even talk to me for almost two months."

Brian stood up straight. "I find that hard to believe, looking at you now."

191

"It's true. I would never have imagined back then that we'd ever feel these kinds of feelings for each other again. I thought they were gone for good." Jim's eyes started welling up with tears. He quickly blinked them back.

"You really *are* serious," Brian said. "So what did you do? How did you win her back?"

"For starters, I learned how to dance."

"What?"

Jim laughed. "It's a long story. Maybe I'll tell it to you sometime. The thing is, I had to be willing to do whatever it took. And I had to learn from scratch what the Bible says about being a good husband. We're not like the animals, we don't have all these instincts that click into place and get us doing the right things at the right times. If we're going to learn them, we have to be taught. Why don't you give me your email address and I'll send you some of the materials my dance instructor gave me?"

"About dancing?"

"No, about marriage. About relationships. About why they fail and what makes them work. But I'd like to share one thing with you right now, something that just might help you salvage what's left of this Italy trip."

"I wish you would," Brian said. "I'm open

to try anything."

Just then Jim caught the hand signal of a father getting ready to take a picture of his family in front of the Tower. He and Brian were standing in the way. "How about we get out of this family's picture first. Let's go stand over there." They moved about twenty paces away. Jim looked around and saw Marilyn standing at the edge of the field, not far from the row of souvenir booths that ran along the main road. She waved, made a little hand gesture to indicate she was praying. Jim wanted to wave back but didn't want to interrupt their conversation. He was close to wrapping up anyway.

"Brian, if I asked you what's really bothering Amanda, what's really upsetting her and making her feel frustrated about your relationship, could you tell me what she'd say?"

Brian thought a moment. "No, I'm not sure I could."

"And how much talking about your problems have the two of you been doing since you got here?"

"You mean how much fighting? We're not doing a lot of talking. But I understand what you're saying. We've been talking a lot."

"And yet with all that talking," Jim said,

"you're not any closer to understanding what's going on inside her, are you?"

Brian shook his head no.

"I think the reason is you're probably doing the same thing I did for years, the same things most guys do with their wives. See, we make the mistake of thinking communication is about understanding our wives' *words.* But the truth is, good communication is more than that. It's about understanding the *feelings* behind those words. It's about listening to Amanda's heart, not just the things she says. And it's definitely not about you making sure she understands and agrees with what you're saying."

"Listening to Amanda's heart," Brian repeated. "I don't think I'm any good at that."

"Maybe not now, Brian. But you can learn this. I'm serious. I was as thick as these medieval walls around here, and I learned how. The starting point, though, is simple. You have to first accept that this is the goal when you and Amanda are talking. It's not making her see your points, it's about understanding her heart, and then not reacting in anger or getting defensive when she finally does open up and share what's bothering her. Man, that part's real important. You get angry, you'll shut her right down, blow the whole thing."

Brian nodded. It seemed the lights were coming on.

"I suggest you go find her, wherever she is, and apologize to her as strongly as you can. Tell her you really want to understand her, and ask her if she'll hit the reset button and give you another chance. If she will, then you just start asking her questions and keep asking her more questions. *What* questions. *Why* questions. Anything that will give you a clue about how she's really feeling. And then shock her by not correcting her or adjusting anything she says. This conversation is not about fixing Amanda. It's about hearing her heart. I can almost promise you, you do this and you'll see progress right away, maybe even a mini-breakthrough."

At some point, while Jim was talking, a tear had slipped down Brian's face. He wiped it away, shook Jim's hand, and said, "I can't thank you enough, Jim. If you'll excuse me, I've got to go find someone."

As Brian walked away and blended in with the crowd, Jim spotted Marilyn walking across the field in his direction, reading something on her cell phone. He met her halfway.

■ ■ ■ ■

Marilyn put her cell phone back in her purse after receiving a text from her good friend Charlotte back home. "Well," she said, "how'd it go?"

Jim gave her a hug. "Pretty good, I think. He listened, and now he's heading off to find Amanda. Not sure how she's doing right now, but I think he's in a better place. If he does what I said, who knows?"

"So, you don't think we have to spend our last two days avoiding each other?"

"I hope not."

She hugged him again. "I'm so proud of you." As they walked toward the cathedral next to the Leaning Tower, she wondered how much this happy mood would change if she brought up the topic Charlotte had texted her about a few moments ago.

25

For the next hour and a half, Jim and Marilyn leisurely toured the two other historical buildings next to the Leaning Tower, the cathedral and baptistery. All the while holding hands. The buildings were magnificent architectural works in their own right, but obviously the Leaning Tower was the thing. She couldn't take her eyes off it whenever they were outside. It was just such an icon; she'd seen it in so many movies and magazine pictures throughout her life. It was hard to imagine she was actually standing there, seeing it with her own eyes.

As they walked, it became clear to Marilyn that Jim was relieved at how well his time with Brian had gone, like a great weight had been lifted off his shoulders and now he could enjoy himself again.

She wasn't surprised; Jim had always been an effective communicator in his business and social settings. But during their small group meetings in their new church back home, Jim rarely shared his thoughts out loud. She'd get to hear him on the car ride home and tried to encourage him to share more often. She didn't know if his reluctance was due to feeling out of his element talking about spiritual things, or if he still felt unworthy talking about marriage issues.

Whatever it was, she kept praying God would build up Jim's courage so that he'd feel comfortable initiating conversations with their two sons back home. Both needed him in their lives, especially now that Jim was becoming the kind of husband she had always wanted him to be. Although she continued to have concerns about Doug, it was Tom who especially needed his father now.

"Are you okay?" Jim asked as they walked out of the baptistery into the bright sunlight. "You seem a little distracted."

Marilyn still wasn't used to this, Jim being perceptive enough to ask about her shifting moods. She liked it, but it still caught her off guard. Instinctively, she reached for her cell phone in her purse and thought about Charlotte's text. Should she bring it up now? "I want to tell you, but I'm just not sure this is the right time."

"Well, now you have to tell me, because

I'll be totally distracted until you do. Is it something bad? I saw you looking at your cell phone as you walked across the field. Is everything okay back home?"

"Everything's fine back home. It's just . . ."

"Just what?"

"I got a text from Charlotte." Marilyn paused, not sure what to say next. Initially, after she and Jim had reconciled last summer, Jim was a little skeptical about Marilyn's friendship with Charlotte, since Charlotte was the woman Marilyn had stayed with when they were separated. But after he'd gotten to know her, Jim liked her a lot.

"So, what did it say? Was it bad news?"

"How much more time until we have to meet up with the group?"

Jim looked at his watch. "We have about twenty minutes."

"That's perfect. Let's go over to that little café, and I'll tell you about it over a cappuccino."

When they were seated at a little round table, Jim said, "Guess this is kind of a big thing, considering all the buildup."

"It's an in-between-size thing," she said. "It's something I've been wanting to talk to you about for a few weeks, but we were so busy getting ready for the trip it never seemed like the right time. Charlotte's text just kind of pushed it to the front." Back home, she'd have never imagined the right time would be sitting here in Pisa, sipping cappuccinos in view of the Leaning Tower.

"So I don't need to feel tense anymore?" Jim said.

"You feel tense?"

"A little."

"I'm sorry, you have my permission to stop feeling tense." She reached across the table and took his hand, hoping what she was about to say wouldn't cause his tension to return. "Did I mention to you that Charlotte started volunteering for a crisis pregnancy center they opened in River Oaks?"

"There's a crisis pregnancy center in River Oaks?" Jim asked.

"I guess I didn't mention it. Yeah, it opened a few months ago. Several Christian churches in the area have gotten behind it. Ours is one of them. I've been seeing something about it in the announcements several Sundays in a row."

"Where is it located?"

"It's in a little storefront on the edge of the business section downtown."

"Doesn't seem like the kind of thing folks in River Oaks would go for," he said.

She knew what he meant. River Oaks was

such an upscale community. "They gave us a little trouble," she said. "The town council, I mean. But after we assured them this wasn't going to be a political thing, that the center's really just there to help young girls who get in trouble, they backed off. Rich girls and upper-middle-class girls get in trouble that way too, you know."

"Did you say 'us' and 'we' just now?"

Oops. She had. Immediately, she felt Jim's hand tense up. "I did, but let me explain."

"Are you involved with this thing already?"

Was this the old Jim surfacing now? It almost seemed like it. "I shouldn't have said it that way. I haven't really gotten involved yet, but I want to. I've just been talking with Charlotte about it on the phone. I guess I said it that way because I already feel connected to what's going on, through all my chats with Charlotte, I mean."

Jim's face and hand relaxed. But his reaction made her realize she was right to approach the subject with caution. After their reconciliation, Jim had agreed she could keep her job at Odds-n-Ends, the little gift shop downtown, which was a major growth step for him. But she had no idea how he'd react to the idea of his wife volunteering at a crisis pregnancy center. The old Jim would have said something like, "No way, you're not getting mixed up with those kinds of people."

"So what do they do at this place?" he asked and sipped his cappuccino.

"Mostly counsel young girls who get pregnant. Their goal, obviously, is to try to gently steer them away from getting an abortion. So they offer free pregnancy tests and ultrasounds and even do some career counseling, if needed. Charlotte loves it there."

"So that's what the text is about? She's wanting you to sign up."

"Sort of. Not sign up to join. Not yet. But they're having an orientation class next week, the day after we get home. She texted me because today is the last day to sign up for that. After the orientation class, you can decide whether you want to be a part of it, the kind of things you might do, and how much time you can put in. But I promise, Jim. I won't sign up until I talk to you about it, make sure you're okay with it. Right now, I'm just asking if I can take this orientation class."

"I don't like the sound of that."

Oh no, here goes. Lord, help me to be patient with this residue of the old Jim. "What do you mean?"

"It sounds like you're asking my permission, like you feel you have to. I can tell this whole thing — talking to me about it — has made you all tense and nervous. I'm sorry, hon," he said, squeezing her hand tenderly. "I'm sorry for all the years I treated you so harshly, all the times I treated you like a child. You shouldn't have to ask my permission for something like this. We're partners now. Friends. You don't have to be afraid to talk to me anymore, about anything."

Tears welled up in her eyes.

"So, I can text Charlotte back and say yes?" She reached for her napkin and wiped the tears from her eyes.

"Of course you can." He looked at his watch. "But maybe you should wait until we've rendezvoused with the group. We're supposed to be at that spot in five minutes." He took the last sip of his cappuccino and stood up.

She did the same. Then she walked around the table, put her arms around him, and gave him a seriously passionate kiss.

26

Jim and Marilyn gathered at the rendezvous spot with the rest of the group, just beyond the tall castle-like wall bordering the Pisa complex. The bus was running late. The tour guide had asked everyone to stay put, saying the bus should be here within the next five to ten minutes.

"I can't believe our trip will be over in one more day," Marilyn said. This afternoon the bus was going to take them one hundred miles north to the picturesque seaside town of Portofino. They'd spend the evening and morning there, then head back to Rome tomorrow afternoon.

"Not one more day," Jim said. "Two more. Don't you remember? I added an extra day so you could drive like a crazy woman on the Autostrada in that BMW."

Marilyn gasped. She had completely forgotten. She reached over and gave him a hug. "Since the bus is late, I think I'll step over there away from the crowd and give Charlotte a quick call. I could text her, but I'd rather tell her in person, if that's all right."

"Sure, go ahead. But keep looking over here. Charlotte can be quite a talker. Don't want you to get too distracted and miss the bus."

Marilyn shook her head. "Now you know that's not going to happen. I won't be five minutes." Marilyn pulled out her cell phone. She dialed the number and waited through a handful of rings.

"Oh my gosh! Marilyn, is that you?"

"It's me."

"You're still in Italy, right?"

"I am."

"I can't believe it. You're calling me from Italy. And you're on your second honeymoon. How's that going, by the way? He treating you right?"

"He's treating me wonderfully," she said. "I couldn't ask for more."

"Aww, I'm so glad. So happy for you, for the both of you. I can't believe you're calling me all the way from Italy. I was just hoping to get a text. Is that what you're calling about, my text?"

Marilyn smiled. Each time Charlotte said "your" or "for," her Boston accent shined through. "It is. But I'm just so excited about how the conversation with Jim went, I thought I'd call you instead."

"So he said yes? You can go to the orientation meeting?"

"He did, and it wasn't even a difficult conversation."

"I thought for sure he'd turn you down flat. I never thought he'd go for this."

"I was pretty surprised, pleasantly surprised, how well he responded. So go ahead and sign me up."

"I will. I'll call them as soon as we get off the phone. Oh Marilyn, this thing fits you like a hand in glove. I'm doing the whole RN bit, of course. But I think you'll make a great mentor. You have such a way of talking, and you're such a great listener. And you have an amazing relationship with your daughter. These girls down here are going to be so blessed once you get trained and plugged in."

"I hope so." Marilyn had never done any counseling before. But Charlotte said they weren't looking for a professional, just someone with a caring heart and a listening ear. Most of these girls came from broken families, and many didn't have good relationships with their mothers.

"You just treat them like you treat your

daughter," Charlotte said, "and you'll do just fine. So where are you right now?"

"I'm standing about one hundred yards away from the Leaning Tower of Pisa."

"No way."

Marilyn walked a few steps over to where she could see it through the big stone arch. "I'm looking at it right now."

"Really? Wait a minute. I'm on my computer. Let me do something."

Marilyn heard a bunch of clicks as Charlotte typed on the keyboard. "What are you doing?"

"I'm Googling the Leaning Tower. Wait a minute, there it is. I'm using Google Maps, you know, the camera view, the one that puts you right there on the street. I'm looking at that arch right now. It's through this big castle wall, right? And you can see the Leaning Tower right through it?"

"That's the one," Marilyn said. "I'm standing right there."

"What's it like? Seeing it up close?"

"It's unreal. But the whole trip's been that way. Every time I see one of those famous landmarks, it's the same feeling. The Colosseum, the Vatican, Ponte Vecchio in Florence, and now this."

"Ponta-what?"

"Ponte Vecchio, it's that fancy old bridge

with all the little shops built right on it. Didn't you see the pictures I put on Facebook?"

"Oh yeah, that's right."

"Well, look, the bus just arrived and Jim is waving at me. I better go."

"I guess you better. It was so nice that you called. You'll be home in a few days, right?"

"Don't remind me. I don't want this trip to end."

"Well, I'll pray that your last few days go by real slow then. You and Jim have a great time, and I'll see you soon."

Marilyn hung up and threaded her way through the crowd to join Jim. After they boarded the bus and began to drive off, Marilyn took one last look at the Leaning Tower, which she could see just over the stone wall.

So unreal.

An hour later, as the tour bus drove northwest along the coast, Jim and Marilyn and the rest of the group were treated to a spectacular Mediterranean sunset. Jim turned to Marilyn and said, "Do you realize where we're going?"

"Portofino, right?"

"Yeah, but this is the *real* Portofino.

Remember that little boat ride we took at Universal Studios CityWalk? That fancy Italian hotel we stopped at?"

Marilyn remembered. How could she forget? Their new church had created a small group for couples who wanted to work on improving their marriages. One of the first things their group leader talked about was the need for them to commit to a date night each week. He strongly recommended the husbands take the lead on making this happen. Jim took this totally to heart. Except for a few occasions, they hadn't missed a single week. "That was our first date after we got back together," she said.

"Well, that fancy hotel — which Universal called Portofino — was modeled after the place we're going to this evening. I've seen some pictures of it. You're going to love it. The real thing is *so* much better."

"I can't wait." Marilyn looked across the aisle. She whispered to Jim, "Do you see that?"

"I've been watching them for the last few hours. They seem to be doing much better."

Brian and Amanda. Not only were they together, they were talking in gentle tones, smiling on occasion, and right now they were actually holding hands. "Thanks to you," she said.

"I don't know about that."

"Well, I do. I'm proud of you for taking the chance. And look, the Lord rewarded your courage."

Jim smiled and squeezed her hand. Seeing the Holbarts gave Marilyn hope for Tom and Jean. Maybe Jim would get similar results, if she could only convince him to follow through and get together with Tom when they got home.

27

About thirty minutes later, they began to see several signs for Portofino. The trip was almost over, and Marilyn still hadn't figured out the conversion from kilometers to miles, but it was clear they were almost there. Their conversation so far had been light and easy. Marilyn decided to take a chance and bring up the idea of Jim talking to Tom, while the evidence of his success with the Holbarts was still fresh.

Since the Holbarts were across the aisle, she kept her voice just above a whisper. "Can I talk to you about something?"

"We've been talking the entire time since we left Pisa, so I guess you want to talk about something a little more serious."

"Not serious, just . . . well, I guess it is a little serious."

"What is it?"

"We've talked about it a few times already. It's about Tom. I was thinking that since your talk with Brian went so well this afternoon, you might feel a little more confident to reach out to Tom when we get home."

"I don't see how they're connected. Brian's a stranger. Tom is my son."

"How does that make a difference?"

"Well, things did go well with Brian, but what if they hadn't? Not a big deal. Worst-case scenario, we'd avoid each other until tomorrow, then go our separate ways and never see each other again. If it doesn't go well with Tom . . ."

"I don't understand what you're afraid of." She shook her head. "I'm sorry, that came out a little edgy."

"Yeah, it did."

"It's just I genuinely don't understand how you think it would go badly. Tom loves you, in a big way." So much so, Marilyn thought, she wondered sometimes if Tom didn't love Jim more than he loved her. "I think he'd be wide open to anything you have to say."

Jim sat back in his seat. She couldn't read his face. Maybe she should back off. She waited a few moments more. "What are you thinking?"

"I'm remembering a number of conversations with my own father that ended badly.

Conversations we had after I moved out, after you and I got married. And I'm remembering the ugly feelings I felt about him after. I don't want Tom feeling that way about me. Ever."

"But Jim, your relationship with Tom is way better than what you had with your father. Don't you think?"

Jim looked out the window. "Maybe. Maybe not. I tried leading my family the way my dad did, and look where you and I ended up. I love Tom, and I'd like to think we could talk about anything, but you know we're not that close, not like you and Michele are. I wouldn't know where to begin."

Marilyn wasn't sure about that, either. But there had to be a way. "Maybe you should just start slow, not start out with a goal of talking about everything in one night. Maybe that first night you don't talk about anything serious at all. Maybe you just go to a ball game or play a round of golf."

"We haven't golfed together in years."

"Well, there you go. You could go golfing together. There's lots of time to talk while playing golf, right?"

"I suppose," he said. "But Harold and I have been golfing for years. We never talk about anything that matters. And I'm not sure Tom could even afford to play golf. Their money seems pretty tight these days."

Marilyn was getting a little irritated. She reminded herself Jim was probably just resisting the idea because he was afraid of failure. She didn't know what to say. She sat back in her chair and decided to drop it.

A few minutes later, Jim said, "I'm sorry. I'm just being difficult. I know what you're saying. I should just start off trying to rebuild the bridge with Tom, the way I had to do with you."

Marilyn smiled and sat up. "Exactly. Just start spending some time together again. Don't force the conversation part. We'll just start praying God will open a door for that at the right time. You just be willing to go through it when he does. Like you did earlier back there with Brian."

Tom was driving home in the dark, exhausted. Tonight was the first time he had to work late at the Java Stop. It had been a surprisingly busy night and ended kind of rough. Two college kids had gotten into a fight, apparently over a girl, which Tom had to break up. Then a middle-aged couple kept complaining about their food not being any good. The bread was stale. The soup was cold. The lunch meat had a funny smell.

Tom finally had to give them their money back just to shut them up. He was sure that had been their aim all along.

He pulled into his driveway, hoping Jean had already put the kids down for the night. He walked down the sidewalk to pick up the mail, saddened by how much came out of the box. It was too dark to read any of it. Hopefully it was mostly junk mail, not bills. As he walked through the door, it was clear by the absence of Tommy's signature greeting that Jean had gotten the kids to bed. She looked up from her television show as he walked into the family room.

"You're home," she said. "You want me to heat up some leftovers?"

"That's all right, I ate something at work."

"From the cafeteria? I thought you hated the food there."

He did, or he used to five months ago when he'd worked there. "You do what you gotta do." Those were the kind of answers he always gave; not quite a lie, not quite the truth. Not that it mattered. He knew Jean would feel just as betrayed and just as lied to when all of this came out. Now with that surprise visit from Uncle Henry yesterday, he had a sick feeling his day of reckoning wouldn't be too far off in the future.

"The kids missed you at dinner and bath

215

time," she said, her eyes back on the television.

Tom noticed Jean didn't include herself when she said this. "Hopefully, it'll only be a few nights a week. But hey, we could use the overtime, right?" Why did he say that? He instantly regretted it. It was far too bold a lie. "What are you watching?"

"Just one of those design shows you hate with all your heart. It'll be over in about ten minutes if you want to watch something together."

"Sounds good. Let me go upstairs and change, put this mail away."

As he walked down the hall, she said, "I left some debits from the grocery store on your dresser."

He groaned. Under the stairway light, he could see lots of bills mixed in with the junk mail. When he got upstairs, he walked right to his dresser to check out the amounts.

Maybe he was just tired. Maybe it was the rough time he had at work. Or maybe it was the stack of bills that had just come in. But it looked to him like Jean had spent a ridiculous amount of money on groceries.

He brought the debit receipts over to the desk and held them under the lamp. "Look at that," he muttered aloud. "Not a single coupon. Not a single stinking coupon." He hurried down the stairs, holding the debit receipts in his hand.

Jean looked up as he came into the room. "What's the matter?"

"What do you mean, what's the matter? These are what's the matter."

"I put them where you asked me to," she said. "Right on your dresser."

"It's not where you put them, it's the amount of money you spent."

"What? I didn't spend any more money than I normally do. Well, maybe a few dollars more. But this is the week I have to buy bathroom and laundry products. They always cost more. But they're the same things I buy every month."

"Well, it's gotta stop. We just can't keep spending money like this."

"Why? Why can't we?"

"Because we can't. For one thing, the electric bill's going to start jumping up as it gets hotter. And food prices keep going up, and gas. You can't tell me this is the same amount we've been spending all along. It seems way higher to me."

"But it's not. Prices are going up all the time, but they haven't gone up that much since the last time I went shopping. And would you please keep your voice down? You're going to wake the kids."

Tom walked closer to her and held the receipts out. "And where's the coupons? I asked you to start couponing. There's not a single coupon on either of these receipts."

"You're right, there's not. I haven't had time yet to start collecting and sorting them. But I will. You asked me to, and so I will. But I don't get it."

"Get what?"

"Why you're so upset right now. I'm not doing anything different than I've been doing for years. Why are you acting like money is so tight? If anything, we should be feeling some breathing room, with you starting to work all this overtime."

"Well, we're not! I can't explain. You'll just have to —"

"Why can't you explain? Why can't you tell me what's going on?"

Tom's anger was about to boil over. He had to leave before he said some things he'd regret. Tonight was not the night to deal with this. Not tonight. "I just can't!" he yelled. "Why can't you just do what I say? Is that such a big deal? Spending a little bit of your spare time getting some coupons together so I don't have to keep seeing debit receipts like this?"

The look on Jean's face changed. She

didn't reply. Tears began to well up in her eyes.

I can't take this, he thought. *I'm not going to let her manipulate me with her tears.* "I've got to go." He tossed the receipts on the coffee table, turned around, and headed back toward the front door.

"Where are you going?" she cried.

"Out. I just need some fresh air." He walked out and slammed the door.

28

The next morning, Jean sat quietly at the dinette table staring at nothing in the backyard. Tom had just left for work without saying a word. He had only gone out for about forty-five minutes last night, but when he came back, he refused to talk to her. They went through their normal get-ready-for-bed routines, minus any conversation.

Somehow, Tom had no problem falling asleep, and she nearly hated him for it. She'd tossed and turned for over an hour and was tempted to take a sleeping pill or a Benadryl but dared not because of the baby. She hadn't been to the doctor yet, but she was certain she was pregnant. That knowledge only increased her anxiety about the difficulties they were having.

It just made no sense. The way Tom was acting. Not just the past few weeks but the past few months. None of it made any sense.

That was what she was thinking about as she sat there sipping cold coffee, staring at nothing in the backyard. Fortunately, Tommy and Carly were sleeping in, which almost never happened. A small mercy from God.

A single terrifying thought had tried to enter her mind last night, but she refused to let it fully form. If she had, she would have never gotten to sleep at all. That same thought had been crouching at the door of her consciousness all morning, waiting to be invited in. Weakened by the lack of sleep and worn down by her conflicting emotions, she could no longer resist its presence.

This phantom thought was the only thing that might explain Tom's bizarre behavior. But it couldn't be true, could it? Not Tom. He would never do something like that, would he? Not to her, not to them. They had talked about this early on during their first year of marriage. She didn't even remember how the subject came up or who talked about it first. But somehow they began discussing how they would react if either one of them were unfaithful to the other.

Although they were both Christians and both believed in God's forgiveness, they felt that if one of them ever betrayed their marriage bed, it would end the relationship for good. They would take that scriptural option that allowed divorce due to unfaithfulness.

Tom had felt just as strongly about this as she did. Partly because Jean wasn't his first love. That honor fell to a girl he'd dated in high school and felt sure he would marry. But she had cheated on him and actually got pregnant by another guy. It crushed his heart. He didn't pull out of his depression until they had met a year later, as freshmen in college.

When they had talked about this, Tom was emphatic. She could still remember the look on his face and the edge in his voice when he'd said it: "Jean, I love you more than I ever loved her. And your love has completely healed my heart. But I'm serious, don't ever think about cheating on me, no matter how hard it gets between us. I've got to know you won't ever go there. Promise me. I couldn't take it if you did."

He went on to say he would never do that to her, no matter what. Then he said, no he'd begged her, if she ever felt tempted to cheat on him because of anything he had done, or any way he was treating her, would she please talk to someone about it and tell them what she was feeling, rather than turn to some other guy. She could even talk to his mom if she wanted.

She knew then just how serious he was, because if there was anything Tom dreaded in life, it was the thought of displeasing his parents. He was almost obsessive about it.

She took a final sip of her cold coffee, trying to find some comfort in this bizarre memory. Oddly, it had given her strong assurance from that moment until now, that no matter what, she could count on Tom remaining faithful.

No matter what.

But sitting here now, her feelings and emotions colliding inside, she couldn't help but wonder if the thing she had dreaded most had actually happened. That Tom's heart had left her for another. What else could explain the way he had been acting lately?

And now, these "overtime hours." Tom had never worked evenings before. He had announced it as something that would be going on "for a few months." If that was so, then they should have plenty of money. Instead, Tom was acting like a maniac, fretting over every penny.

Why else would he be worried about money now with all this overtime, unless he was spending it on some other woman?

■ ■ ■ ■

About two hours had gone by since Henry Anderson had his quiet time. The thing that had been bothering him all evening yesterday, and had kept popping up during a restless night of sleep, became the preoccupying theme in his morning devotions. He was pretty sure he knew why.

God wasn't okay with him helping his great-nephew Tom hide what he'd been doing these past five months. Henry didn't believe in covering up things. Never did. In his almost seven decades of life, nothing good had ever come of that. And he was certain God had not orchestrated things to get him to intersect with Tom at the Java Stop just so he could be a co-conspirator in Tom's scheme.

As he walked into the kitchen to speak with Myra, he was greeted by the wonderful smell of fresh baking bread. "Now there's a smell you can never get too much of." He came up behind her and gave her a peck on the cheek. "So glad you bought that bread machine."

"That coffee's still pretty fresh," she said, "if you want to pour a cup. Of course, it's decaf, so it won't give you that kick if you're needing a good kick about now."

"Decaf is fine. I'm kicking pretty good, don't think I need any more help. Can I talk to you a minute?"

She turned around to face him. "What's on your mind? I could tell last night something was bugging you. Have a pretty good idea what it is."

"It's this thing with Tom and Jean," he said.

"Yep, that was it. I didn't think you'd be able to sit on that very long."

"I can't believe I agreed to do it in the first place. I was just so shocked and so unprepared for what he said."

"Don't be so hard on yourself. It would have shocked me too." She leaned up against the counter. "I wonder how he's going to react to the news that Jean's pregnant."

"My guess is, pretty badly. But I don't think it'll be near as bad as Jean's reaction to Tom's news." He sat on a dinette chair nearby. "The whole thing's just horrible."

"Oh what a web we weave . . ." she said. "So what are you going to do?"

"I told him I wouldn't say anything to anyone else but you without talking to him first. So I've got to abide by my word." He stood up to fix that cup of decaf.

"So you're going to drive back over there?"

"Don't see as I have a choice. Figured I'd find out what time he got off work today and be there to meet him when he came out."

"What if he has to close?"

"Then I'll just have to go there in the dark. But I don't think calling him first is a good idea. Then he'd have all day just to stew on it. Get himself all worked up before I get there."

"So how will you know when he gets off work?" she said.

"Thought I'd just call over there and hope one of the other employees answers. If they do, I'll just ask them what time the assistant manager is working till tonight. If they ask why, I'll just say I need to talk to him." He stirred the creamer into his coffee.

"And what will you do if Tom answers the phone?"

Henry didn't know what he'd do then. Right now, he thought hanging up sounded like a pretty good idea. But he doubted God or Myra would agree with that. "I'm just gonna pray that doesn't happen."

29

The following day was Jim and Marilyn's last day in Italy, but the excitement of what she was about to do helped offset the lingering sadness about this wonderful trip coming to an end. In less than twenty minutes, she would be leaving Florence and driving the BMW they had rented this morning back to Rome on the Autostrada, traveling at least one hundred miles an hour. Jim had said, "One hundred miles per hour at the most." Marilyn had gotten him to back off that . . . a little.

It was already midafternoon. Per the deal they had struck at breakfast, Jim had driven the Beemer at normal speeds on the way here, taking the scenic route. They had stopped to take pictures and sightsee a little at the four charming medieval towns between Rome and Florence, the ones recommended by the doctor who had recently purchased one of Jim's properties back home.

That was great fun, but Marilyn had to admit she was a tad distracted, almost wanting to push the day along. After a full week of sightseeing throughout the Italian countryside, *this* was the experience that had captivated her thoughts as soon as the alarm went off this morning.

"Do you want me to drive us out to the highway?" Jim said. "Then I can pull over and we can switch places."

"No, how about I drive us out to the highway, and you give me directions?"

Jim laughed. "I had a feeling that's what you'd say. Here's the keys." He handed them to her and walked around to the passenger side.

She got in, moved the seat forward, and repositioned the mirrors. "I was sad all they had to rent was an automatic."

"I'm not. You haven't driven a stick shift since before the kids were born."

She turned the car on. "But that's part of the fantasy, hearing the engine rev up as I shift through the gears."

"Sorry to disappoint you on that. But my fantasy included us getting back in one piece."

They weaved through the narrow streets

of Florence then drove along the beautiful Arno River as they headed out of town. She loved the feel of this car. It turned so tight, and the steering responded to every little move she made. And so much power, especially compared to her car back home. Jim reminded her of the dangers of drifting into any other lane but the left one once they hit the highway. Older, slower cars kept to the right lane. But she would be driving forty miles an hour faster than some of them, and could very easily plow right into the back of one before she knew it.

Finally, they reached the ramp and she began to floor it.

In seconds, they were at fifty. Then sixty, seventy, eighty, before they had even reached the end of the ramp. The car they had rented showed both kilometers and mph on the dashboard. "You're okay," he said. "No cars coming. Now just ease on out there."

Was he going to be doing that the whole time? Acting like some nervous coach? She looked in the rearview and side mirrors and quickly zipped into the leftmost lane. Eighty-five, ninety.

"Whoa," he said. "You call that *easing*?"

"No, I call that driving. And I call what you're doing *annoying.*" She looked over at him. Good, he was smiling. "I thought you said you were going to trust me," she said.

"I will. I mean, I do. Really, I'm okay. Now would you look at the speedometer? You're about to miss the magic moment."

She glanced down. There it was, ninety-five, ninety-six. She pushed the pedal a little harder. There . . . it happened. "I'm doing it! Do you see it? One hundred miles an hour." The car wasn't even vibrating. Outside her window, she could tell she was driving fast, but it didn't seem like she was going that fast. She looked over at Jim. This was so exciting.

And so far, no other cars on the road.

"I think you could easily go 120 or 130 with a car like this," she said.

"But we're not, right? You said just a little bit over 100, right?"

"I did. I'm just saying . . . this is an incredible car. And I'm having an incredible time." She looked over at him. "And you are an incredible husband." She reached over and patted his hand.

He quickly lifted her hand and placed it back on the steering wheel. "I'm so glad you're getting to do this, but remember my fantasy? Getting there in one piece?"

She smiled and glanced back at the windshield, then down at the speedometer. One hundred and four, one hundred and five.

She was having the best time.

Henry Anderson sat in his car in the parking lot of the Java Stop. He had intended to come here yesterday, after he and Myra had talked about it. He had even called the restaurant and found that Tom got off at 4:00. He was just about out the door when Myra stopped him. "We're both such dummies," she'd said. "You can't go visit Tom today. You're supposed to take me to the doctor at 4:30. We can't cancel it. Took me over a month to get this appointment."

So the plan got bumped until today.

And here he comes, Henry thought. He glanced at his watch. Right on time. Today Tom got off at 5:00. *Lord, give me the right words to say.* He got out of his car and walked toward Tom's, which was parked around the side. Tom didn't see him until he was just about ready to get in. "Hey, Tom. Sorry to surprise you like this."

"Uncle Henry." He stepped back, clearly not expecting company. "What . . . what are you doing here?"

Henry walked around to Tom's side, stayed back a few steps. "I wanted to talk with you about what we talked about the other day."

Tom put his hand on the car door handle.

231

"Now's not a good time, Uncle Henry. I've gotta get going or I'll get stuck in traffic."

Henry knew that wasn't quite true. Traffic was a little heavier than normal from here to Tom's house, but nothing like rush hour on I-4. "This will only take a minute," Henry said. "It can't wait."

Tom took his hand off the car door. "What is it?" The look of dread on his face suggested he already knew.

Henry tried to express with his eyes the love he felt for Tom and the compassion in his heart for the mess he'd gotten himself into. "I'm not comfortable doing what you asked me to do the other day."

"What part?"

"The part about not telling anyone you got laid off five months ago. The part where you asked me to love you by doing that. See, that goes against everything I believe about love. Love tells me to always do the right thing for someone, the thing I know is in their best interest. Even if, sometimes, it's also the hard thing."

Tom looked down on the pavement, shook his head. "I had a feeling this wasn't gonna work." He looked up. "So who are you gonna tell? Or who have you already told?"

"I haven't told anyone except your aunt Myra. Just like I said. And I'm not really thinking of telling anyone else at the moment."

"You're not?" A slight expression of hope.

"No, because that's not the right thing. The right thing is to ask you to reconsider and tell the person you should've told right off the bat. And I don't mean your dad."

"You mean Jean."

"It's just not right, Tom. Think about the things that were said at your wedding. I was there. I remember. The preacher quoted the verse when Jesus said you were no longer two but one. If I recall, one or both of you even mentioned something about that in your vows. You wrote your own, didn't you?" Tom sighed, nodded. "How does what you're doing — what you've been doing these past five months — line up with that?"

"I am going to tell her, Uncle Henry. I said I would. I just want to wait till I get a job, a good one."

Henry took a step closer and gently said, "That's no good, Tom. That's not being honest with her, not even close. She needs to know what's going on. Now. Today. Look, I'll go over there with you. Right now, and help you two work this out."

Tom looked like he was about to be sick. "I can't. I can't do it. Not like this."

"Why?"

"Because she'll totally freak out. I don't just mean a little bit. I know her. You don't. With all due respect, your coming over to help won't help at all. And besides, my parents are coming home tomorrow from their Italy trip. I'm supposed to pick them up from the Orlando airport at 3:30 tomorrow afternoon. Is this what you want them to come home to? My wife having a total meltdown, possibly throwing me out of the house?"

"You really think that's what she'll do?"

"Oh yeah . . . or something worse."

Henry took a deep breath. He wasn't sure what to do or say next.

"Can't you just give me a little more time? Let my parents get home and settle in before this whole thing blows up?"

"I suppose we can wait a few days more," Uncle Henry said. "That may be wise."

"I appreciate that," Tom said. "I'll start to work on a plan, figure out some kind of way to break this to her, figure out the best time."

Hearing this gave Henry no confidence at all. It was this "figuring out things" that got Tom into this mess in the first place. "I don't know, Tom. I think you need some help to do this right. You haven't been thinking straight, Son. For a good long while.

Something that's helped me for years in hard situations is getting my close advisors involved. There's a Bible verse that says, 'There is safety and wisdom in a multitude of advisors.' Doesn't sound like you have any advisors right now. But you need 'em. We all do at times. So, I'll give you a few days. But sometime during those few days you and I need to meet again, when we're not so rushed, and talk over a few things."

Henry could see Tom didn't much like that idea. "That's my deal, Tom. If you want me to wait. And it's nonnegotiable."

30

Their plane touched down on the runway at the Orlando International Airport right on time, then bounced once and touched down again. Everyone gasped, then a collective sigh of relief as the plane stabilized and began to slow down.

"Talk about bumpy rides," Jim said.

Marilyn finally eased up her stranglehold on the armrests. "That may have been the worst airplane ride I've ever been on." The turbulence had begun to shake the plane almost two hours ago while they were still out over the Atlantic. It had come on suddenly, causing one man in a business suit to bang his head as he walked back from the restroom. An RN three rows back had administered first aid and said he probably would need a few stitches to close the wound properly after they landed.

Marilyn turned in her seat and looked at him now. His head was bandaged, and he held an ice pack on the wound. A flight attendant sat across the aisle, filling out an accident report. Marilyn felt the plane swerve to the right and looked out the window. The airport was just ahead on the right. "I can't wait to get off this plane."

Jim reached for her hand. "Sorry I couldn't arrange for a better ending to our trip than this."

"It's not your fault."

"I know. But still."

"It won't spoil my memory of this trip," she said. "Nothing can. I think this is the best vacation we've ever been on."

"Nothing else even comes close," Jim said.

"How are we getting home?"

"Tom is supposed to be picking us up," he said.

"Then I'm sure he'll be there. He's like you, totally organized."

"I told him we could rent a car, but he wouldn't hear of it."

Marilyn looked at her watch. "So what time is it here?"

"Just a little before 3:30 in the afternoon."

"You're kidding. I'm ready for bed," she said.

"I moved my watch back hours ago, to help me get used to the time change. I suggest we do our best to stay up as long as we can. Otherwise, we'll be struggling with jet lag for days."

Marilyn yawned and lifted her watch toward the sunlight coming in from the window, then reset the time. "I really want to see the grandkids, but I'm not sure I have the energy for that right now."

"You don't need to worry, Tom's coming alone. When we talked about this before we left, he told me he'd be coming right from work."

What a relief. She looked out the window again in time to see their plane turn toward the gate. In a few minutes her fairy tale would end. But now that they were back, other than being tired to the bone, she was actually looking forward to being home and seeing all her loved ones again, hearing all their little stories about what they had done over the past ten days.

There probably wouldn't be that much to tell, she thought. She and Jim had been on a delightful adventure filled with fascinating sights and sounds, making memories she would cherish for the rest of her life. But she knew life back home had probably bumped along like it always did, full of predictable routines and sameness.

Life changes very little in a ten-day span back home. And for the most part, she was glad.

The interior of the Orlando International Airport could have been designed by Disney's Imagineers. It almost looked like part of a theme park. The layout, the decor, the palm trees and tropical shrubs, all the gift shops and fancy souvenir stores. It even had something like a monorail system ferrying ticketed passengers across the tarmac between the security area and the gates.

Tom used to do a little traveling with his job at the bank. He remembered how nice it was flying back into Orlando, compared to most of the other airports he'd been to in the US. As he eyed the crowds flowing out of the monorail into the main lobby, he tried to let the theme park ambience soothe his shattered nerves.

But it wasn't working.

He was so tense, he'd actually caught himself chewing his fingernails, a habit he thought he'd licked back in high school. A few moments ago, he scanned the big electronic board, which confirmed his parents' plane had landed. Fifteen minutes ago. But as the last of the present group of passengers walked by, it was obvious his parents were not among them.

Great, he thought. More waiting.

It was exhausting trying to maintain a cheery façade. Since his conversation yesterday with Uncle Henry, an oppressive gloom had descended on him, and it was all he could do to keep from giving in to despair. This must be what it felt like for a prisoner on death row, on the eve of his appointment with the electric chair. In fact, that was exactly how Tom had felt last night at the dinner table with Jean and the kids.

Meatloaf, instant mashed potatoes, string beans, and Diet Coke. Not what he'd have picked for his last meal.

Jean, of course, kept asking him questions, trying to get him to open up and let her in. As he had for the past five months, he carefully dodged her questions, answered her with ambiguities, or else changed the subject altogether. He could see it was frustrating her, but what else could he do?

He was buying time. An invisible clock was ticking down to his doom.

Just then, Tom's thoughts were interrupted by a fresh crowd disembarking from the monorail. His eyes zeroed in on the scene, scanning for familiar faces. There they were. Did they see him? Yes, they did. His mom waved, her face as happy as he'd ever seen it.

Okay, remember, business as usual. Smile,

*ask questions, talk about the kids, and avoid
eye contact, especially with Mom.*

"There he is, Jim. Do you see him?" Marilyn waved.

"No . . . wait, there he is," Jim said. "See, it's just Tom."

They hurried along, keeping in step with the flow of the crowd. "I hope he remembered to switch with Jean," she said, "and bring their SUV. We'd never fit all that luggage into his little car."

"I'm sure he remembered," Jim said. "You know Tom."

She did. Jim was right. He'd have remembered. It felt good to be home, even just to be on solid ground again, especially after that last part of their flight. The crowd began to disperse as they reached the main lobby area. Now she could see Tom plainly. She waved again, and he waved back. He smiled, but instantly she could tell, just by looking at his eyes.

Something was wrong.

Tom walked toward them, closing the gap with his arms outstretched. They greeted each other and exchanged hugs. Tom immediately insisted she let him pull her carry-on bag. They headed toward the baggage claim escalator, with Tom asking a flurry of questions about their trip. But the more he talked, the more convinced Marilyn became.

Something was wrong. Something was seriously wrong.

31

Jean quietly opened the front door to let Michele in. "Carly is still sleeping, but I can't imagine that going on much longer. She's been down for two hours already."

Michele stepped past her into the foyer. "How about Tommy?"

Jean closed the door. "He's coloring in the family room and watching a cartoon on the Disney channel. But I'm sure he'd love it if Aunt Michele wanted to interrupt that. I know you're great with kids, so do whatever you're in the mood for." She looked at her watch. "Hopefully, I won't be gone more than an hour. I've never been to this doctor before, so I don't know if she's one of those who fills up the waiting room or gets you right in there."

"Don't worry if you go over a little," Michele said. "After you called, I called Allan, and he's fine with us just grabbing some dinner out when I get home. So don't rush on my account."

"Well, before too long Tom will be home from picking your folks up at the airport. He's just planning on dropping them off at their place in River Oaks, then coming straight home."

"There's an idea," Michele said. "I'll call my mom after I leave here, see if they want to join Allan and me for dinner. I'm sure her cupboards are bare from being gone ten days."

"Sounds like a good idea," Jean said. "Well, I better be going. Thanks again for coming on such short notice. I just called the doctor's office yesterday, and they're squeezing me in at 4:00." She reached for the doorknob.

"Jean, Tom knows you're going to the doctor, right? You did tell him about the pregnancy test."

Jean stopped, then turned slowly to face Michele. She shook her head no.

"You're kidding. You didn't tell him?"

"I couldn't, Michele. I don't have time to explain. I wanted to, I really did. But Tom's been —" She had to get hold of her emotions. "He's been so difficult lately, way more than usual. I decided just to make an appointment with the doctor first. But I promise, I'll tell him tonight when I get home."

"I'm not mad, Jean. Just concerned. I really think you guys need some help. Allan and I've been going to the same church my folks started going to after they reconciled last summer. It has a lot of ministries geared to help families. My parents are going to a small group set up to help married couples."

"Tom would never be in a small group with your parents. He'd rather jump off a bridge."

Michele laughed. "They've got several of those groups and one pastor totally devoted to married couples. Really, you guys should check it out. It's only twenty-five minutes from here. And it would be so nice if we were all going to the same church."

"I'll think about it," she said. "But really, I've gotta go." She gave Michele a quick hug then walked out the door. She couldn't imagine how a conversation like that would go; she couldn't even talk to Tom about being pregnant.

Jean almost tripped on the curb leading up to the doctor's office. She had to calm down. They were sure to take her blood pressure inside; it was probably through the roof right now. But she had no reason to be upset. She'd been through this kind of exam twice before; it was no big deal.

As she stepped through the doorway, she knew what was really bothering her: Tom, and his reaction to the news.

She walked into the waiting room. Flashes from conversations when she'd told him the news about Tommy and Carly came to mind. Both times, Tom had been elated. He'd made Jean feel like a queen. That wasn't so long ago; Carly wasn't even two years old. How had Tom changed so much in so little time?

Was it her fault somehow? She'd been wrestling with this for days but couldn't come up with anything she had been doing differently, any irritating habit she had started. Was it her looks? She'd never felt secure about her appearance. But she had lost all the pregnancy weight and even let Tom pick out her hairstyle. She never wore outfits he didn't like.

No, stop this. There was only one explanation that made any sense, and she knew it. It was a wife's worst nightmare — that she had lost him to someone else.

"Can I help you?"

Jean didn't even hear the glass window slide over. She looked down at the receptionist smiling at her. "Uh, sorry. My name is Jean Anderson. I have an appointment with Dr. Evans at 4:00."

The receptionist scanned the computer screen. "There you are. Is this your first time with us?"

"Yes."

The girl reached behind her, slid out a clipboard from a cubbyhole, and handed it to Jean. "Could you fill this out, both pages, and bring it back to me?"

"Sure." Jean took the clipboard and found a seat in the mostly empty waiting room. At least she wouldn't be left in here too long. She spent the next ten minutes filling out the forms then gave them back to the receptionist.

The receptionist looked them over. "Thanks. Do you have insurance?"

"Yes, with my husband's work. Let me find the card." She hadn't used the insurance card in so long. Well, that was one thing to be thankful for, how healthy they had all been. "Here it is."

The young woman took it and was just about to run it through a card reader when she said, "Um, it looks like your card's expired. See the date here?"

Jean looked at it and saw that it was. "I'm sorry. I don't know how that happened. They must have given my husband new cards at work and he forgot to give me mine. Could you call the number there on the back? I'm sure they'll tell you the new expiration date."

The girl handed her the card back. "I'm sorry, but you better. I'm not sure they'd give that information to me."

"Oh, you're right. All these new privacy laws. Just give me a sec." Jean backed away from the window and dialed the number, then worked through the automated system until she was talking to a human being. "Yes, my name is Jean Anderson. I'm here at a doctor's office, and we just realized my insurance card is out of date. My husband is insured at work. He must have forgotten to give me the new card."

"What's the policy number?" the woman asked. Jean gave the woman both the policy and Tom's member number and was put on hold.

"I'm sorry," the woman said a few moments later, "but that member number is no longer valid."

"I don't understand." Jean reread her the number. The woman confirmed that was the number she keyed in. "Can you try it again? It has to work."

She heard the keyboard clicking over the phone. "I'm sorry. I'm getting the same message. It's an invalid number."

"But that doesn't make any sense," Jean said. "Is the policy number right? The number for the bank?"

The woman looked it up and said, "The bank's policy number is still valid. It's just your member number that's not."

"What does that mean?"

"It means the bank your husband worked at is still insured with us. I'm afraid, for some reason, his insurance with them has lapsed."

"You said the bank he *worked* at. He still works there."

"I wouldn't know about that, ma'am. You'll have to take that up with him. And why his insurance has lapsed. According to my records, it happened over five months ago."

"Five months ago. But how can that be? Tom never said anything to me about losing his insurance."

"As I said, you'll have to take that up with him."

"Oh, I intend to. So . . . what you're saying is, as of this moment, our family is uninsured?"

"I'm afraid so."

"And you're absolutely sure there's no mistake?"

"None that I can see. Is there anything else I can help you with?"

"No, thank you." She hung up.

What in the world? She turned and stepped back up to the window to face the receptionist. "I don't know how this happened, and I don't think there's anything I can do about it now, but it looks like somehow we've lost our medical insurance. I guess I'm going to have to cancel my appointment today."

"I'm sorry," the young woman said.

"Thanks." Jean turned and headed toward the door. A sickening feeling began churning in her stomach.

Tom, what have you done?

32

Life was so much simpler when he lived here.

Tom sat in the driveway at his parents' house in River Oaks — his old house — looking through the windshield. He'd never appreciated it then. This house was just the place you came home to after school, where you ate your meals. Most of his friends lived in houses just as nice, so he never got the sense of how huge it was. Now it looked like a palace. Three families could share the space and not get in each other's way. Tom's place was barely one third the size, and he couldn't even afford to keep it afloat.

He'd never achieve a fraction of his father's success.

He looked up at the wraparound porch, saw his mom waving through the living room window. She had that same concerned look on her face. During the car ride from the airport, he tried to keep the conversation centered on their Italy trip. Thankfully, his dad was in a talkative mood. But his mom kept trying to redirect the conversation back to Tom. How was he doing? How was Jean, how were the kids? Was everything okay?

No . . . everything wasn't okay.

Tom had given her short answers, then quickly asked his father more questions, trying to shift the focus off himself. It had worked. For now. He pulled out of the driveway, waved one last time, and drove off.

The car almost drove itself through the glorious streets of River Oaks. Tom had made the drive so many times he didn't need to pay attention. Before long, he'd be back in their Lake Mary subdivision — an equally familiar place but, lately, one that felt like anything but home.

Jean had pulled over at a nearby parking lot to use her cell phone. She was driving Tom's car so he could use their SUV to pick up his parents. She'd left the hands-free gizmo in the SUV. Her hands trembled as she worked through the contact list to find the number for Tom's bank. She didn't want to call Tom right now. After what she'd learned at the doctor's office, she wasn't sure she could trust anything he'd say. "Hi, this is Jean Anderson. My husband Tom works there at the bank, in the IT department."

"Would you like to speak to him? Do you know his extension?"

"No, not right now." She laughed nervously. "I mean, I know his extension. I just don't need to speak with him at the moment. Could you connect me with whoever handles medical benefits?"

"I can do that," the girl said. "That would be our HR department. I'll put you through."

A few moments later she was talking to someone else, a man.

"Hi, my name is Jean Anderson. My husband works there. I was just at the doctor's office, and they told me something strange. Somehow, our medical insurance got canceled. They said it happened five months ago. Did the bank cut employee benefits for some reason?"

"No, Mrs. Anderson. In fact, after the merger six months ago, our health insurance benefits actually improved."

"Really?"

"Yes, except for a few dozen layoffs, everyone around here is pretty pleased with the changes."

"Did you say six months ago?" she asked.

"Yes. That's when the merger became official."

"Did anything significant happen a month after that? That's when the insurance company said our policy lapsed."

There was a short pause. "Well, most of those layoffs I mentioned happened around then. What did you say your husband's name was?"

"Tom Anderson. He works in the IT area."

"Yeah, we had a number of layoffs in that department. Guess there was a lot of overlap over there. Here, let me check." She heard some keyboard clicks. "I'm sorry, Mrs. Anderson. But your husband's name is not listed as one of our current IT employees."

Jean's heart sank. How was this possible? "You mean Tom was laid off? Five months ago?"

A longer pause. "I don't know what to say. It looks that way. I don't work in that area, but I could put you through to the IT supervisor if you'd like."

"No, that won't be necessary. Thanks for your help." She hung up.

Tom had been laid off? Five months ago? This was horrible. But it didn't make any sense. Why wouldn't he say anything? He'd been driving off to work every day for the last five months, just like he always did. If he wasn't going to work, then where was he going? Where was he spending all that time?

Tears streamed down her face as the next question formed.

And with *whom*?

It took Jean more than twenty minutes and all the napkins in the glove compartment to finally regain her composure. She was glad she hadn't made that call to Tom's employer while driving.

Fear and confusion filled her heart. She had to calm down, reason things out. Tom had lost his job. Okay, that happened sometimes. The economy was in bad shape. Lots of people had lost their jobs. But it had happened five months ago, and he hadn't told her. Why, why hadn't he told her? Why would he keep something like that from her? She couldn't think of a single reason.

It suddenly felt like she was married to a complete stranger.

She glanced down at the digital clock on the dashboard. Tom should be getting home in about twenty minutes. She was only ten minutes from home now. *The kids.* She had no idea what she'd do or say when she confronted him. But she knew she didn't want the kids there when it happened. She quickly dialed Michele's number.

"Hello?"

"Hi, Michele."

"What's wrong? You sound upset. What did the doctor say?"

"I didn't even see the doctor. I —"

"You didn't?"

"Let me explain." She released a sigh. "Oh Michele, it's just awful." She had to get control of herself. "I didn't see the doctor, because our insurance was canceled five months ago."

"What? Why?"

"Why? Because Tom was laid off five months ago. That's why!"

"What? You're kidding. I'm sorry, of course you're not kidding. How did you find out? Did he tell you this?"

"No, I found out the first part at the doctor's office. And I just got off the phone with Tom's bank. They confirmed it. The insurance was canceled because he was laid off five months ago, after that big merger."

"And he didn't say anything about it? Oh Jean, I'm so sorry. I can't believe he'd do something like this. What's he been doing all this time?"

"Exactly." That was the question, wasn't it? "Listen, we don't have a lot of time. I'm heading home now, and Tom should be home in about twenty minutes. I don't want the kids there for that. I hate to ask you this, but could you watch them a little longer . . . somewhere else? Could you get their things together and get them ready to leave?"

"Sure," Michele said. "I'll do it right now."

"I just realized, this is going to ruin your dinner plans with your folks."

"No, it won't. I never called them. I wasn't able to reach Allan to make sure he'd be okay with it."

"Thanks so much for helping me out here. I don't know what I'm going to do, or what's gonna happen in the next twenty to thirty minutes . . ."

"I'm so sorry, Jean. Allan and I will be praying for you. It's okay if I tell him, right?"

She put the car in gear. "Sure, tell Allan. Everyone's gonna find out about this soon enough." She hung up. *Find out about this.* The words repeated in her mind. Find out about *what* exactly?

She had no idea. She only knew she had no desire to listen to any of Tom's lies or excuses.

33

"Was that . . . ?"

Tom had just turned onto the main road leading into his subdivision, lost in thought. But he could've sworn Michele's car had just gone by the other way. He glanced through his rearview mirror, trying to get a better look, but it was too far away. After turning a few more corners, he pulled into his driveway. He decided to check the mail before going inside. He wished he could think of a dozen other things to do first.

Tonight was the night he would tell Jean everything, after the kids went down.

He still couldn't think of what to say or how to introduce it. Every scenario he came up with ended badly. He pulled the mail out of the box and forced himself to walk back to the house. As he came up the curved walkway, the front curtain moved slightly, as if someone had peeked out. Probably just Tommy.

He unlocked the door, halfway expecting to be tackled at the knees by his son. But the house was quiet. Oddly quiet. Could the kids both be upstairs napping? It was pretty late in the day for that. "Hello? I'm home." He walked down the hall.

Was that . . . crying?

Sounded like Jean's voice, just around the corner. "Hello?" He walked into the family room. Jean was sitting at the dining room table, holding her face and a wad of tissues in her hands. Tom rushed over. "Jean, what's wrong? Where's Tommy and Carly? Are they okay?"

She looked up, but her eyes weren't filled with grief or sorrow. He saw rage.

"How could you?" she said. "How could you do this?"

"Do what? What have I done?" He pulled a chair out.

"What did you do today?"

"What do you mean? I just got back from picking my parents up at the airport. But you knew that."

"Before that!" she shouted.

What was going on here? "You know . . ."

"Tell me."

"Jean, what's wrong? Why are you acting this way?"

"Tell me."

"Tell you what?"

"What were you doing before you picked your parents up at the airport? And don't lie to me. Could you do that just once? Tell the truth. You remember how to do that?"

Could she know? Had she found out? "I don't know what you're talking about. You're not making any sense."

"What were you doing before you picked your parents up?"

What should he say? It seemed like she had found out. But how? He glanced around the room, stalling for time. If he kept up the lie, and she had found out, she might lose it altogether. "Jean, I wish you'd just tell me what's going on. Why are you so upset?"

She put her hands on the table. "You're not going to answer me, are you? You want to lie to me, I can tell. You're so good at it. Really, you've become a master. You want to just keep it going. But now you're wondering if I discovered your little charade on my own, and what kind of trouble you'll be in if you lie to me right now."

"Jean, I don't know what to say."

She stood up. "It's called the truth, Tom. It's not hard. For most people, anyway." She walked to the hutch, pulled out a fresh tissue from a Kleenex box, and blew her nose. "Were you with her?"

260

With *her*? "Jean, what are you saying? With who? Was I with who?"

"See? You can't even answer me straight about that. You keep answering my questions with questions. That's what liars do, to avoid giving straight answers. I read about that online. Did you know that? They have websites to help spouses figure out if their husband or wife is cheating. I read a list of all the tactics lying spouses use. You've mastered them all."

Tom felt an odd sense of relief. She thought he was having an affair. Maybe this wasn't going to be so bad after all. When she realized the truth, that is. "Jean, I'm not seeing anyone. I never have, and I never will. You know how I feel about that."

For a moment she didn't answer. "And I'm supposed to believe that?" she said, pulling out another tissue.

"Of course you are. It's the truth."

"Oh, and you, you're the guardian of truth? Is that it?"

"Jean, would you come over here and sit down? I do have something to tell you. Something pretty bad. But it's not what you're thinking, not even close."

She turned around and leaned against the hutch. "I'll stay right here."

"I guess you found out somehow about

261

my job situation." It was a relief just saying it. "I've been wanting to tell you the truth about this for so long now."

"You have? You've been *wanting* to tell me? Well, at least there's that." She took a deep breath.

"How did you find out?"

"I went to the doctor today and —"

"You did? What's wrong?"

"Let me finish."

Then it dawned on him: the insurance.

"Guess what I found out?"

"We don't have insurance."

"And why don't we have insurance?"

He looked to his left, through the sliding glass door to the backyard. "Because I lost my job five months ago. But I'm sure you know that by now."

"Look at me when you say it."

He turned to face her. "When I say what?"

"Look me in the eyes and tell me what you should've told me five months ago. I want to hear you say it, looking at me."

"I . . . I lost my job, Jean. Five months ago. And I've been hiding it from you and lying about it ever since." Suddenly, a wave of emotion rose up inside him, and tears welled up in his eyes.

For several moments, she just stared at him. Then she said, "Why?"

262

"It wasn't my fault, Jean. It was Jared, you remember him, right? We sat across from each other at the Christmas party last year? He and his wife. When this whole merger thing went down, Jared stabbed me in the back and stole my job." She was shaking her head. That's not what she meant. He realized that now. "You mean, why didn't I tell you?" He took a deep breath; he had to get this right.

He was just about to explain when she said, "Do you have any idea what you've put me through these past five months? I've imagined everything from you don't love me anymore to you must be seeing someone else. I've felt sick and tense every day, walking on eggshells around you, and you haven't noticed it for a minute. It's like I'm invisible. You come home every night — from who knows where — and you're totally focused on yourself, till the moment you leave the next morning. I have no idea what happened to the man I married."

She walked over toward the sliding glass door, talking toward the glass. "You treat me like one of the kids! You think I can't handle the truth so you had to protect me. Well, guess what? I haven't felt protected, I've felt shut out and ignored. I've even been struggling with guilt and shame because I'm not good enough for you. I've gone out of my way cooking your favorite meals, trying to cheer you up. I've gone out of my way trying to keep the kids quiet, so they wouldn't set you off."

She turned to face him. "Do you have any idea how it's been for me all these months?" A new look came over her face. "You know what? I don't want to hear it, any of it. Not now, anyway."

Tom was stunned. For several moments, he didn't answer. What could he say? "But I want to tell you," he finally said. "The whole story."

"Well, I don't want to hear it."

"Then what . . . what do you want me to say?"

"I don't want you to say anything. I'm exhausted. I feel sick inside. Just looking at you makes me nauseated. I actually want you to leave."

"Leave?"

"Yes, leave. I want to be alone."

"For how long?"

"I don't know. A few days anyway. I just . . . I need some time alone."

Tom stood. He wanted to protest, to insist she sit back down and hear him out. They needed to talk this out. But it was clearly pointless. "I don't want to leave you like this, Jean. Not like this."

"Well," she said, "you're not going to be the one to help me. That's for sure. So please just go."

He turned and walked back toward the hallway. Just before he reached the stairs, something dawned on him. Walking back into the family room, he said, "Will you at least tell me why you went to the doctor?"

"To confirm something I already know."

"What's that?"

"That I'm pregnant. Now, will you please go?"

34

About an hour later, Jean received two texts.

One from Tom, which initially she didn't read. She forced herself to. Ignoring it became a total distraction. It said: "I love you, and I'm beyond sorry. I know you're not ready to forgive me yet. I hope you can soon. Tom."

Was that supposed to make it all better?

The second text was from Michele, asking if it was safe to call yet. Jean texted her back and said: *I asked Tom to leave, and he did. Give me about thirty minutes?*

Michele got right back and said, *Sure.*

Jean spent the next thirty minutes sitting on the sofa, staring at the wall. All her tears had been spent, for now. She felt equal parts numb and exhausted. Her deepest fear in this whole thing had been that Tom was unfaithful. She had never imagined he had lost his job. That was a blow, but it was something she felt she could deal with.

Could just the layoff explain the way he had been acting these past few months? To her, that didn't make any sense. Why not just tell her something like that? True, she probably would've lost it a little; had a couple of bad days wrestling with her fears. But then she would have bounced back and gotten to a place where she was trusting God for their future. If he had told her right away, she could have started finding out about government programs that would help them through. But instead, he'd treated her like a two-year-old. He didn't see her as an equal or even as a grown-up.

Okay, she worried about things, but like most people did. Average fears. The kids getting hurt or sick, roaches and spiders, riding next to semitrucks on the highway.

So why hadn't he told her when he got laid off five months ago? She could understand if he'd waited a day or two, maybe trying to pick "the right time." She'd have been mildly upset at a delay like that. But there was no rational excuse for what Tom had done. Five months.

And that was her problem.

She reached for the phone and called Michele. "How are the kids doing?" she asked.

"They're doing fine. Allan's playing with

267

them on the rug."

"I'm glad. But, can I ask you something, Michele? Do I seem like a basket case to you? The kind of person who freaks out all the time and can't handle any pressure?"

"No," Michele said. "You seem pretty average to me — emotionally, I mean."

"Well, that's why I asked your brother to leave."

"For good? Are you guys splitting up over this?"

"Not over this. If by *this* we're talking about Tom losing his job and lying about it."

"Isn't that what this is about?" Michele asked. "Did Tom do something else, something worse?"

"I don't know if that's *all* this is about," Jean said. "That's my problem. How can you trust a word someone says if they can lie about something that big every day for all that time?"

Michele didn't answer right away. "That is a problem," she said. "What else are you afraid of? That there's something else he's not telling you?"

"Yes. I'm afraid that he's . . . I'm afraid what's really going on here is . . ." Jean began to cry.

"Jean, I can't see Tom being unfaithful to

268

you. Is that what you're worried about?"

Jean wanted to believe her, desperately. But how could she know for sure?

"My brother's done a stupid thing, a really stupid thing. And I'm not even going to try to defend it. But I really don't think that's what's going on here. It would totally shock me if it were true."

"It doesn't shock you that your brother lost his job five months ago, didn't tell anyone about it, and drove off to . . . *someplace* . . . every day as if he still worked there?" Michele didn't answer. "See what I'm saying? If he can do that, how can we know what else he's capable of?"

"I can see your point," Michele said. "But there's something else I want you to think about, Jean. As part of the big fix in your relationship with Tom."

"Assuming it can be fixed."

"Assuming that," Michele said.

"So, what is it?"

Michele hesitated. "I shouldn't . . ."

"Shouldn't what?" Jean could tell, she wanted to say something she thought would hurt her feelings. "What is it, Michele? Really, I want to know."

Michele took a deep breath and tried to measure Jean's readiness to hear what she wanted to say. "I'm not saying this to hurt you. And after living most of my life under my father's rigid outlook on life, I get how easy it can be to feel pressure just to get in line."

"What are you trying to say, Michele?"

"You've got to stop being such a doormat with him."

"With Tom?"

"Yes, with Tom. You've been letting him walk all over you these past few years. You've got to start speaking up when things bother you. Not just sit there and take it. You don't have to be nasty. The Bible talks about being gentle when we correct each other. But it sounds like you just sit there and take it, and don't say a thing. That's not what I've been taught a Christian wife's role is supposed to look like. That's not how our pastor described it to Allan and me in our premarital counseling. He said God made Eve as Adam's helper because Adam needed the help. Then he said we're not helping our husbands if we sit there and say nothing when they go off track."

"You're right," Jean said. "You're absolutely right."

"So when you're praying," Michele said, "don't forget to pray for a new backbone."

Jean tried to smile. "I will."

■ ■ ■ ■

Henry and Myra Anderson, sitting in their favorite chairs, sipped coffee as they watched *Wheel of Fortune*. Myra heard the sound first, but she didn't need hearing aids like Henry. "Someone just pulled into the driveway," she said. They rarely got visitors, unannounced ones anyway. She got up to investigate.

Henry hit the pause button on the remote and sat up.

Myra peeked out the front window. "I'm not sure, but I think that's Tom's car."

That got Henry's attention. He stood and walked toward her.

"It is," she said. "He's getting out, and he's dragging a suitcase."

"A suitcase? That can't be good." Henry walked over and opened the front door just as Tom turned into the walkway. His face was all red, his eyes puffy, his shoulders slumped with the weight of the world.

"Hey, Uncle Henry. I'm sorry to do this, show up like this uninvited. But I didn't know what else to do or where else to go."

"Come on in, Tom. You're family. You're always welcome here." He put his arm around Tom as he came close and just let

271

him sob.

Myra walked up and put her arms around him too. The suitcase fell backward to the floor. "You poor thing," Myra said and patted his back.

Henry walked over to the hutch and grabbed a box of tissues. After a few moments, Tom regained some of his composure. He picked up the suitcase.

"Don't worry about that," Myra said. "You come on over here and sit down. Had anything to eat for dinner? I could heat up some leftovers. Made some chicken parmigiana, plenty of it left."

Tom shuffled over to the sofa. "Thanks, but I can't eat."

Henry sat nearby in his chair. Myra said, "Well at least let me get you some iced tea or cold water."

"Some cold water maybe, thanks."

She headed for the kitchen.

"So, I guess your conversation with Jean didn't go so well," Henry said. "I thought you were going to wait a few days. You change your mind?" Henry had hoped to get with Tom beforehand, to help him work through how to handle it.

"She didn't give me a chance. God didn't give me a chance." He exhaled a deep sigh, looked down toward the floor.

"What do you mean?"

"Just like he sent you to the restaurant the other day, he sent her to the doctor's office this afternoon. She found out we lost our health insurance five months ago. Then she called my old employer, who confirmed I got laid off at the same time. Why didn't God give me a chance? I was gonna tell her. Tonight, I was gonna tell her." Myra walked back into the room and handed Tom the water. "With her finding out about it this way, she doesn't want to have anything to do with me. She wouldn't even give me a chance to explain. She just threw me out."

Lord, Henry prayed, *please give us wisdom here.* Henry sat a moment, not sure what to say. A Scripture verse played through his mind: "For the Lord disciplines those he loves and he punishes each one he accepts as a child." It was somewhere in Hebrews. Was that what this was? Was God lovingly disciplining Tom here? "I'm not pretending I have all the answers, Tom. But I do know one thing — despite how this happened, God still loves you. Jean may have thrown you out, and she may even feel like she has good reason. But God hasn't rejected you. You know that, right?"

Tom looked up at him. Tears filled his eyes

again. "Feels a whole lot like rejection to me."

35

It was good to be home.

It wasn't so good doing laundry. Marilyn had been at it for almost an hour. Ten days of luxurious living in the Tuscan countryside could almost make a person forget that all these clothes you packed would face a day of reckoning when you got home. Jim had suggested she wait until tomorrow, but then she'd have it hanging over her head until then.

Besides, she had an extra hour to kill. When they had gotten home, Doug had called saying he'd like to go out to dinner with them but that it would take an hour to get home. He was driving back from Flagler College in St. Augustine, where he hoped to attend in the fall. She couldn't believe it — her little baby was graduating high school in just a few weeks.

Then she and Jim would officially be empty nesters.

Another reason to get the laundry done was that it kept her moving. If she sat for even a little while, she'd fall fast asleep. For her body clock it was already past midnight, and it felt like it.

She moved a load from the washer to the dryer and put a fresh load in the washer. She decided to make sure Jim hadn't fallen asleep on the bed. He was supposed to be getting showered and changed. She looked at her watch. Doug should be getting home in about ten minutes. She decided to sneak over to the little apartment above the garage, to survey the damage.

Doug had moved up there last year. He'd been keeping up with things a little better, but that was with Marilyn's constant super-vision. What would she find after being gone ten days? As she cleared the final step, she braced for the hit. The door opened, and to her great surprise, everything looked . . . fine. A little lived in, but that was all.

From here, she could see only the living area and kitchen. She hurried across the carpet to peek in his bedroom. My, my. Her little boy was growing up. The bed was made, the clothes hung up, even his shoes were in the closet. "Good for you, Doug-las." She headed back through the front door, down the stairs, then across the walkway toward the main house.

Jim would love this. They both had noticed a positive change in Doug since he'd gotten a job at a grocery store a couple of months ago. She walked through the French doors into the great room, then around the stairway toward their bedroom suite on the first floor. She could hear Jim singing in the bathroom.

"How's it coming?" she said.

"Almost done, just gotta do my hair."

That sounded funny to her.

"Can you pick out a shirt for me? All the ones I like are in the trip laundry."

She came up from behind as he stood at the mirror and gave him a hug. "You smell nice. Doug should be here any minute."

"I'll be ready. Any idea where we're going?"

"How about we let Doug pick?"

"Fine," he said, "as long as it's not Italian. Think I want something nice and American for a change."

Marilyn laughed. "I'm with you on that."

"I could even go for a nice burger," Jim said.

A hamburger actually sounded pretty good to Marilyn. Maybe she'd suggest that to Doug. "Here's something nice." She told him all about what she'd found in Doug's apartment. When she finished, her phone rang. It was her friend Charlotte.

"Don't get that," Jim said. "You guys will be talking for twenty minutes."

She slapped his arm. "No we won't." She headed toward Jim's side of the walk-in closet as she answered the phone. "Hey, Charlotte."

"So you made it home okay?"

"We're home but, listen, I can't really talk. We're about to go out for dinner."

"This'll only take a sec. Just confirming you're still going to the orientation meeting with me tomorrow. You know, at the crisis pregnancy center."

Marilyn had forgotten all about it. "Yes, I'm going. Not sure how awake I'll be." She selected the shirt she wanted and walked it over to Jim.

"Hope it's okay, but I went ahead and also signed you up for counseling training Saturday morning. If you don't want to go, you can cancel it. But the spots were going fast."

"I guess."

"Whatta ya mean, you guess. You'll be great at it."

"I'm sure that's fine."

"Good, then it's settled. Well, you all have a nice dinner. So glad you got back all right."

■ ■ ■ ■

Forty minutes later, they were sitting down with Doug at the Beef Joint, a local mom-and-pop place that made great burgers the old-fashioned way. It had a condiments bar with every imaginable thing you could ever want on a burger. Marilyn was already in her seat; Doug was heading this way and Jim was still fashioning his masterpiece at the bar.

Doug looked great, and he was so excited about some news he'd picked up at the college. Back at the house, he had given them both a warm hug when they'd greeted.

Doug slid into the booth. "So, what was your favorite thing of the whole trip?"

"Let's see . . . probably just having all that time with your dad. Either that, or driving that BMW one hundred miles an hour on the Autostrada." She pretended as if she were still deciding.

"You drove a BMW one hundred miles an hour?"

Marilyn nodded.

"And Dad was okay with that?"

"It was your dad's idea. He set it up."

"No way." Jim walked up and sat next to Marilyn. "Dad, you let Mom drive a hundred miles an hour in Italy?"

"Let's pray over the food, and then I'll answer that." Jim led them in a short prayer of thanks. He looked up at Doug. "Yes, I did. But I was a nervous wreck."

"He was," Marilyn added. "But he had no reason to be." Jim and Doug began to devour their burgers. She was hungry, but she'd also gained six pounds on the trip. *I'll start working on that tomorrow,* she thought as she bit into the burger.

For the next twenty minutes, they exchanged stories. Of course, it wasn't exactly a free-flowing dialogue. Jim and Marilyn talked all about Italy; Doug's side of the conversation was more like an interview with one-sentence answers and follow-up questions.

The only disappointment came when Jim asked Doug if he'd made it to church on Sunday. A long pause was their answer. Doug quickly apologized. "The guys were over late Saturday playing Xbox. Sorry, I overslept."

To help Jim resist the urge to turn the conversation into a lecture, Marilyn remembered something they hadn't talked about yet. "You still haven't told us about your time at the college. You said you had some good news."

"Oh, right. I had a great meeting with the guidance counselor. While you were gone, my acceptance letter came in. So I made an appointment —"

"You got accepted?" Marilyn said. "I'm so excited for you!"

"That's great, Doug," Jim said. "I'm proud of you. You worked hard to get your grades up this past year. See? It paid off."

"It did. And here's the thing. Turns out, I can graduate almost a year early if I take courses during all the summer semesters. You'll even save a little bit, Dad, if I do this. The classes will cost the same, but you won't have to pay as much room and board since the summer semesters are shorter."

"You want to graduate early?" Jim asked.

"Sure, if I can. The thing is, I'd have to move into the dorm just a week after my high school graduation."

Marilyn's heart sank. "You mean, you wouldn't be moving out in the fall? You'd be leaving us in June? That's less than six weeks."

"But it's only an hour and a half away, Mom. I'd be coming home for visits all the time."

Marilyn doubted that. More likely, once Doug left home they'd see him less and less. He was already so independent. She set her burger down on the plate.

Suddenly, she had lost her appetite.

36

Later that evening, Henry invited Tom outside on the patio with him. A sliver of light remained in the western sky. The temperature was a pleasant seventy degrees. Myra had poured them glasses of fresh iced tea. "Have a seat, Tom. I was thinking maybe we could have that chat. The one we were going to have before you talked with Jean."

Tom sat in the wicker chair, set his glass on the round end table between them. "What's the point now? The whole thing is so messed up."

"I don't think things are as bad as they seem, Tom. I don't know for certain why God let it play out this way. I'm sure he has his reasons. But things aren't just unraveling here. I believe God is still in total control of everything going on, even now."

"If that's true," Tom said, "then I guess he must be trying to punish me for the lousy way I've handled this."

Henry smiled as that verse about God disciplining those he loves came to mind again. "You might be on to something there, Tom."

Tom looked up, puzzled. "You think God really is punishing me?"

"Maybe," Henry said. Then he quoted the verse in Hebrews. "Actually Tom, the whole chapter where that verse sits — I think it's chapter 12 — is all about God's discipline. I've been disciplined by God more times than I can count. Every Christian has. We might not always recognize it, and because we don't, we often don't learn the lessons God's trying to get through to us. But because he loves us, he stays at it until the lights finally come on."

Tom reached for his iced tea. "You're saying this whole mix-up with Jean is . . . God loving me?"

Henry nodded. "The Bible says God disciplines those he loves. He's not like earthly parents, who discipline their kids when they get fed up or embarrassed by what they're doing. His only motivation is love. And that his child learns the lesson he's trying to teach him." Henry sat back in his chair and waited a few moments to let all this sink in.

Tom set his glass down on the table and stood up. He walked to the edge of the patio and stared out toward the backyard. He was breathing so heavily that Henry could hear him from where he sat. This went on for a minute or two. Henry felt like maybe he should say something comforting.

Finally, Tom turned, blinking back tears. "I think you're right, Uncle Henry. I've been making excuses this whole time for every wrong thing I've done. Ever since I got that pink slip from the bank. All these lies to Jean and everyone else. Blaming everybody but myself." He looked down at the ground. "I don't even know why I did it. In the beginning, I thought it was to protect Jean. But as time went on, I knew that it wasn't the real reason." He walked slowly along the back edge of the patio, where it bordered the grass.

Henry stood and walked toward him. He felt a strong nudge about where this conversation should go next. "Who are you protecting, Tom? Do you know?"

Tom shook his head, not really looking at Henry. "I don't know. I just . . . I thought it was Jean, but after the lies kept piling up, it became more about me not getting caught in all these lies. Or what Jean and my folks would think when they found out the truth.

Oh man . . ." He reached up and began massaging his temples. "They're going to find out now." He took a deep breath. "My parents, they might already know." A long exhale.

There it was again, Henry thought. It confirmed his suspicions. Tom seemed to be retreating inside himself. Henry had to do something to reach him before he slipped into full-blown despair. He put his arm on Tom's shoulder. "I think I know why you did it, son."

Tom looked up. "You do?"

Henry nodded. "It's because you're an Anderson man. It's our legacy. A sad one, but there it is." Tom was listening but clearly didn't understand. "The thing is, if you don't learn this lesson, you'll pass it on to little Tommy, just as surely as your dad passed it on to you, and my dad passed it on to us. Aunt Myra and I've been seeing this thing play out for a while. You're already headed in that direction with little Tommy."

"I am? What direction? I don't get it. What are you saying?"

"Let's go back over to those chairs a minute, and I'll explain. It won't take long." Tom followed him back to the wicker chairs. Henry took a long swallow of his iced tea.

"What do you mean, I'm an Anderson

man? You're saying it like it's a bad thing."

"I'm talking about the way you were raised. You had no say in it, but it happened just the same. It was the way my dad raised me and your grandfather, the way your grandfather raised your dad, the way he raised you. Tell me something: during all those months of lying, who were you more afraid would find out, Jean or your dad?"

"Jean," Tom said without hesitation. "I see her every day. There was a lot more danger in her finding out than my dad. I only ever see him every week or so. If Jean found out, I knew it would be all over. There's no way she would keep this thing between us. What am I saying? She's probably already told them."

"Told who?" Henry knew the answer.

"Told my . . ." Tom stopped. He saw it.

"Your folks?" Henry said. "More specifically . . . your dad?"

Tom nodded, lowered his head. "He's going to think I'm a total loser. I really screwed things up. Now, he's gonna know." Tears rolled down his cheeks. "About the job, the house, the cars, the maxed-out credit cards." He looked up. "We're going to lose everything, Uncle Henry. Everything."

The tears came stronger now. He looked

down at the ground again. "He told me to get that certification, right after I graduated. But I didn't listen. He told me not to buy the house when I did, not to get that second car. He's gonna blow his stack when he sees how much debt I've racked up on those cards." He looked up at Henry. "We don't even believe in credit cards, did you know that? They're a trap. You know how many times I heard that growing up? Hundreds. Now look. I'm in a hole so deep I'll never get out."

His head fell into his hands. Henry heard him say, "I'm a screwup. A total screwup."

Henry rubbed his back gently. It was hard to be an Anderson man.

37

The next day, a Saturday, Marilyn drove into the quaint downtown section of River Oaks, right past Odds-n-Ends, the little store where she worked. She was excited to get back into her routine, which began on Monday. She wondered what kinds of things Harriet, the owner, had ordered since she had left for Italy. All kinds of new summer goodies. She couldn't wait to see them.

She angled into an open parking space near a little bistro. Michele's car was already there. They had planned this lunch before the trip; Michele wanted to make sure she heard all about Italy while things were still fresh in Marilyn's mind.

As Marilyn got out of the car and walked toward the front door, she felt a little concerned. It was something in the tone of Michele's voice when they had confirmed things on the phone an hour ago. Marilyn wanted to ask then but decided to wait, since they were spending this time together now.

The restaurant was fairly crowded. Michele waved to her from a table in the back. She was smiling and stood to greet Marilyn as she reached the table. "Look at you," Michele said, "the world traveler comes home." They hugged and sat in their chairs. "So, how was it? I want to hear everything."

But there it was, in her eyes. Something was troubling Michele. Something big.

Over the next forty-five minutes, while Marilyn ate two perfectly grilled lamb chops over long grain rice, and Michele enjoyed her plate of thyme-and-garlic marinated shrimp, they talked all about Italy. Michele insisted that Marilyn walk her through the entire trip, day by day. It was great reliving all those moments again and being able to share them with her daughter.

"You and Dad sound more like a couple on their first honeymoon, not a couple of old fogies in their forties," Michele teased.

"That's how it felt. Every single day. Your father was amazing. I feel closer to him now than I have in twenty-seven years."

Michele sipped her café au lait. "I'm so happy for you, for both of you. You've come so far since last summer. I really thought it was over back then, that there was no way back for you guys."

"So did I," Marilyn said. "But God had mercy on us. A lot of couples our age dread the empty-nest years. But now, I'm actually looking forward to them. I just didn't think they were gonna be here so soon."

"What do you mean? Doug's not leaving for college until the fall."

"I guess he didn't tell you."

"Tell me what?"

Marilyn told her about Doug's plans to leave home early, right after his high school graduation. "But let's not dwell on that now," she said.

There it was again, that look in Michele's eyes. Something was bothering her, something she didn't want to talk about. "What is it, Michele?"

"What is what?"

"Something's wrong. I can tell. I can always tell. What is it?"

Michele sighed. "I don't want to talk about it now. You need to know, but not now. You're just getting back from your trip. We're having such a great lunch. Let's leave it be for a little while."

"Michele . . . you know that's not gonna work. Not with me. I won't be able to concentrate on another thing you say if you don't tell me." Michele sighed again. A double sigh. Must be pretty bad. Marilyn began to tense up.

"I suppose you're right. You're going to find out soon enough anyway, with something this big."

This big? What could it be?

Michele took a deep breath. "I guess I should just say it. Tom was laid off from his job at the bank five months ago."

"What!"

"There's more. Since then, he's been lying to Jean and all of us about it. Jean just found out yesterday, and not because he told her. She found out the hard way. She went to the doctor's office, to confirm that she's pregnant. That's when she discovered they lost their health insurance."

"Jean's pregnant? Does Tom know?"

"He does now. They had a big blowup yesterday. She confronted him when he got home from the airport."

This was terrible. "How far along is she?"

"We don't know. She wasn't able to see the doctor because of the insurance thing. I can't believe Tom would do something so stupid."

"How did he lose his job? Was he laid off, did he get fired?"

"I really don't know, Mom. I haven't

heard the whole story yet."

The waiter came up and asked if they had saved any room for dessert. Both thanked him but said no. Marilyn couldn't even think about eating anything else now. "But I would like some coffee, please."

"No more for me," Michele said.

What a mess, Marilyn thought. "Do you know what Tom was doing that whole time? If he wasn't going to work, where was he going?"

"I don't know that one either," Michele said. "I'm going to check in on Jean, see if she'd like to talk more about it. Last night she just wanted some time alone. I do know this . . . it's got her wondering whether or not Tom has been unfaithful. Like maybe there's more going on here than just losing his job."

"I don't believe that," Marilyn said. "Do you? I can't see Tom throwing away his relationship with Jean and the kids like that."

"I don't want to believe it. But I can't imagine lying about losing your job for five months, either. Then going off every day, pretending to go to work. Jean said, how can you trust a word someone says if they can lie about something that big every day for all that time?"

The waiter walked up and poured Marilyn's coffee.

This was so awful. They weren't talking about just anyone; they were talking about Tom, her son. "Do you think Jean would talk to me?" Marilyn loved her daughter-in-law deeply. They had a good relationship, but not a close one. She'd always blamed Tom for that. He was so standoffish, so controlling. Just like his father had been for so many years. He had probably forbidden Jean from sharing any of their "private business." The poor thing, Jean was probably an emotional wreck right now.

"I don't know, Mom. She might. But maybe you should let me test the waters on that first. She started opening up to me while you guys were gone. I think she *needs* to hear from you, especially after what you've been through with Dad. If anybody can help her sort through the deep emotions she must be feeling, it's you." Michele reached her hand across the table and squeezed her mother's fingers. "I know talking to you always helps me."

"Thanks, hon," she said, reaching for a napkin. "I love talking to you, any chance I get. And I do want to talk to Jean, as soon as God opens a door. Give me a call after you see how she's doing."

"I will."

Marilyn took a sip of coffee. "But I think even more important than me having a talk with Jean is your father having a talk with Tom."

"I'm so glad you said that," Michele said. "I've been wishing Dad would talk to Tom for months. I even talked to Allan about it."

See, Marilyn thought. Even Michele knew Tom and Jean were in trouble. It was a feeling Marilyn hadn't been able to shake for months now. It hung over her head like a cloud for hours every time they visited. It was why she'd kept pressing Jim to reach out to Tom in Italy, to spend more time with him.

Oh my. Jim.

What's he going to say when he hears about this?

38

Marilyn drove with a heavy heart to their home on Elderberry Lane. She wasn't thinking about Italy anymore. But as she turned the corner onto the little service lane running behind their home, she couldn't help but smile at what she saw. "I can't believe it. He remembered."

Standing above the white privacy fence were the long, thin — and now very familiar — tops of five Italian cypress trees. They had only talked about this once on their trip, how much she loved these trees that lined the roadways and villa driveways throughout Tuscany. Pushing the garage door opener, she pulled into her spot in the garage. She almost didn't have the heart to tell Jim about her conversation with Michele at lunch.

She got out of the car and walked through the garage, through the side gate, and into the backyard. Jim was bent over, his shirt drenched in sweat, furiously digging five large, evenly spaced holes along the side fence. He hadn't seen her yet. Next to him in a cluster were the five trees, with burlap sacks tied around their root balls. They looked much too heavy for Jim to lift by himself. She hoped that wasn't the plan.

As she got closer, she saw he wore earbud headphones attached to an iPod in his pocket. She was about to tap him on the shoulder when he stopped digging and turned around. He had seen her shadow.

"Well, what do you think?" he yelled over the volume in his ears. He stood back and waved his arms like a showman introducing a line of dancers.

She threw her arms around him, sweat and all. "I love them!"

"Honey, I'm a mess." He dropped the shovel and pulled out his headphones.

"I don't care. I can't believe you remembered."

"Of course I did. I said I would. Figured I'd do it right off the bat, before I got sucked back into our routine."

She released her hug. "You're not going to move those huge things into those holes by yourself, are you?"

"No, Doug's gonna help me. He gets off work at 4:00. That's when your orientation meeting is, right? With Charlotte?"

"That's right." She looked at her watch. It was an hour and a half away. Now she wondered if she should cancel. How could she pay attention to anything with this crisis going on between Tom and Jean?

"Are you still going?"

"I . . . uh, I think so."

"You sounded so excited about it before," he said.

"I know. I really do want to go. It's just . . ." She sighed.

"What's the matter?"

"Something's come up. Something I found out about at lunch with Michele."

"Something between her and Allan?"

Marilyn shook her head no. "Something Michele told me. Could you use a break? I really need to talk to you. How about I go in the house and pour a Coke. You can clean up a bit and I'll fill you in."

"You want me to take a shower? I'd like to finish digging first, if that's okay. Might take me twenty minutes."

"This can't wait. Can we talk now? Maybe you could just dry off with a towel, change your shirt."

"Sure, hon. Sounds serious."

"It is."

■ ■ ■ ■

After she'd left Jim by the fence, Marilyn spent most of her time praying about what to say, but even more about how Jim would take it. She set the sodas on the bar and pulled out a stool.

A few minutes later, Jim came in and sat beside her. "Okay, what's up?"

"Before I tell you, I want to say I probably won't have answers to most of your questions. This thing just happened, last night, I guess. And Michele still doesn't know most of the details."

"Well, you've certainly got my attention." He lifted his glass and took a long swallow.

Jean reached for hers but didn't drink. "I don't even know where to begin. You know how we tried not to talk about our kids' problems on our trip?" Jim nodded. "And you know how that didn't work out very well?"

"Some of the time it did."

"Well, you're right. But I couldn't get one of our kids completely out of my mind."

"Tom?" She nodded. "So this is about Tom and Jean? What's the matter? What happened?"

She looked in Jim's eyes, trying to read

299

them. "It looks like our son has done something very foolish. When Michele first told me, I couldn't even believe it."

"I'm listening." His face grew serious.

"He was either fired or got laid off from his job at the bank."

"Well," Jim said, "I guess he got fired, if you're saying he did something foolish."

"Jim, you need to let me finish."

"I'm sorry."

"The foolish thing isn't about how he lost his job, but *when*." Jim looked properly puzzled. She continued. "It happened five months ago."

"Five months ago! Five months ago! What are you saying?" Jim set his glass down.

"He lost his job at the bank five months ago, but he didn't tell anyone. Not even Jean."

"You're kidding. That's . . . that's absurd. Why wouldn't he tell anyone?"

"We don't know, not yet."

"Well," Jim said, "what has he been doing all this time?"

"Apparently, he's been getting up every day pretending to go to work, keeping the same routine he always had."

"That's just . . . that's crazy. Where was he going? What's he been using for money all this time?"

"I don't have all the answers, remember? I really don't know. I guess he's been on unemployment."

"Well, they can't live on that. Not with *that* mortgage, and those car payments. He wouldn't last two months on unemployment with his bills, let alone five."

"I don't know, Jim. I guess we'll find out those kinds of things in a little while."

Jim sat back in his stool, propped up his legs on the footrests. He was shaking his head back and forth, staring at some point in the kitchen. "This is just crazy. What an idiotic thing to do. What was he thinking? He's probably gonna lose the house, the car. Maybe both cars. Five months, that's a long time. And he didn't tell anyone? What possible excuse could he have for not telling anyone?"

She realized he wasn't really asking questions at this point, just venting his confusion and frustration. But she was concerned about where his heart would go with this information.

He looked out toward the backyard and continued, as if Tom was standing nearby. "C'mon, Tom, you can't be serious. That's not how I raised you. You take responsibility for your mistakes, you don't bury them under the rug. You deal with them. Did you

301

think you'd get away with something like this?" He turned back to Marilyn. "It's like something a little kid would do. Isn't it? Not something a grown man would do."

Little kid, Marilyn thought. Yes, a little boy. A picture flashed in her mind, her little Tom. He was such a sweet child. All she could think of now was the pain he must be feeling, and the confusion.

"Marilyn, are you listening?"

"Yes, I suppose it does seem immature," Marilyn said. "And if you ask me, pretty out of character for him. Of all our kids, Tom was the most responsible. Even when he was a child. I almost never had to tell him to do something twice. He always did his chores, always followed through." She couldn't see Michele doing something like this, either. Now Doug? That really wouldn't surprise her at all.

"There's gotta be more to the story," Jim said. "I didn't raise Tom to do something as crazy as this. It would be easier to believe he shot somebody."

Marilyn didn't like hearing Jim say the phrase "I didn't raise Tom," as if he had raised Tom on his own. That was the second time he'd said this. But in a way, it was partly true. She had always struggled with the heavy expectations Jim had placed on

Tom growing up. She regularly felt like Jim was too hard on Tom. But Tom never seemed to mind. He adored his father.

But still, Marilyn regretted the fact that she had never spoken up about it. It was wrong, clearly. Look at all the bad fruit showing up on the tree now. Maybe if she'd had more courage back then and pressed these issues with Jim, she could have begun to steer him in a healthier direction.

"Where are they now?" Jim asked. "Tom and Jean, what's the status of things?"

"Michele said there was a big blowup last night when Tom got back from the airport."

"So Jean just found out about it?" Jim said. "How?"

Marilyn took a few minutes to explain what she understood, then said, "From what I gather, Jean put Tom out of the house, at least temporarily."

"Good for her," Jim said. "Where is he now?"

That sounded a bit harsh. "I don't really know." She was more worried about Tom than angry.

Jim stood up and started walking toward the bedroom.

"Where are you going?"

"To get my cell phone," Jim said. "I've gotta call Tom, get to the bottom of this."

"Stop right there," Marilyn said. "You'll do no such thing."

39

Tom was buttoning up his shirt in Uncle Henry and Aunt Myra's guest room. He had to be at work at the Java Stop in less than an hour and needed to leave early to make the drive from New Smyrna Beach to Lake Mary.

Although his life was in ruins, the thick depression that had consumed him for so long seemed to have lifted somewhat after his conversation with Uncle Henry that morning. For the last few hours he'd felt something he hadn't felt in a long time: the nearness of God. Because after that talk, Tom had driven to the beach, found a fairly secluded stretch, and just started walking. The longer he walked, the clearer things became. It was true that his so-called friend Jared had betrayed him. But everything that happened after that, the mess he'd made reacting to that betrayal, was entirely of his own making. As the pile of troubles and

305

consequences from his string of poor choices mounted up in his mind, he realized this wasn't something he could ever untangle by himself.

Before he'd left the house, Uncle Henry had walked up and said, "It's for things just like this that God sent us a Savior. You need to turn it all over to him, Son. My advice would be to humble yourself by admitting that you're powerless to get yourself out of this mess. Seek his plans for your life instead of your own. You could even begin to thank him for using this trial to turn you back to him. No one fixes messes like God. I know this firsthand."

As he'd walked along the shoreline, Tom finally had a break-through. With tears rolling down his cheeks, he told God he really wanted to get it right . . . with Jean, with everybody. Whatever that meant. Whatever he needed to do. For however much time it took.

Thinking about that moment now, he walked over to the bed. He sat on the edge to put on his shoes. He heard a noise in the hall and looked up. It was Uncle Henry.

"How you making out?"

"I'm doing all right," Tom said. "What you said this morning really helped. That walk on the beach did too."

"When do you have to leave for work?"

"In about fifteen minutes."

"Well, I've been talking with your aunt while you were gone. We both think you might need some help patching things up with Jean. Not just with Jean, but with your father too."

"My father? You think he and I need some . . . patching up?"

Uncle Henry came through the doorway. "Well, maybe not patching up so much. But I think — we both think — your problems with Jean actually go upstream a bit. They're connected to a breakdown in your relationship with your dad. Something I think neither one of you is seeing."

"Well, I'm fine with whatever you want to do, Uncle Henry. Right about now, I could use all the help I can get." He bent down and tied his shoes. "You think at some point, though, you could call Jean for me? See if she's okay with me coming home after work, or whether I need to come back here?"

"Sure, I can do that. If she wants you to come back here, you're welcome to use this room for as long as you need it."

Tom looked up into Uncle Henry's kind eyes. "When you talk to her, please make her believe there's nobody else. Because of all my lies, she's actually wondering if that's what's going on here. But I promise you it's not. It never dawned on me this whole time that she'd think that. This is just about me losing my job, and for some stupid reason thinking it might be a good idea not to tell her till I got a new one. But it's gotta be eating her up inside, wondering if I've been unfaithful."

Uncle Henry sat in the upholstered chair in the corner. "Why do you think she thinks that, Tom, that you've been unfaithful?"

"I don't know. I suppose it's because I've also been treating her like crap this whole time. And because she isn't buying the idea that I would keep this charade going for five months if it was just about losing my job. Even saying it, I can't believe it myself. It was such a dumb thing to do. That's so clear now. But at the time, it felt like the only thing I could do. I still don't know why I did it."

Uncle Henry nodded, like he was understanding something beyond what Tom had just said.

"What is it?" Tom said. "What are you thinking?"

"Everything you're saying is confirming what Aunt Myra and I talked about. The *real* reason you did all this. The core motivation."

"What are you saying?"

"It's about your dad, Tom. There's something broken in your relationship with him. And with God's help, I'm hoping we can get that fixed."

"My dad?" Tom stood up. "I wish I could stay and talk, but I really gotta go."

Uncle Henry stood up too. "I'll walk you out to the car and explain a little more." Tom turned down the hallway. Henry followed behind him. "I'm not saying your dad's to blame for everything you've done wrong here. I think you know that."

"I'm not seeing how my dad's to blame for any of it, to be honest." He came into the living room. "He wouldn't have approved of anything I did if I'd asked him."

"No, I'm sure he wouldn't. But what I'm talking about goes deeper than that. It has to do with our family history, something that's been missing in your relationship since you were a child. Something your dad probably never even thought was all that important. Of course, he wouldn't have. None of the Anderson men got this. I wouldn't have, either, if I'd have stayed in the fold."

None of this was making too much sense

to Tom. He stepped into the kitchen to thank Aunt Myra and say good-bye, then headed through the front door toward his car. "I really want to hear more about this, Uncle Henry. I honestly do. But if I don't leave now, I'm gonna be late."

"That's okay. Don't worry about it. Probably better if I take this up with your dad first anyway." He patted Tom on the shoulder as he got into his car.

A few moments later Henry stood by the front window and watched Tom's car drive off down the road. "You were right, Myra, about all of it. I'm certain of that now."

Myra walked up beside him, just in time to see Tom's car turn the corner.

He put his arm around her shoulder. "I suspect he barely got any encouragement at all from Jim throughout his childhood."

"You never did from your father, you or your brother."

"No, we sure didn't. And neither did Jim. It's tragic how few fathers realize the power of their tongue."

"To build their kids up or tear 'em down," she said. She gave Henry a little squeeze then pulled away. "I gotta finish up in the kitchen." Talking over her shoulder, she said, "In some ways, getting rejected by your dad when you picked me was the best thing that ever happened to us."

Henry, still looking out the window, was thinking the same thing. The very same thing.

"When are you going to talk to Jim about this?" she said from the kitchen.

"Think I'm going to call him now, maybe take a drive over there before dinner."

40

For the last hour, Marilyn had sat next to Charlotte at the Women's Resource Center orientation meeting. The director, Arlene Ryan, seemed to be wrapping things up. But already Marilyn was completely sold on everything she'd heard. She was so glad she had come.

She almost hadn't, but Jim had insisted she go, after promising her he wouldn't attempt to contact Tom while she was gone. He'd agreed with her — this whole thing had upset him too much, and he'd only make things worse if he stuck his nose in right now. They would pray and talk about it later, see if there was anything they could possibly do.

"So, are you gonna do it?" Charlotte leaned over and whispered.

"Definitely," Marilyn said. "I would love to be a part of what's going on here."

The resource center was a quaint little

place, like a small doctor's office. A little on the plain side, but it was clean and nicely decorated. There were about ten other women listening to Arlene's presentation. Marilyn would be a part of the counseling team, but, as Charlotte assured her beforehand, this wasn't some kind of heavy psychotherapy thing. Arlene had made a point of saying they weren't equipped to provide professional counseling, even calling the volunteers "client advocates." Their clients were mostly young women in a crisis who, for the most part, needed a mother's love and advice. But for a variety of reasons, they weren't getting it.

The question was, could they — these client advocates — step in and fill that role? Could they help guide these girls to make the kinds of decisions they should be making at a crucial time like this? Then Arlene went on to spell out what that guidance looked like in a practical sense. Marilyn nodded her head the entire time. She also experienced a significant measure of gratitude for the relationship God had given her with Michele. And a renewed burden for the gaps that still existed in her relationship with Jean.

The meeting wrapped up after twenty more minutes. Coffee and light refreshments were served. Marilyn walked right over and turned in her signed form at the registration table. Charlotte had already signed up a month ago. As an RN she had more medical duties, mostly involving ultrasound. She really had only come to encourage Marilyn and, apparently, talk her up to the director. Marilyn saw her talking to Arlene right now, pointing in her direction. Charlotte smiled and waved her over.

As Marilyn approached, Arlene stuck out her hand. She was a lovely lady, dark-haired, slender, maybe a few years younger than Marilyn. "So you're Marilyn Anderson. So glad to finally meet you. Charlotte talks about you all the time." They shook hands.

"I was totally inspired by what you said," Marilyn said to Arlene. "I'd really like to help out here any way I can."

"Charlotte thinks you'd make a wonderful mentor for our girls," Arlene said.

"I hope so. I've always found it easy to talk with my daughter and all her friends."

"That's because she's such a great listener," Charlotte said. "And she never judges."

"Of course," Marilyn continued, "I don't have any experience talking girls through a crisis like this."

Arlene walked over to a table and picked

up a small booklet, then returned. "I wonder if you wouldn't mind reading this over in the next few days. It's something we prepared to equip our advocates." She handed it to Marilyn. "This should give you a good idea of what's involved."

"I definitely will."

"In fact," Arlene said, "if you can finish reading it by Monday and are still enthusiastic about doing this, I might like to put you with one of the girls right away."

Marilyn wasn't sure she liked the sound of that. She had told Jim she would run everything by him before committing to anything specific. "Right away?"

"Well, in a few days anyway. We're really short staffed at the moment. I talked with Charlotte about it, and she thinks you're almost ready to go right now."

Marilyn shot Charlotte a look meant to convey "What have you gotten me into?" Charlotte just raised her eyebrows and smiled.

"But I'm not even trained yet," Marilyn said.

"Oh, I don't know about that," Arlene said. "You've successfully raised three children through high school, right?"

Marilyn thought for a moment about the troubles waiting for her at home. Had she successfully raised her children? At the moment, she found herself wishing she could go back and do some things differently. Very differently.

"Yes, but —"

"Then I'd say you're probably closer to being trained than you know. I'm sure all we'd be doing is some tweaking and fine-tuning. Besides, for the first session, you'd be shadowing one of our more experienced mentors. You'll pick up a lot just watching her."

That sounded a little less scary.

"I don't mean to rush you, Marilyn," Arlene continued. "Really I don't. You think it over, read the booklet, talk it over with your husband. See if God puts faith in your heart for this. That's how we do most things around here. A whole lot of walking by faith."

"I suppose I can do that," Marilyn said.

"Here's my card. My cell number is on the back. Call me in a couple of days, and we'll talk."

Another volunteer came up to talk to Arlene. Marilyn took that as an opportunity to make her exit. She gently pulled Charlotte over to the table with the coffee and cookies. "What did you tell her about me, Charlotte?"

"Just the truth. About how kind you are, how caring you are, what a good friend you are, how wise you are."

"Do you know anything about this first girl they want to put me with?"

"Sorry, I don't. But I know you'll do great, and like Arlene said, starting out you'd just be shadowing the more experienced mentors."

"I don't know if I'm ready for something like this right away. I thought I'd have a month of training, or at least several weeks."

"Don't worry, hon. Arlene is real nice. Just do like she told you. Think about it, pray about it, talk it over with Jim, read that booklet there. Don't get all worked up. I think this is one of those things, you know? Where we make such a big deal about it in our heads, then it turns out to be something so simple. They're real relational around here. That's all they're looking for, for you to be who you already are with some of these girls."

Marilyn breathed a sigh of relief. Maybe she was getting all worked up over nothing. She didn't have to decide right now. And she wouldn't do anything without talking it over with Jim and getting his input. They were a team now; she didn't have to face decisions like this on her own anymore.

Jim . . . she'd better get home.

Whether she was ready to start counseling a young unwed mother was nothing compared to the full-blown family crisis of their own back home.

41

"Hello? That you, Jim?"

"It's me, Uncle Henry. Where are you calling from?"

"Just standing here in my driveway, but I was planning on heading over to your house. If you're there, that is."

Jim got a picture in his mind of a vintage yellow '68 Chevy Impala with a black vinyl top, and his uncle standing right beside it. "Oh, I'm here. But not sure this is such a good time. Just finishing up a big tree project with Doug."

"Doug? Tell him I said hi. You know, it's gonna take me about thirty minutes to get over there from here. If you're just finishing up, maybe you'll be done by the time I get there. What do you think?"

"Guess it's kind of important then?"

"Kind of," Uncle Henry said. "You up on all that's going on with Tom and Jean?"

"Tom and Jean? Hold on. Let me get to

where I can talk." Jim put his hand over the phone and took a few steps toward the veranda. He turned back to his son. "You're doing great, Doug. Just keep filling in all those gaps with that rich, black soil. I'll be back in a minute. Just going to talk over here with Uncle Henry a minute." When he got beneath the shade of the veranda, he continued. "Uncle Henry, do you know what's going on? We just got in yesterday. Michele told Marilyn about it, but she didn't know any details. Sounds like a real mess."

"I believe I know a good bit of it. Actually, that's why I want to come see you. Tom is staying with us for the time being."

"He is? I heard Jean put him out of the house. I was worried about where he'd end up."

"Well, he ended up here. He's at work now. Just left a little while ago."

"Work? I thought he got laid off."

"He did, from the bank. This is a temporary job, as he calls it, at some coffee and sandwich shop not far from where they live. Just started working there a little while ago, I think."

Jim couldn't believe his son with a bachelor's degree in finance was working at a coffee shop. "There's so much I don't know about what's going on, Uncle Henry. I'd really like to talk with you. I'm sure Doug and I can get this project behind us before you arrive."

"Good. Then I'll get in the car and start driving."

"Has Tom told you why he did this? It seems so crazy to me. I still can't believe he'd do something so idiotic. Marilyn and I were talking about it a little while ago. Neither one of us can figure it out. The Tom we know would never do something like this." Jim heard Uncle Henry's car start up.

"Well, if you don't mind, I'd like to talk about all this in person. With you and Marilyn. Is she there, by the way?"

"No, she's not. She's at some volunteer orientation meeting. But I expect her home real soon."

"Good," Uncle Henry said. "She should be in on this conversation. Let's hold off talking about this any more until I get there. I'll be there in thirty minutes."

The drive took more like forty-five minutes, and by then the temperature had cooled off a bit, allowing Jim, Marilyn, and Uncle Henry to meet out on the veranda by the pool. Doug had left to go hang out with some friends.

Marilyn had just gotten home a few minutes ago. Jim could tell she was all set to brief him on her big meeting until he interrupted her, saying it would have to wait. Uncle Henry had come and needed to speak with both of them about Tom and Jean.

That got her attention.

For the next twenty minutes over glasses of iced tea, Uncle Henry gave them a play-by-play account of Tom and Jean's situation. He answered most of their follow-up questions too, although there were a few things he still didn't understand himself. The more he talked, the less sense Tom's conduct — even his thinking — made to them.

When Uncle Henry had finished, Jim said, "Please tell me you have some idea as to why Tom chose this path. I've been racking my brain, and I'm coming up empty. I can't even imagine what his finances look like right now."

"I imagine they're in pretty sad shape," Uncle Henry said.

Jim looked over at Marilyn. "I hope this doesn't come back on us somehow. We don't have enough reserves to bail him out."

"Let's don't get ahead of ourselves, Jim,"

she said. "Let's hear what Uncle Henry has to say."

"You're right." He turned to face his uncle again. "So let's have it. Why are we in this mess?"

Henry took a sip of his tea, rubbed his forehead. "This is going to take a bit of doing, getting all this out."

"Don't worry about it, Uncle Henry," Marilyn said. "We're in no hurry. Take your time."

He looked up at Jim and said, "The short answer for why we're in this mess is that Tom made a bad decision to hide something he was ashamed of. From Jean, from you guys, from everyone. And once he started, he kept it going, one lie after another, whatever it took to keep the perception intact that everything was fine, same as it ever was."

"But Tom knows lying is wrong," Jim said. "He's known that since he was a kid."

"Yeah, he does. And he's taken responsibility for that. First with the Lord and soon with everyone else. And he knows there's gonna be consequences for this. He's broken trust with everybody. The reason I'm here, the reason I want to talk to you two, is because Aunt Myra and I think there's something bigger going on here than what's on the surface. Something that has to do with what's broken in this entire family."

Jim leaned forward in his chair. "You're saying I'm the reason Tom did this? Because of the way I raised him?" Marilyn reached over and patted Jim's forearm.

"Hold on there, Jim. When I say broken, I'm not just talking about you and Marilyn, and the way you raised your kids. This thing's been broken a long time. Goes back at least as far as my dad and the way he raised your dad and me."

Jim sat back. He had to calm down. Uncle Henry was a praying man. He had come all this way to say something, and Jim needed to hear him out.

"Maybe I could open this up and make sense of it by telling you a little story about myself. You know I was a math teacher, right? Did that for over twenty-five years till I retired. But you probably don't know that when I was a kid, math was my worst subject. And it continued to be during my first two years of high school. I flunked geometry and had to retake it. I was sure one month into that second time around I was gonna flunk it again. One reason I was doing so bad was my teacher. He talked like he was sure I was gonna fail. The only bright spot was I knew more than half the class was failing right along with me. The teacher had arranged our chairs according to our grade. All of us who were failing sat in the back."

"That's a crummy thing for a teacher to do," Marilyn said.

"Yes, it was. Then one Monday morning, all that changed. Sitting behind the teacher's desk was a new teacher. Our old one had been reassigned to another district. We felt like the people in Paris who'd just been liberated from the Nazis in World War II. Something that new teacher said that morning changed my life, literally. I now know something I didn't know then. He was actually doing something very biblical with me and the entire class."

"What did he do?" Jim said.

"He stood before the class and said, 'If anyone fails this class, then I have failed.' And he made a commitment that morning to do whatever it took to see that every single one of us passed the course. He pledged to see that we learned and even enjoyed this subject to the best of our ability. Whether that meant staying after school to tutor us or even coming in for a special session over the weekend, he dedicated himself to make sure every single one of us made it. And that's exactly what he did, week in, week out, till the semester was over. And you know what happened? He posted our grades on that last day of class, and we all passed. Every single one of us."

"What grade did you get, Uncle Henry?" Jim asked.

Uncle Henry's eyes watered as he said, "I got my first A in math, the first one in my entire life. I felt so proud. And all because one man committed himself to our success."

He took a deep breath, then looked Jim right in the eyes. "That first teacher was just like my dad. That's how he treated me and your dad our whole childhood. And that's how your dad treated you. But it's not God's way. That day in geometry class with that new teacher, I got a glimpse of the fatherhood of God, and it changed my life. For the first time, I began to understand the deep need all children have to receive encouragement and blessing from their parents and the powerful effect it can have on them when they get it. It's something we all crave and long for as children but so few of us ever receive. I didn't, not at home. Not even once. But I did that day, and it changed my life."

Jim felt a wave of emotion rush over him. He had never been treated that way grow-ing up. Not even once. He'd never felt accepted by his father. Never felt like he measured up or could ever earn his approval. Nothing he did was good enough, no matter how hard he tried. If he did ten things right but missed one, that's what his father would jump on. Even in high school, when Jim finally started excelling in sports, he never heard his father say, "Great job, son" or "I'm proud of you."

Jim's father had died never having uttered those words.

Not even once.

"Jim . . . are you okay?" He heard Marilyn's kind voice, but it seemed as though it came from across the room.

He couldn't help it. Jim felt like that boy searching the stands for his father, only to be disappointed again. "Dad, *why?*" he muttered as unstoppable tears made their way down his face.

And then, uncontrollable sobbing.

42

Jim didn't know why, but he cried for the longest time. A few times he thought he was coming out of it, then more flashes and images from his past floated up and he'd start right up again. At some point, he stopped seeing pictures from his own childhood and was even more tormented by Tom's. All the times he'd treated Tom the same way his dad had treated him.

Riding him, driving him, pushing him to excel.

For a moment, Jim caught his breath. *I wasn't just like my dad, was I?* He tried to think of times when he'd encouraged Tom, times he'd told Tom how proud he was of him.

He couldn't think of any.

Not one.

He cried the hardest after that.

"He'll be okay, Marilyn," Uncle Henry said softly. "This is a good thing. God can do more in a man's heart at times like this than listening to a hundred sermons."

Marilyn left for a few moments, saying she would refill their drinks and get a trash bag. She had already left once to get a box of Kleenex. A sizable pile now occupied the center of the glass table. When she returned, Jim finally had enough breath and enough calm to say something lucid. He looked at Marilyn's face then at Uncle Henry's and said, "Tom feels what I felt so many times. I just carried the deep hurt from my dad into our relationship. I am . . . my dad! Oh Lord."

The tears came again.

Five minutes later, his tears finally seemed to be spent. He wiped his eyes with fresh tissues and blew his nose and said, "Now what was all that about?" But he knew the answer. He had experienced this once before, when God had broken his heart over the way he had treated Marilyn all those years.

Now he saw the way he had treated Tom, what had been broken in their relationship and, clearly, what needed fixing.

"Are you going to be okay, hon?" Marilyn asked.

"I'm going to be more than okay." He looked at Uncle Henry. "Just so I'm clear on this, the reason Tom lied about losing his job for all this time, the real reason, the deepest reason, was that he was afraid of me finding out how badly he had failed?"

"I believe so," Uncle Henry said. "He cared about Jean being disappointed with him and her worrying about how they'd make it too. But the more I talked to him, the clearer it became. He was mostly hiding it from her because he knew once she found out, you'd find out too. Again, not just about the job loss, although that's probably the biggest thing. But he told me they're probably gonna lose the house and at least one of the cars, and that their credit cards are maxed out."

"Credit cards?" Jim repeated. "Maxed out?" Henry nodded. Jim shook his head in disbelief.

"He must be in torment," Marilyn said.

"But why didn't he ask for help?" Jim said. "Before it got so bad? No, never mind. That's a stupid question now. But see, this brings up something I really don't understand. How can we bless and encourage our kids about things they're doing wrong? Won't that cause them to stop trying hard to succeed? How do they stay motivated to keep pursuing the right goals? It sounds like you're saying we should reward them before they reach the finish line. What would motivate them to keep running?"

"Those are good questions," Uncle Henry said. "They're probably the questions most parents are thinking about when they withhold encouragement and blessings from their kids. But my high school teacher didn't give out As to everyone up front and say, 'Here you go. You get an A and you don't even have to do the work.' We still had to do the work, all of it. But his encouragement and blessing and his total commitment to our success provided strong motivation for us to do all we could to reach that finish line ourselves. That's how God's grace works. It goes before us, comes in behind us, and holds our hand along the way. If a child has that kind of support from a parent, he can become anything God wants him to be."

The fog was beginning to lift. Jim looked at Marilyn. She was smiling. She knew he was getting it. "You've been trying to tell me this for years, haven't you?"

"Something like that," she said. "But I'm seeing it a lot better now myself. And there's something else I'm seeing a lot clearer."

"What's that?"

"You're not the only one to blame for how Tom turned out. I had some real concerns about the way you were treating him, for years. But I hardly said a word. I was too afraid of you, but I should've let my love for Tom and his welfare override my fears. I should've spoken up . . . so many times."

"I probably wouldn't have listened."

"Maybe not, but I still should've tried." She looked at Uncle Henry. "Does Tom know this? Have you shared all this with him?"

"No. I introduced a little of it today. But I really felt like God wanted me to share it with the both of you first. I'm thinking it might be better if Tom heard this from you, Jim. Not me."

"I agree," Jim said. "I really want to have that conversation with him now."

"Do you think I should be the one to talk to Jean?" Marilyn asked. "Where is she in all this?"

"I'm not sure," Uncle Henry said. "Tom asked me to talk to her, but really, it wasn't about this."

"What about, then?"

"He wants me to convince her this has nothing to do with him seeing anyone else."

"Are you sure it doesn't?" Jim asked.

"Pretty sure," Uncle Henry said. "As best as I can discern, he's telling the truth about that."

"So can I talk to Jean about this . . . other stuff?" Marilyn said. "I've been wanting my relationship with her to go deeper than it's been anyway."

"I think that would be a great idea," Uncle Henry said.

"Maybe I'll do it with Michele," Marilyn said. "What do you think? Jean has started opening up to her lately."

Uncle Henry nodded. "I think God's giving us some wisdom here."

Jim reached for Marilyn's hand, smiled. "Sounds like a plan then."

Uncle Henry stood up. "Guess I better head over to Jean's, see if I can take care of that conversation in person. Jim, can you walk me to my car? Just a few things I want to mention about your talk with Tom."

Marilyn gave Uncle Henry a warm hug. "I don't know how we can thank you and Aunt Myra for all your help. I don't have the words. What you've done for Tom and what happened here . . ." Tears filled her eyes. "You don't know how long and how often I've prayed for a breakthrough between Jim and Tom. And for Tom and Jean. I have real hope for that now, Uncle Henry." She gave him another hug.

"You're welcome, Marilyn. I'm just grateful whenever God lets me be a part of what he's doing." He walked across the pool area and through the back gate toward his car. Jim followed right behind. When they got there, Uncle Henry said, "When I get home, to help you get ready for this conversation with your son, I'm gonna send you some Scriptures to read in an email."

"You're doing email now?" Jim asked.

"A little," he said.

"What are the Scriptures about?"

"Well, I just want you to see a little more from God's perspective on this idea. It's really all over the place in the Bible. The Old Testament patriarchs like Abraham, Isaac, and Jacob all did this with their children. At different times, they'd gather them together, lay hands on them, and bless them. They'd say all kinds of encouraging things about their future, meaningful things God wanted them to hear. Many in the Jewish culture still practice this idea of parents blessing their children, but we don't see too much of it going on in the church today."

"Maybe it's because you only see it in the Old Testament," Jim said.

"That's not really true. I see a real clear example of this with Jesus and his disciples at the Last Supper. Think about it . . . at that point, they weren't getting anything right. They were arguing between themselves about who was the greatest. Peter was telling the Lord that he couldn't wash his feet one minute, swearing that he'd die for him the next. Jesus knew that very night Peter would deny even knowing him three times, and all of them would desert him. You should read some of the amazing things Jesus said about his disciples that night. All kinds of things that expressed encouragement and faith about their future. I'll send you those Scriptures. It'll help build faith in your heart for Tom, since things look pretty bleak right now."

Uncle Henry opened the car door and got in, then rolled down the window. "Aunt Myra and I will be praying for you guys."

Jim reached in and patted Uncle Henry's shoulder. "Everything Marilyn said back there goes for me too. I don't know how to thank you for all your help, Uncle Henry."

"It's my privilege, Jim. I really mean that. We love you guys like we love our own kids. You be sure to call me and let me know how things go with Tom."

"I will."

43

Jean had just hung up the phone with Tom's Uncle Henry. She wasn't thrilled about it, but it looked like he was on his way over. And he was just a few blocks away. Apparently, that was who Tom turned to after she asked him to leave the house yesterday. She had always liked Uncle Henry, but right now she was physically and emotionally exhausted.

She hadn't slept well last night, understandably. And it took forever to get Tommy and Carly down for their afternoon nap. She was actually thinking of taking one herself when Uncle Henry called. He promised he'd only stay a few minutes, but she doubted she'd be in any mood for a nap after hearing what he had to say.

She walked out to the kitchen to fix herself a cup of coffee. Tom had texted her three times today. All varying expressions of remorse, regret, and his undying love. She didn't respond to them. Partly because she didn't know what to say, because she didn't know what she felt inside. Mostly, she felt numb. The closest thing she could compare it to was the way she'd felt the day after her mother died.

After fixing her coffee, she heard the low bass sound of a car pulling up in the driveway. That was quick. She hurried back out to the living room, hoping to catch Uncle Henry before he rang the doorbell and woke the kids. Through the front window, she watched him exit the crazy yellow car he drove. Quietly, she opened the front door.

"Hey, Jean," he said a little too loudly as he came up the sidewalk.

She gestured for him to keep his voice down. "The kids are still sleeping. If we do this right, they'll stay asleep till we're through. Come on in." After he stepped in the foyer, she said, "Care for some coffee?"

"No, thanks. Had all the caffeine I can drink for one day."

"Let's go talk at the dining room table," she said. "So there's no chance the kids will hear us." She led the way. She set her coffee down at her usual spot and pulled out the chair. "Can I at least get you some ice water?"

"That would be nice, thank you." He sat

in the chair across from hers. "Aunt Myra and I are so sorry for all you're going through. And I'm not here to judge you or put any pressure on you, one way or the other."

"I appreciate that. It really has been pretty bad. I knew Tom had been acting off for quite some time now, but I never imagined this." She came back with the ice water and set it beside him, then sat in her chair. "So Tom spent the night with you guys."

"He did. Truth is, I found out about him losing his job a few days ago, by accident."

"How?"

"I just showed up at the coffee shop he started working at, and there he was."

"Tom is working in a coffee shop?"

"He just started there a little while ago. But yeah. He's there now, as a matter of fact."

She couldn't picture Tom doing something like that under any circumstance. But really, at this point, why should anything surprise her?

"He wanted me to ask you whether he could come home tonight, or whether he should come back to our place."

She sipped her coffee. "You drove all this way to ask me that?"

"No, that's just a small thing. I brought it

up just so I wouldn't forget to ask."

"Well, you can tell him I'm going to need at least another night or two. I know we have to face each other eventually and talk this out. But I'm just not there yet."

"That's fine. I understand. The other reason I came over, the main reason, is to tell you I don't believe Tom has been unfaithful to you, Jean. I really don't."

Wow, she didn't expect that. "You don't?"

"I really don't. I don't believe that's what's going on here. As an elder in my church, I've dealt with men who were unfaithful. Sadly, several times. But I can tell, Tom's not lying about that. I can't offer you proof, just my discernment and judgment."

Jean couldn't help it; her eyes instantly filled with tears. "Excuse me." She got up and grabbed the box of tissues on the counter. "I thought I was all done crying."

"That's okay. These are big things you're dealing with."

She came back to the table and sat down. "Then why did he lie to me all this time about losing his job? That just makes no sense to me. Look, I just found out about that part of this charade a little while ago and I'm already doing okay. It's a little scary, but I'm not freaking out or losing it."

Uncle Henry sat back, smiled briefly. "I

can understand why that would confuse you. And I'm not making excuses for Tom by anything I'm about to say. But there actually is a very credible reason why Tom thought he couldn't tell you. I just spent time with Jim and Marilyn going over this, and they think this makes a lot of sense. A whole lot of sense. In fact, we think we're on the verge of a breakthrough that could turn everything around for Tom. For both of you."

She had no idea what he was talking about, but if Jim and Marilyn were behind it, and they thought it might bring about some kind of breakthrough with Tom, she was definitely interested. "Could you explain a little about what 'this' is?"

"I could. But if you're open to it, Marilyn said she would like to share it with you."

Jean nodded her head. "I'd be happy to get with Marilyn. I've wanted to talk to her for months, ever since she and Jim got back together. But Tom would never allow it. He'd never let me talk about our problems with anyone."

"Well, I think you'll find Tom is in a whole new place about that. God's done a major work in his heart since the two of you last spoke. Tom's not gonna mind you talking with his mom about this. I guarantee it. In fact, he doesn't know it yet, but he and his father are about to have a conversation real soon that will change their relationship forever."

Could that be true? Tom . . . in a whole new place? And getting help from his dad? Marilyn was going to be helping her? She'd wanted them to get help for so long. She reached for the box of tissues as the tears flowed freely again.

Uncle Henry reached his hand across the table and gently patted her forearm. "It's okay, Jean. You've been suffering with this awhile. But I think God's about to mend something that's been broken in this family for a very long time."

44

Tom walked out to his car in the parking lot of the Java Stop, just after locking up for the night. It'd been a long day but a fairly busy one, which had kept his mind off most of his troubles. Uncle Henry had sent him a text that afternoon, which he hadn't read yet. Now seemed like a good time. He was pretty sure he knew the topic.

After getting in the car, he opened his phone and read: *Tom, looks like you're staying the night at our place again. But made real progress. I'll tell you more when you get home.*

Tom wasn't surprised that Jean wasn't ready for him to come home just yet. She hadn't responded to any of his texts today. He wondered what Uncle Henry meant by "real progress," hoped it was at least close to his own idea. He thought about calling him but decided to wait until he got back to New Smyrna Beach. Uncle Henry didn't like people driving while talking on their phones.

Tom pulled into the driveway thirty minutes later, and the house was dark except for a lamp in the living room. When he opened the front door, Tom found Uncle Henry reading a book in his favorite chair. "You're home, Tom. Come in. Aunt Myra couldn't hold out anymore."

Tom looked at his watch. It was only 10:30. He remembered they usually headed to bed before 10:00. "Thanks for waiting up for me," he said. "I would have hated to be kept in suspense till morning. You mentioned in your text you made some progress."

"I did. But come on in and have a seat. You can sit in Aunt Myra's chair there. Unless you'd like to get some kind of snack first."

"That's okay. We have all kinds of snacks there at the end when we close. Have to throw most of them out, since the owner wants things fresh every day." Tom set some things down on the coffee table and took a seat.

"Seems a shame to throw good food out. Can't he donate it somewhere?"

"Oh he does. Gotta whole bunch of charities that are supposed to come in on a

343

schedule to haul it away. But sometimes they don't show up before we have to go. So I'm donating some to you guys. This white box here? Might want to check it out for breakfast tomorrow."

"Thanks, Tom, that was thoughtful. Well, what do you want to hear first? My talk with your mom and dad, or with Jean?"

Tom dreaded hearing about the talk with his folks. "You've been busy. Let's start with Jean. How did that go?"

Uncle Henry closed his book, set it on the end table. "Pretty good, I'd say."

"Did you convince her there's nobody else?"

"Pretty sure I did. But you were right, she found it hard to believe this whole charade was just about losing your job. It gave me an opportunity, though, to set up a conversation between her and your mom."

"My mom? I don't follow you."

"Yeah, I guess that has to do with my other big piece of news. My talk with your folks. Met with them before I talked with Jean. That talk went very well. Very well indeed. This might make more sense if I told you about that one first."

"Guess you better start there, then," Tom said.

Tom found himself bracing the armrests

for the next fifteen minutes as Uncle Henry walked him through that conversation. The more Uncle Henry talked, the more Tom relaxed. He didn't know why he was so tense, or what he expected or feared, but by the end of Uncle Henry's briefing, Tom felt mostly hopeful inside. His dad seemed to take the news pretty well, much better than he had anticipated.

Of course, it wasn't as if Uncle Henry had shared all the gritty details of Tom's situation. He had probably just summarized things in general terms, maybe even glossed over a few things that would shock his father. Tom wasn't in the clear yet. He was sure when he and his father talked, he'd be asking Tom for a whole lot more details, to make sure he was getting the bottom line.

That thought caused Tom to grip the armrests again.

"So you see," Uncle Henry said, "your father is in a totally different place about all this. I think you need to open your heart to the possibility that God wants you both to start writing a new chapter in your relationship."

"I hope so, Uncle Henry. I really do." Tom couldn't quite make that leap yet, though. "So how does my mom factor into this? You said she's going to be talking with Jean."

"That's right," he said. "She wants to help Jean see the way your dad raised you guys and how it stacked the deck against you, made you feel like you could never quite measure up to his expectations. And how that played into your motivation to keep this whole thing hidden until you could present your situation out in the open, all fixed up."

Tom liked the sound of that and hoped hearing it would do Jean some good. It also reminded him of another thing he needed to apologize to her for: being so secretive all the time about their problems and forbidding her from opening up when she felt like they needed help. "So, when are these conversations supposed to take place? Do you know?"

"I'm gonna let your dad handle all that," he said. "But I'm sure it will be soon." He sat up in his chair and picked up his book. It appeared he'd said all he had planned to say. "You have any more questions you want to ask tonight?"

"I do, but they can keep. Besides, I'm exhausted. Thanks, Uncle Henry, for doing all that. It sounds pretty encouraging compared to where things were."

Uncle Henry stood. "Glad to do it, Tom. I better turn in then, so I'll be ready for church in the morning. You're welcome to attend with us if you'd like."

"I might just do that," Tom said. "I think Jean and I need to be going somewhere else anyway. Someplace where we can make a fresh start."

45

The next day, Jean drove her SUV down the little tree-lined service lane that ran behind Jim and Marilyn's big house on Elderberry Lane, then pulled into the driveway. It had been over a month since they had visited as a family.

She looked in the backseat. Carly was already zonked out. Little Tommy smiled at her, but he was blinking pretty slow. She had initially asked to have the ladies meet at her house, where she could put the kids down for a nap, and now wished they had listened to her. But Jim had some reason for wanting to meet Tom at their home in Lake Mary.

Marilyn had pointed out that they had converted one of the guest bedrooms upstairs to a kids' room to accommodate Tommy and Carly whenever they visited, which was true. In some ways, that room was nicer than the kids' rooms in their own house. Jean loved coming here anyway; it was such a beautiful house in every respect. Like walking through the pages of *Southern Living* magazine.

As she lifted Carly out of her car seat, Michele's car pulled up beside her. Seeing her dilemma, Michele quickly got out.

"Here, Jean, let me help you." She ran around the other side of the car.

"Thanks."

"Hey, Aunt Michele," Tommy said, "when did you get here?"

"Just now, Tommy. Can I help you get out of your car seat?" He nodded and lifted his hands. She unbuckled him and pulled him out.

Jean started walking through the garage, carrying Carly. In the car, she had opened her eyes for just a moment; now she was out again.

"Would you like me to get this diaper bag?" Michele asked.

Jean stopped in her tracks. "Oh yes, please. I totally forgot about it." Why was she so nervous? She knew Marilyn and Michele were just here to help her. And she so wanted the help. She'd been waiting for years to get closer to them. Now that the day had finally arrived, she was all keyed up inside.

She made her way through the garage, then out the door leading to the main house. She heard the overhead garage door close. There was Marilyn, standing by the French doors in the great room, waving and smiling. As Jean and Carly neared, Marilyn opened the door to let them through.

"Oh look, the precious thing," Marilyn said quietly, her face instantly the grandma. "I want to eat her up, she looks so good."

Jean walked past her, not wanting to give her up to Grandma just yet, not until her nap was through. "I'm just going to take her right upstairs, if that's okay."

"I know it has to be," Marilyn said. "But I haven't seen her in over two weeks. It will be so hard." A few moments later, in walked Michele carrying Tommy. "Oh, look."

Michele had been stroking his cheek, and he looked drowsy enough to fall asleep. "I'm just going to follow Jean upstairs," she whispered.

"Make sure you set the gate across the top of the stairway nice and tight," Marilyn said.

"I will."

After the kids were all safely tucked away, Jean and Michele tiptoed down the stairway. Marilyn had things all set up in the living room. The coffeepot and three matching mugs lay on a tray on the coffee table, next to a small platter of blueberry scones. Pleasant instrumental worship music played softly in the background. Jean paused at the foot of the stairs to take in the scene.

How many times over the last several years had she wished for a visit like this with Marilyn and Michele? Although not under circumstances like these. Hopefully, this might be the start — as Uncle Henry promised — of a new beginning for their family, and this scene might be repeated again and again in a far more relaxed atmosphere.

"Have a seat, ladies," Marilyn said.

"Where?" Jean asked.

"Anywhere is fine. Don't worry about getting crumbs on the rug or the furniture. After Jim and I got back together after Michele's wedding, and Jim promised I wouldn't have to host any more hoity-toity parties, I told him this living room was no longer going to be treated like a museum. It is now officially — like all the other rooms in the house — a place we can enjoy."

After fixing her coffee and snagging a scone, Jean sat in a plush chair across from Marilyn. "I love these," she said then took a bite. A piece broke off, bounced on her lap, and fell to the floor. "Oh no."

"My vacuum cleaner does an amazing job," Marilyn said. "So don't worry about that. Why don't you both eat while I give you an update about what's happened? And what's supposed to be happening right now with Tom and Jim."

"Okay, but first I need to say something." Jean set her coffee down. "I'm so sorry you and Jim had to come home to this nightmare. You didn't even get a chance to unpack before you got slammed with this thing. It was horrible timing. I hope we haven't ruined your vacation."

"You haven't," Marilyn said. "We had a great trip, and we made the most wonderful memories. But Jean, you and Tom are family. Nothing is more important. After we get through this challenging time, I'll invite you both back just to chat about our trip and look at all our pictures."

"I'd love that," Jean said.

"Me too," said Michele.

Marilyn picked up her coffee cup and tucked her feet beneath her on the couch cushion. "Jean, I want you to know how sorry I am. No, how sorry both Jim and I are, for what Tom has put you through these last five months. We don't blame you or see you at fault for any of it. When we first heard about it, we were totally shocked. It seemed so unlike the Tom we know, to do something like this. Jim even said he'd have more easily believed it if you told us Tom had shot somebody." She took a sip of coffee. "I was almost going to say, that's not how we raised Tom to be. But after hearing what Uncle Henry had to say, I'm not so sure that's true."

Jean wasn't quite sure what Marilyn meant but decided to just keep listening.

Marilyn continued. "I'm sure you've seen how much Tom admires his dad."

"Maybe just a tad," Jean said.

"I think the saying 'The apple doesn't fall far from the tree' was made for Dad and Tom," Michele said.

"Well," Marilyn said, "the fact is, it's been a cause of great concern for me. Really, for several years. I've watched how Tom has treated you and the kids in family settings and, to be honest, most of the time it's really bugged me."

Jean wanted to ask why she'd never said anything, but she thought she knew the answer.

"Then last summer," Marilyn said, "after everything came to a head between Jim and me, I kept hoping Tom would see how much his father had changed, and get the message that most of Jim's example — the things

Tom had been following all those years — was wrong, because Jim had repented of them completely. And that maybe Tom might —"

"Do the same?" Jean said.

Marilyn nodded.

"I was hoping and praying for the same thing," Jean said. "But it didn't happen."

"So then I started asking Jim about it," Marilyn said. "Asking him to initiate some dialogue with Tom when we got home that would bring all this to the surface. We talked about it on our Italy trip, even though we both made promises to ourselves not to talk about family problems."

"That's kind of ironic," Michele said. "Don't you think? That God was setting up something to bring all this to light at the same time?"

"I guess it is, in a way," Marilyn said. "But I'm glad Jim didn't have that conversation with Tom yet. Not until we heard what Uncle Henry shared with us yesterday. Because now we see the situation a lot more clearly, and we can get at the root of this thing that's broken in our family."

"What is 'this thing' you're talking about?" Michele said.

"It's what your father is talking about

right now with Tom. Let me try to explain it."

46

Tom paced back and forth across his living room rug like a restless lion in his cage. Every few minutes he stopped to peek out through the curtains. His dad was supposed to arrive any minute. It was the first time Tom had been home in two days. Somehow, home had lost all its familiar warmth. It didn't help that Jean and the kids were already gone by the time he'd gotten there. That was part of the agreement.

That was the language she'd used, an *agreement.* Not a good sign, Tom thought. Didn't sound like she was moving toward reconciliation. If anything, it sounded like something legal.

And why had his dad asked to meet here at the house, of all places? This was the last place Tom would have picked to have this talk. It represented the biggest of his many failures.

He still remembered the conversation

vividly, back near the end of 2007.

"Tom, you don't want to buy that house," his dad had said. "Not now. Believe me. You do, you'll regret it."

"I have to buy now, Dad. You don't understand. You've been telling me to wait for over a year. The bubble's gonna burst, you say. Has to. The market can't sustain prices like these. Well . . . look at the market now. They want fifty thousand more than they did six months ago for houses like this. In three more months, I won't be able to afford a two bedroom in this neighborhood."

His dad had just looked at him. Didn't say a thing. Just gave him that half-disgusted look, like he'd raised some kind of idiot. That day, Tom had decided not to stand there and take it. "Dad, I appreciate what you're trying to say. Really. But this time, you don't know what you're talking about. You're not paying attention to the housing market anymore. You're working with commercial real estate. A totally different animal."

"You think so," his dad replied, raising his voice a few notches. "Well, some things don't fluctuate with the market. Like common sense. I don't care if a thousand realtors and mortgage guys are telling you to buy now, they're out of their minds. All of them. It's simple economics, supply and demand. House prices are super inflated right now. You got all these people getting mortgages with zero down payment, no closing costs, some even borrowing more than the house is worth. I'm telling you, it's totally absurd. The whole thing's gonna come crashing down like a house of cards. Be smart, wait till that happens. *That's* when you should buy. Not now. But hey, you've got it all figured out. What do I know? Do it your way. But if I'm right and you're wrong, don't say I didn't warn you."

Tom looked out the front window again. His dad's car had just pulled into the driveway. "Well, Dad, you were right, and I was wrong," he mumbled. "About the house and everything else." Tom sighed, pulled away, and walked toward the front door. He dreaded this moment. Especially the look in his father's eyes.

A flash went through his mind. *Leave. Leave now. Slip out the sliding glass door in the dining room. You don't have to do this.*

But he did. Of course he did.

He glanced at the mirror hanging in the foyer, saw what he always saw. Stood up straight, set his shoulders back, and reached for the knob just as the doorbell rang.

This was it. The door opened.

"Hi, Tom."

Tom stood there a moment, took a deep breath, and looked into his father's face. When he did, he was taken aback by what he saw. So unlike anything he expected.

Tenderness, kindness.

And then, "I'm so sorry, Son. For everything you're going through."

Now tears. Tears in his father's eyes?

"Dad, I . . . I really screwed it up."

His father stepped forward as Tom collapsed into his arms and just sobbed. Strong arms wrapped around him and pulled him close. "It's okay. It's all right." He felt those arms squeeze him closer still. "I'm here for you. It's okay." This went on for several minutes. A thought went through Tom's head. They were standing outside in full view of the neighbors. But it no longer mattered. He was holding the man he'd been wishing his entire life would hold him this tenderly.

Finally, he regained some composure and lifted his head up. "Maybe we should step inside."

"Okay," his father said, "you lead the way."

Tom stepped aside so his father could come in all the way, then closed the door behind him. "Should we meet in the family room? You can head in there, I'll be right in. There's some fresh coffee in the kitchen, if you want some." He ducked into the half bath beneath the stairway to wash his face and blow his nose. He stood there looking at the roll of toilet paper, wondering if he should bring it with him. He hadn't expected that outburst by the front door and couldn't be sure it wouldn't happen again. Then he remembered the Kleenex box on the hutch.

When he came out, his father was sitting on one end of the sofa. "I just grabbed a glass of ice water, if that's okay."

"Sure, Dad. Think I'll do the same." Tom went out to the kitchen, poured himself a glass, then sat in his usual chair diagonally across from his father. "I guess we have a lot to talk about."

"Sounds like we do," his father said.

"I suppose Uncle Henry briefed you pretty good on where things are at with me. I mean, my financial situation. But feel free to ask any questions. You can't help me if you don't know what's really going on." It felt good saying that, because Tom realized he genuinely meant it. He was all done hiding things from this man, and he could tell by just looking at his dad that this was going to be unlike any conversation he'd ever had with him.

"I guess my first question, then, is . . . how bad is it for you guys?"

"It's pretty bad. For starters, there's no way we're going to be able to keep the house. I haven't even told Jean that yet, but I'm pretty sure it won't come as a surprise. The best we can hope for is a short sale instead of a foreclosure. At least one of the cars is gone. Maybe both. I'm hoping to trade them in, maybe get an older minivan, and just have one car payment. But we're underwater on both, especially the SUV. Our credit may be too shot to even do a car deal now."

"How about . . . your credit cards? What have you got on them?"

Tom hated going there, but there was no way around it. "I know you don't even believe in credit cards, unless you can pay the balance off each month. But I got stuck. Well, trapped is more like it. See, at first —"

"Tom, it's okay. You don't have to defend what you did. I just want to understand what you guys are facing now."

What was going on here? His dad had said this so gently. Could Tom really just tell him everything now, without fear? He paused, checked his father's facial expression, then continued. "I got just over five thousand on two cards." His father winced when he heard the amount, but that's all he did.

"And this new job, at the coffee shop —"

"It's just temporary. It's full-time, but it doesn't come close to covering our expenses, not in this house. It's just buying us some time."

"Putting your finger in the dike," his father said.

"That's one way of putting it. I'm using the time to study for my IT certification. That's another thing you were right about. I should have gone after it right after I graduated, or at least when I first started at the bank. It keeps coming up in these interviews, the fact that I don't have it. So I'm planning on working at this coffee shop while I study and get ready."

"How long do you think it will take, to get ready to take those tests?"

"A few more months. But the truth is, even if I got a great IT job tomorrow, we're in such a deep hole, I don't see us ever getting back to square one."

"Well, don't worry about that now. I know things look bleak —"

"Real bleak."

"Okay, real bleak. But from what Uncle Henry tells me, you've gotten squared away with the Lord on all this. Right?"

"Yes. Well, almost. I'm still not right with Jean yet. She and I still need to talk."

"But I mean, you've repented of all the lying and deception."

"Definitely."

"Uncle Henry thinks you're committed to doing whatever God tells you to do from here."

"If I knew what that was," Tom said. "Then yes, I am."

"Well, see, you've taken care of the most important things," his father said. "Nobody fixes things like God. Once we humble ourselves and start looking to him for direction, and we're willing to do whatever he tells us, he can start turning everything around again, working it all to our good and to his glory. I know all about this now, Tom. Firsthand. You'd be amazed at what God can do, even in a matter of months. That's why I'm here this afternoon. You know that, right? Not to judge but to help you. Maybe share a few of the things I've learned. Some of it from last summer, when I almost lost your mom. Some of it I just learned yesterday from your uncle Henry."

"He mentioned he had something kind of big to talk to you about."

"Well, he did. And it was big. I'd like to

share it with you if you're okay with that."

"I'm all ears," Tom said.

47

Jim sat forward in his chair. He'd been rehearsing how to get into all this with Tom but hadn't been able to settle on anything specific. Maybe God didn't want him to work so hard. Just before he'd left River Oaks to come here, Marilyn had said, "Just be yourself. Your new self. Talk from your heart, not your head." And then she'd added, "Think of this as just the first of a bunch of conversations you and Tom are going to start having."

But Jim really wanted to get this one right.

"You want a refill on the water?" Tom asked.

"Yeah, that would be nice." Jim was about to stand.

"I'll get it." Tom reached for his glass and walked to the kitchen. "I can hear from out here if you want to start explaining what Uncle Henry said."

Jim took a deep breath. The thing was, he

wanted Tom to see his face when they talked, see his eyes. "Are you in any kind of hurry?"

"No, not at all."

"Then I'll just wait till you get back."

It didn't take long. Once they were in place again, Jim decided to just step out of the boat. He'd either walk on the water or sink like a stone. "Tom . . . I wasn't a good father to you."

"What? No, Dad. Yes, you were."

"No, I mean it. I did the best I could with what I knew, what I believed. But you . . . you didn't experience anything close to the fatherhood of God. That's what you needed, what God wanted you, your sister, and your brother to experience."

"What, is that what Uncle Henry told you? That's the big revelation? That you were a lousy father? I'm not buying it, Dad. You didn't make me decide to lie the last five months. You aren't responsible for the mess I've made of everything. You've been a great example to me, for the most part. Hard-working, faithful, diligent. You're honest, you've got integrity. You've been a great steward, following all those principles all those years. So don't do this, okay? You're not to blame for this, and I'm not a victim."

This was going to be harder than Jim

thought. It wasn't coming out right. "Okay, I need to back up a little. I'm not trying to say you aren't responsible for your choices."

"Good, because it kind of sounded like you were."

"But . . . if you agree with that, then you've got to allow that it works both ways."

"I don't follow."

"That I'm also responsible for my choices . . . as a father. And I made some bad ones. A long time ago. And I kept making them for a long time. Pretty much until . . . now."

"What are you saying, Dad?"

"I'm saying the way I raised you, the things I emphasized and modeled . . . all those years. I . . . I majored on minors. Not the things that mattered most to God. I focused on the things that mattered most to me."

"But they were biblical things. Right? So they couldn't be all wrong. I don't know why you're trashing everything you've ever done now. The whole way you raised us. It's not right. It still feels like you're blaming yourself because I screwed up."

Jim sat back, said a quick prayer. *God, give me wisdom here. I want to reach his heart.* A picture flashed into his mind. "Tom, how many of your matches did I see?"

"What?"

"Growing up, your karate matches?"

Tom's expression suddenly changed. He looked down at the rug. "I didn't take karate, Dad."

"See, that's even worse," Jim said. "Okay, mixed martial arts. How many did I see?"

Tom looked up, and his eyes filled with tears. "None. You didn't see any of them. Mom went to most of them, but you were always . . ."

"Too busy. Say it. I was always too busy."

But Tom didn't say it. He wiped his eyes with a tissue. Jim took a deep breath. It was going to be hard keeping it together for the next few minutes. "Here's another question. Think about this one, Tom. Might take a minute. How many times do you recall hearing these words from me: 'I'm proud of you, Son.' How many times? Do you remember?"

Tears rolled down Tom's cheeks.

Now they filled Jim's eyes. He tried blinking them back but couldn't. He had to keep going. "How many times after you did some chore or some job for me did I say, 'Great job, Son'? That's it, just . . . 'You did a great job' without pointing out some little thing you missed, some little item you forgot?"

Tom reached for more tissues.

"See," Jim said, "here's the thing." His voice was breaking up. "I can't remember ever saying those words to you, Son. *Ever!*" He yelled that last word. It startled Tom. But Jim felt so angry at himself. "That . . . that's what I'm talking about. See . . . your heavenly Father was at every one of those matches. He saw you get every ribbon and every trophy. And he wanted me there too. He wanted you to be able to look up in the stands and see me smiling and waving at you. Whatever else I was doing? Didn't matter. Not compared to being there with you.

"And you know something else?" Tom was actually sobbing now. Jim was barely able to keep talking. "God was proud of you at least a thousand times while you were growing up, and he wanted me to be the one to tell you. But I missed out on all those holy moments, because I had a different idea of what being a father was supposed to be. I see that now. I did what my father did, and what his father did, and who knows how long this sick thing has been going on."

Jim stopped. He had to catch his breath. "But it stops here today! With you. And with me. Uncle Henry says it's never too late to start obeying God. And God's love is powerful enough to cover a multitude of sins. Yours and mine. So you and I are going to

369

begin a new Anderson legacy today, one where fathers treat their sons right, the way God wants them to be treated."

Tom stood up, still sobbing, and walked over to his father. He bent down and sat on the floor beside him. Jim reached down and gently put his hand on Tom's shoulder. "I am proud of the man you've become."

"You can't mean that," Tom said, and buried his face in his arms.

"I do mean it," Jim said. "God's forgiven you, and so have I. For all of it. You don't need to feel ashamed anymore." Tom continued to cry, making Jim feel so helpless. "We'll figure this thing out . . . together. I wasn't there for your matches, Tom, but I'm here now. And I'm not going anywhere." Jim massaged his shoulder gently. "You might feel like you're losing this match. Like it's totally hopeless. But it's not. And if I were in the stands right now, I'd be your biggest fan. No matter what happens."

They sat there in silence for several minutes, both sobbing.

After they got their tears under control, they cleaned up as best they could. Tom stood and held out his hand to his dad. They threw their arms around each other, neither wanting to let go. Finally, Tom moved back into his chair and whispered, "I appreciate everything you said, Dad. More than I can say. But I still don't get how you can say you're proud of the man I've become. Not after all this, the way I handled this situation."

"I'm not condoning the lies and deception, Tom. And you know God doesn't, either. I guess what I'm trying to say is, if I had raised you all along with the right kind of encouragement and support, if I'd been there for you and really took the time to listen to you when you struggled, we probably wouldn't be in this situation right now, and you wouldn't be facing all these financial challenges alone. Instead you had to spend all that time and energy trying to impress me and win my approval. You should have known all along that you already had it, and you had nothing to prove."

Jim got up, brought his glass to the counter. "After all this crying, guess I need another refill of this ice water."

"Here, I'll get it," Tom said. He brought both glasses to the refrigerator.

Jim sat at a bar stool by the counter. He glanced over and noticed an old broken picture frame lying on its side. Something about it looked very familiar. He reached over and picked it up. "My gosh," he said. "Would you look at that?"

Tom turned to see what he was talking about. "Oh, that," he said. "Tommy accidentally knocked it off the wall in the hallway a little while ago. I just haven't had time to put it back up yet. When it fell, it yanked the anchor right out of the wall."

"I haven't seen this thing since . . . since just after your grandpa died." Jim looked at his father's scowling face. He had been mad about something that day. What was it? He looked at himself, standing behind his father in the photo. He wasn't smiling either. In fact, Tom was the only one smiling. "You were, what, four years old when this was taken?"

"That's what Mom said. The same age as little Tommy now. I'll get that put up again real soon."

"Don't hurry on my account," Jim said. "Are you going to fix this broken glass? And this frame looks pretty crooked."

"I wasn't planning on it," Tom said. "That's exactly the condition it was in when you gave it to me, right after Grandpa died. I didn't want to change anything about it. It's the only picture of the three of us together. The only one."

The way Tom talked, you'd think it was some kind of family heirloom. "You know the story behind this portrait, don't you?"

"No, I don't think I do."

"Well, pull up a stool here, and I'll tell you."

48

Tom joined Jim on a bar stool by the kitchen counter. Jim handed him the broken portrait. It was an unsightly thing; he was surprised Jean would even allow something this banged up to hang on her wall. He watched the care Tom used as he held it, realizing this meant a great deal more to him than it probably did anyone else in the family. "Do you remember the day we took this picture?" Jim asked.

"Vaguely," Tom said. "In fact, it's so vague I'm not even sure it's a real memory."

"That's probably not a bad thing," Jim said. "My memory is pretty clear."

"Not a good day, huh?"

"Not really. Your grandfather, as always, was way too busy to sit still for something like this. I had been after him for weeks to meet with us at the photography studio. He kept saying yes, but then he wouldn't show up. He did it again that day. I had to get on

374

the phone from the studio and basically get in his face about it. I mean, really get angry. That's not something I ever did with my dad, so he knew I was pretty serious. But he also didn't appreciate me talking to him that way, so he let me have it with both barrels as soon as he arrived for the shoot."

"I guess that explains the serious looks on both your faces."

"I think so," Jim said.

"Jean thought maybe you guys were doing something like those old pictures from the 1800s. You know, the ones where nobody smiles."

"Might just as well have been. Didn't do a lot of smiling when your grandfather was around. But hey, you were smiling."

"I was, wasn't I?"

"Of course," Jim said, "I had to bribe you to get that smile."

"What do you mean?"

"I had to promise to stop by McDonald's after we were done and get you a Happy Meal toy."

Tom leaned back on his stool. "I remember now. It was Rufio, from the Peter Pan movie. He was the only one I didn't have in the Peter Pan collection."

"We bought you a ton of those things over the years."

"I still have them all. In a box under my bed."

"You're kidding."

"Every single one. Now that we're talking about it, I think I'll dig out a few for Tommy. He's certainly old enough to enjoy them now."

"I'll bet some of them are worth some money," Jim said. "Might want to look into that."

"Could be. Wouldn't that be great if they were hot right now? Maybe they can get me out of debt."

Both men smiled at that. Felt good to be smiling again. Jim reached for the broken portrait; Tom handed it to him. Jim asked, "Do you remember much about your grandfather?"

"Not really," Tom said. "Didn't he die a little while after this picture was taken?"

"It was a few years after," Jim said. "The reason you don't remember him much is he moved up north shortly after this photo. Your grandmother had already died by then. He remarried a lady who had a full family, and she persuaded him to pretty much focus on them instead of us. I hate to burst your bubble, Tom, but the truth is, I sent this portrait to him that first Christmas he moved away. Know where I found it?"

"You mean after he died?"

Jim nodded. "It wasn't on the mantel of the fireplace or on the edge of his big mahogany desk. I found it at the bottom of a box in his garage. That's why the glass is broken and the frame is bent. I was so discouraged, I was gonna throw it out. But then I thought about you, saw your little smiling face here in this picture. Thought you might like it someday."

Tom shook his head. "And all this time, I've been treating it like some family heirloom. Jean and I have actually had arguments about it."

Jim laughed. "About this?"

Tom nodded. "I was such an idiot. I wouldn't even let her fix the broken glass or buy a new frame."

Jim set the broken portrait back on its side, slid it toward the wall, away from the edge of the counter. "I tell you what . . . since you're so broke, you tell Jean I'll put up the money for both the glass and the new frame."

"She'll like that. Of course, after hearing that sad story, she might not even want to put it back up on the wall."

Hearing that gave Jim an idea. A really good one. An excellent one even.

"What are you smiling about?" Tom asked.

"Just something."

"Can you tell me about it?"

"I will, but I want to talk it over with your mother first."

Tom released a pent-up sigh. "I wonder how the other talk is going right now."

"You mean with your mom and Jean and Michele?" Tom nodded. "I'm sure it's going well," Jim said. "I think this whole thing is being orchestrated by God to help you guys get back on track. When are you and Jean going to talk?"

"I was hoping we could do that this evening, if she's not too exhausted. I'd sure like to move back in here tonight."

"I wouldn't be surprised if things worked out that way."

Tom stood up. "I don't know about you, but I'm getting a little hungry. Don't know what kind of plans we'll be making for dinner, but I could use a little snack. Want to munch on some pretzels? Got some nice sourdough ones around here somewhere."

"I'd love some," Jim said.

Tom opened the cupboard door next to the refrigerator. Then he peeked his head out and looked back at his father. "Since we're sharing secrets this afternoon, I got one of my own."

"You mean besides the one about pretending to have a job for five months?" Jim smiled.

"Yeah, besides that one." He pulled the box of pretzels out and closed the cupboard door. "Do you remember that coffee shop robbery that happened around here just over a week ago?"

"I heard about it. In fact, Doug showed me this YouTube video about it last night. All his friends are trying to guess who this mystery guy is, the one who broke up the robbery. He said there's a growing list of theories."

"What does Doug think?"

"He says it's gotta be some covert ops guy or maybe an FBI agent working undercover, with the kind of moves he used to take the robber down. Why else wouldn't he want his face on camera?"

"What do you think?"

"Me? I don't know. Your mom and I were in Italy when it happened. Why?"

Tom got this look on his face, followed by the biggest smile.

"No . . ." Jim said. "No . . . that's not you. Is it?"

Tom nodded. "It is."

"Really?"

"Really."

"You're not kidding?"

"I'm not kidding."

"You stopped an armed robber in broad daylight?"

"Knocked him to the floor, got the gun out of his hand, sent him running for the door."

Now Jim was smiling. "I can't believe it. But why did you take off? Everybody's trying to figure that out. I saw the video. You got your hand up blocking your face like you're some mafia don and you're almost running out the door."

"Dad, think about it. What would've happened if I stayed around and talked to the police and the news media?"

Now Jim understood. "Does Jean know?"

"No. Think I should tell her?"

"Well, I wouldn't lead off with that part of the story, but that's one of the big lessons, one of the big changes you want to start making with her."

"Tell her everything?" Tom said.

"Yep, everything. You may need to use some wisdom and timing, but the days of keeping things from her have to be over and done."

"Agreed," Tom said. "So . . . what do you think? About what I did?"

Jim got off the stool, walked over to Tom,

and slapped him on the back. "That's my boy! Now pass the pretzels."

49

Tom tapped his foot as he stood on the wraparound porch of his childhood home on Elderberry Lane. He had just rung the doorbell, although he could have walked in. Considering all that had happened, he felt the need to ask permission. The love of his life was somewhere on the other side of the door. A woman he had treated horribly for the last five months. She deserved, at a moment like this, any extra added measure of respect he could give.

When he'd called the house a half hour ago after meeting with his dad, his mom had answered. Apparently Jean was experiencing some strong emotions at the moment and couldn't come to the phone. But his mom said the meeting had gone very well. She agreed to convey Tom's request to meet with Jean this evening and talk things out. He wanted to pick her up at the house and drive her to the beach for a walk. Something they used to do all the time before the kids were born.

Jean had said yes. His sister Michele had instantly volunteered to watch Tommy and Carly for as long as they needed.

So Tom was here now, on the porch, hoping this final meeting of the night would go as well as the others. Everything that had happened so far amazed him. Weeks ago when he'd considered his "day of reckoning," the only scenarios he could conjure up had been tragic and ended in total heartbreak. They weren't in the clear just yet, and many things could still go wrong, but faith was building in his heart, confirming what Uncle Henry had said, really what the Bible had said: God gives grace to the humble.

That was the only thing that could explain what Tom was experiencing now.

The door opened. Tom was shocked to find Jean standing there in front of him. Her eyes were red and puffy, but he supposed his probably were too. Other than that, she looked beautiful. The first thing he noticed after the puffiness was the softness in those eyes. They instantly melted his heart. He hadn't seen that look since before this whole ordeal began.

Tom was just about to say something

when he heard "Daddy!" It was Tommy screaming from across the living room.

He ran toward Tom and jumped up like he always did. Tom scooped him into his arms. Carly had seen him too and began to whine from her high chair.

"Where you been?" Tommy said. "You been gone forever."

"Not forever, just two days. Daddy was on a little trip."

"Did you go far away?"

"No, not too —" Tom looked at Jean. "Yes, Tommy. Daddy went far away. Very far away. But I've come back now, to you, Carly, and Mommy."

"I don't like you to go far away."

"I don't either, Tommy. So I won't go that far away . . . ever again."

Tears filled Jean's eyes. Hers stirred the same reaction in him.

Michele was standing nearby and caught this exchange. She walked over, holding out her hands. "Here, Tommy. You stay with me for a few minutes. Let Daddy come in and see Mommy, okay? Remember we said they're going to take a little drive?"

"Will they go far away?" he asked as he transferred to Michele's arms.

"Not far, Tommy," Jean said, wiping the tears from her eyes. "And we won't be gone very long, either. And tonight, Daddy will be home, right . . ." She began to choke up but pushed through. "Right where he belongs."

For the most part, they didn't talk during the half-hour drive to New Smyrna Beach. As they'd gotten in the car, Tom suggested that they wait until they were on the beach to talk things through. To help them achieve this goal, Tom had loaded a playlist of Jean's favorite Coldplay songs on his iPod.

It was a rule with Jean: you don't talk when Coldplay was coming through the speakers. You sing.

Well, she didn't sing very much during that car ride, though she couldn't help herself in a few places. But on the interstate, just about the time they saw the first sign for New Smyrna Beach, she had reached across the seat for Tom's hand. He enjoyed her singing, but feeling her hand in his was way better.

In less than fifteen minutes, they were pulling into a little parking area near the beach. It was the same spot Tom had come to yesterday during his soul-searching walk. The beach was even less crowded now. The sun had begun to set, but at this time of year, that would still give them plenty of time to talk before dark.

"Do you want to leave your sandals in the car or bring them with you?" Tom asked.

"I guess we could leave them," she said. "I'm guessing the sand isn't very hot this time of day."

"No, it should be nice and cool. We could even walk in the first few inches of the water if you want. The temperature was perfect yesterday."

They walked along the wooden deck connecting the parking area to the beach. As they did, Tom decided to reach for her hand. She took it and even squeezed back. A great sign, he thought. Hope continued to build in his heart that tonight could be the start of a brand-new beginning for them.

They continued in silence as the deck ended and they crossed the soft sand. Since the sun was behind them, it didn't matter which direction they went. It wouldn't be in their eyes either way. Tom led them toward the south; there were a few less people in that direction.

For some unexplainable reason, Tom felt like they could begin talking once they reached the water's edge. He began to rehearse what he would say first, then stopped himself. His dad had given him some advice about this moment before they'd parted in Lake Mary.

"You don't need to say a lot," he'd said. "Say what's in your heart, because right now your heart's in a pretty healthy place. Jean needs to hear the brokenness you feel inside over all this, not long-winded paragraphs of explanation. She needs to know how serious you are about making some fundamental changes in your relationship. Mostly, she needs to feel your love, and that she can have hope that things between you are really going to change this time."

50

"Where do you want to start?" Jean broke the ice first. She quickly added, "Are you sure we're going to get used to this water pretty soon? Feels pretty cold to me."

"Just give it a minute. If you don't get used to it, we'll go up there," Tom said, pointing to the hard-packed sand that ran parallel to the water. "I guess I should go first. But Jean, stop me at any point if you want to ask something or say anything. I won't mind."

"Okay."

"I think these last few days have been the worst and best days of my life. I feel like I've been walking around almost dead inside for months. All these lies. Spiritually, it's like I was dead. The Lord seemed a million miles away. And so did you, and everyone else."

"I can relate to that. Not feeling far away from the Lord so much, but from you. It's

like I didn't even know who you were anymore."

"I'm sorry about that," he said, squeezing
her hand. He stopped and looked at her. "I
never should have lied to you, hon. Not the
first time or any of the lies that followed.
You didn't deserve to be treated like that.
I'm . . . so sorry."

"I believe you."

"Do you?"

"I do. After listening to your mom explain
what Uncle Henry said, as crazy as it is, it
started to make some sense. But still . . . it
hurt. Especially that you didn't think you
could talk to me about this back when it
first happened."

A small wave splashed over their ankles.
"So what do you think? Want to head out of
the water?"

"No, you're right. I'm getting used to it."

"I don't have a good excuse, Jean. I think
I fooled myself that these lies were for you,
to protect you from worrying about how
we'd make it financially. I was pretty scared
when it first happened. I didn't see it coming at all."

"I imagine you were. But did you really
think I was that weak and fragile? That I'd
fall apart if I knew the truth?"

"That's just it, I know you're not. I guess

I told myself that it would be too much for you, so I could hide my real reason for not telling you the truth."

"Which was?"

Tom sighed, looked down at the water. It was embarrassing to say it now that he understood. "I didn't want my father to find out what happened."

"So all these lies were never really about me?"

"I don't think they were. Only to the extent that I knew if you knew the truth, you'd want to get advice from my folks, maybe even some financial help, which meant . . ."

"Your dad would find out," she said.

He nodded. "It's pathetic now. Just hearing myself say it out loud. I feel like such a total idiot."

They walked for a few moments in silence. "He would have, you know," Jean said. "Found out, I mean. You were right about that concern."

"Because you would have told him?"

"Maybe," she said. "Maybe I would have told your mom, or Michele. I'd like to think he'd have found out because you would've told him, Tom. We're family, or at least we're supposed to be. Families are supposed to go through hard times together, help each

390

other out. Not hide and put up false fronts."

"You're right," he said. "I mean that. That's one thing that's gonna change from now on. No more hiding. No more making you feel like you're betraying me when you want to ask for help. I have no idea what would've happened if I'd been honest from the start, but I know it would have been a whole lot better than what I put us through these past five months."

"I'm glad to hear you say that," she said, "because there's something I need to confess to you along those lines."

"You do?"

"Yeah. It's something Michele helped me see. I haven't been a good partner to you. Not just the last five months but, really, our whole marriage."

"What do you mean?"

"I've just been a doormat. As a wife, I've been way too quiet. So many times you did things I didn't like, didn't agree with, or simply didn't understand. Instead of talking about it, I kept quiet. I prayed, but I should've done more. I should've talked to you, like I'm doing now. So, I hope you're enjoying this kind of conversation with me, because from now on I plan to speak up when something bothers me."

■ ■ ■ ■

Tom let her words sink in as he watched a middle-aged couple walking from the other direction. They stopped talking a few moments to let them pass.

"Honestly, Jean, I'm glad to hear you say that. Here's another thing that's gonna change," Tom said. "Effective immediately, we both know what's going on in our finances. I'll keep paying the bills and doing the checkbook if you want, but I want us to talk about where things are at, at least once a week."

Jean smiled. These were huge things for Tom to admit to and concede. Now seemed like the right time to ask something she'd been dreading. "So . . . where are we at now, financially? How bad is it?"

"It's pretty bad."

He went on to explain how they'd probably lose the house. They were too far behind in their payments already to make it up, and too far underwater to break even if they sold it. The best they could hope for was a short sale. He tried to explain what that meant, but she was too distracted by the thought of losing her home to make any real sense of it. They'd probably have to trade in both their cars and become a one-car family, and an older model car at that, maybe a minivan instead of an SUV. Surprisingly, the hardest thing was to hear how much Tom had put on the credit cards. "Over five thousand dollars," he said.

She couldn't take any more of this. She wanted him to stop. The more he talked, the more depressed she became. Things were much worse than she'd imagined. So many dreams were being smashed. Even normal things she'd always taken for granted were probably out of reach now. The kids needed new clothes; she had been noticing a new outfit at Belks. She could just see herself riding around in an old minivan.

And where would they live? She fought back tears as she pictured moving into some dumpy old apartment. Those days were supposed to be behind them. The days of strange neighbors living on both sides, thin walls separating them. Somebody's mean watchdog barking every time the kids went outside.

Tom continued explaining a few other things, but she didn't really hear him. Silently she prayed, asking God to give her strength not to react in anger when he was through.

A few minutes later, he stopped talking. "So, is that all of it?" she asked, hoping the answer was yes.

He nodded. "Pretty much. I'm so sorry about all this, especially that you're just finding out about it now, in one lump. I've had months to adjust to the loss." He put his arm around her shoulder. "So what are you thinking about?"

For some strange reason, her heart softened toward him. She drew closer and whispered, "I'm sorry you've had to carry all this weight by yourself for all this time." She surprised herself saying this. She genuinely meant it. She hugged him tightly for the longest time. Whatever the future held, at least now they would face it together.

They walked a few minutes longer. She glanced around and for the first time noticed the scenery of the beach more than the heaviness of their conversation. She felt the wind on her face, the bigness of the sky, the colors of the sunset. The soothing sound of the waves lapping against the sand.

"The beach is a good place to bring big things," Tom said. "They never seem quite as big after awhile." He took in a deep breath.

And he was smiling. She hadn't seen him smile in such a long time. It was like the weight of the world was suddenly off his shoulders. *Lord, don't let it now settle back on me,* she prayed.

"Hey, let's do something we haven't done in a long time together," he said.

"Okay, what?" Did he want to build a sand castle? Run into the water?

"Let's head over to those sand dunes and pray together for a little while. Just sit down and run all these things by the Lord, ask for his wisdom and guidance, maybe give us peace so we don't get eaten up inside worrying about how it's all going to work out."

Pray together? This really was a different day for them as a couple. "Sure," she said. "I'd like that."

As they walked to the sand dunes, Tom said, "Before we pray, Jean, there's something else I'd like to apologize for: the way I made you feel about our new baby."

"Well, I haven't really even confirmed with the doctor that I'm pregnant yet."

"I think we both know you probably are," he said. "The point is, I know this is a crazy time we're going through right now, but I really am excited about the baby. And I don't want you to feel stuck out there by yourself, worrying about how we're going to make it. God's the one who gives life, and if he's decided to let it happen now, we'll just have to trust he'll make it all work out somehow."

She was so relieved to hear this. Then he added, "Let's make that the first thing we pray about."

So, they did. And then they prayed for a full twenty minutes more. When they were done, Jean felt as light as a feather, and closer to Tom than she had felt in years. On the way back to the car, she said, "There's something else I'd like us to change, since you're in such an agreeable mood."

"What's that?"

"It would be a little bit of a drive, but I was talking with Michele, and I'd like us to start going to the same church your parents are going to. Michele and Allan are going there now, and she said they're really focused on helping families. They even have small groups for couples who want to strengthen their marriages. Our church is okay, but we've been going there for years and I still don't feel like I know anybody. We've just gone through this whole big thing, and I never once felt like there was anyone at our church I wanted to turn to for help. Are you open to that?"

"Wide open."

"Really?"

"Yeah. I think it would be great to all be

going to the same church together too." When they got back to the car, Tom added, "Here's something else I'd like to change." He walked around to her side and opened her car door.

"You're going to open my car door from now on?"

"Yes, just like Dad does for Mom. But that's not what I'm talking about."

"What then?"

"You and I need to start having date nights again. Every week, like we used to before the kids were born. We'll see if Allan and Michele can babysit, or else my folks."

"But we don't have any money for dates."

"Then . . . we'll come here," he said. "The beach doesn't cost a thing."

She got in the car, then he walked around and got in the driver's side. Before he started the car, he leaned over and kissed her. Then he kissed her again, for much longer, and held her face gently in his hands. When they parted, he said, "I love you, Jean Anderson. Thank you so much for giving me another chance."

She didn't know what to say. "You're welcome" seemed out of place.

Before she could answer, Tom said, "We've been through a tough time. And I know it's not over yet. But I promise you, and I'm being as serious as our wedding day when I made my vows, I *will* become a better man. A better husband to you, a better father to our kids. Whatever I've got to do. You're worth it, whatever it takes. I know God wants this, and he'll help me to change."

51

The house was finally quiet. Michele and Allan had gone home. So had Tom and Jean and the kids — thankfully, all together. Tom and Jean had been too exhausted to give a detailed update about their time on the beach, but it was obvious to Marilyn by the expressions on their faces that it had gone well.

God had answered their prayers, it seemed, in a big way.

Now there was only one thing left to do — make pancakes. Big fluffy pancakes with real butter and lots of genuine Vermont maple syrup. That's all Marilyn wanted to eat. Sometimes in life, that's all you needed. To appease Jim, she had agreed to include scrambled eggs and bacon. For him, the smell of bacon frying in the house accomplished the same thing as eating pancakes did for her.

She decided to text Doug to see which of

the two comfort foods he wanted. Knowing him, he'd want full servings of both. She didn't feel like being alone, so she finished her text with the words, "Come on over and keep your mother company while I cook." Jim couldn't; he was finishing up in the shower.

Ten minutes later, with the smell of bacon filling the downstairs and the first stack of pancakes on the plate, Marilyn heard the back door open. Must be Doug, she thought. She turned around to find him standing there, texting on his phone.

He looked up. "Hey, Mom, smells great in here. Could you make me a plate with some of everything on it? If you don't mind, I'm not gonna eat with you guys."

"Why not?"

"I'm kind of in the middle of something over there. I'd like to keep working on it."

"What could be more important than eating pancakes with your mother?"

Doug laughed. "Well, it's just . . . I'm going to be so busy these next two weeks leading up to graduation, then the week after that I'm gone, heading off to college. Thought I'd get some of my packing out of the way. Just the things I won't be needing between now and then."

Leaving? For college? In three weeks?

The words didn't penetrate at first. Doug's move had been nagging at her, but with all the craziness of this past weekend with Tom and Jean, she'd kept putting off thinking about it. Doug's plans to leave early for college, to start taking summer classes. For a moment, she just stared at him.

"I found a stack of empty boxes lined up on shelves on the far side of the garage," he said. "Okay if I use them?"

Leaving. Doug is leaving us. He's leaving me. My little boy, he's going away. He won't be here anymore.

"Mom? Can I use those boxes?"

It's too soon. It happened too fast. I'm not ready for this.

"Mom? I think it's time to flip those pancakes. They smell like they're burning."

I'm not ready for you to go.

"Mom?"

Doug's face, his beautiful face, blurred as tears welled up in Marilyn's eyes.

"Mom, are you okay? What's the matter?"

"It's nothing, Doug. I'm okay. I just need . . . I just need a minute." She set the spatula on the counter, turned the burners off, and left the kitchen, heading for her bedroom. She passed Jim on the way.

"Marilyn? Are you okay?" He looked at Doug. "What did you say to her?"

She heard him reply, "Nothing. I just asked if I could use some boxes in the garage."

She walked through the bedroom, into the bathroom, closed the door, and began to sob. "I don't want my baby to go, Lord. I'm not ready."

The next morning, a Monday, Tom was called in to the Java Stop to work the breakfast and lunch shift. Business had been steady but nothing close to a rush. Right now, they were cleaning up after the breakfast crowd and prepping for lunch. The café was empty except for one young woman off by herself in the corner.

Tom was just mentioning to his crew that he was going on break when his phone rang. Hmm, he thought, it was Doug. Doug never called him. He answered the phone as he stepped outside. "Hey, little brother, what's going on?"

"I guess the real question is, what's going on with you guys?" Doug said. "I've been busy all weekend since Mom and Dad came home from their trip, but when I stopped in it seemed like big things were going on in the family. When I asked Mom and Dad, they gave me vague answers, but it was obvious, whatever it was, it has something to do with you guys. I tried calling Michele but just got her voice mail."

"Well, at least you thought of me last."

"No, it's not like that. It's just —"

"I'm just kidding, Doug. Don't worry about it. So, what do you want to know?"

"I guess, is everything okay? Are you and Jean okay?"

"We are now. But we've definitely come through a rough patch. It was mostly my fault. Really, all my fault. I'd be happy to tell you about it sometime, but it's kind of a long story. Not sure I want to give you the quick version over the phone."

"No problem," Doug said. "As long as you guys are doing okay. But I guess that explains some things. Like why Mom is so emotional right now."

"What do you mean?"

"I don't know. Last night she kind of lost it on me. After everybody left, she started making pancakes."

"Sometimes in life, you just need pancakes. That's what Mom always said."

"Yeah. Well, I guess last night was one of those times. The thing is, she asked me to eat with her, but I was kind of busy packing up. You know, I'm leaving for college in less than three weeks. Taking summer classes."

"I heard."

"Anyway, she just burst into tears, left the kitchen with everything half done, and went to her bedroom. I waited for her, but she didn't come out for the longest time. Dad finally finished up what she was making and told me not to worry about it. He said she was just going through a hard time. I figured it had to do with what you all had just been through."

"I don't know, Doug. My guess is that what you're describing had nothing to do with Jean and me."

"Then what is it? Did I do something? If so, I'm clueless."

How could Tom explain this? He didn't want to come off sounding like the older brother giving a lecture. "It's not so much something you did, but something you're doing."

"What does that mean?"

"You're leaving, Doug. It's that simple. It's not wrong, not something you have to apologize for or feel guilty about. But it's a big deal for a parent, especially for a mom, when their kid leaves home. Especially when it's your last kid leaving."

"You think that's what it is?"

"I know that's what it is. Think about it. For you, it's the start of this big new adventure. But for Mom, it's the end of an era. You won't be there anymore, and you're not just across the backyard in that apartment, you'll be an hour and a half away. It's a sad thing for a parent to go through. Even though they know it's right. When the time comes, it's just hard. Shoot, if I started thinking about little Tommy or Carly leaving home, I could get all worked up about it right now."

Doug didn't answer for a moment. "I feel like a jerk now."

"Why?"

"Just before she lost it, she asked me if I would eat with her. I told her I was kind of busy packing these boxes up. She said, 'What could be more important than eating pancakes with your mother?' "

"Yeah," Tom said. "That's not good. She was hurting pretty bad right then."

"So, what do I do?"

"Just go out of your way to be kind to her, be patient with her now that you know what she's going through, and the next time she asks you to eat pancakes with her, don't say you're too busy. Even if you're not hungry . . . sit down and eat some pancakes."

52

Jim and Marilyn meandered through their morning, totally exhausted from the weekend. It was hard for Marilyn to fathom how much progress had been made with Tom and Jean in the last few days. It felt more like a week had passed since they'd gotten home from Italy. She tried to focus mostly on that, not on how she felt about Doug leaving for college. Except for that situation, everything seemed to be leveling out in the Anderson family.

Jim was supposed to take the day off, but there was one important appointment he couldn't reschedule. He said it would only take an hour, but the poor thing had to get all dressed up for it.

She flopped down into the big overstuffed chair in the living room and looked at Jim as he came out of the bedroom in his suit and tie. That man still looked so good.

"Hey, hon," he said. "When I get back,

could we take a walk? There's something I'd like to talk about with you. It's kind of a big thing. A good thing, but a big one."

She wasn't sure she was ready for any more big things right now. Even good ones. "Sure. I'll be right here."

Two hours had passed.

Jim and Marilyn had just parked the car near the riverfront park in downtown River Oaks, the place where they'd had Allan and Michele's wedding last fall. Jim had suggested they come here. It was afternoon, but it was a cloudy day and the park was filled with shade trees. On the short drive here, he said he had something big to discuss with her and thought it would be nice to take a walk as they talked.

Jim let go of her hand, so he could use both hands as he unfolded what he had to say. "There's really two things. One small, and one huge. They both involve Tom and Jean. Which one do you want to hear first?"

"Give me the small one first." They had reached the river, so they turned right and began to walk parallel to it. The breeze was much stronger here.

"Okay, I got this idea at Tom's house. Did you ever notice that picture they had hanging up in their hallway, the one with me,

Tom, and my dad?"

"You said *had;* isn't it still there?"

"No, Tommy accidentally knocked it off the wall. But you know the one?"

"Yeah," she said. "The one where you and your dad look mad? The one with the bent frame and broken glass?"

"That's the one. Well, I found out that Tom treasures it, like some kind of family heirloom."

"Why?"

"I didn't realize this, but it's the only picture he has with my father in it. And I guess because I gave it to him after the funeral, he thought it was something special. Anyway, I had to burst his bubble a little and tell him the real story behind it. Then I thought, after all this talk about the crummy way my dad treated me, and the way I treated Tom, and how he started treating his family following the same bad example. Well, I've repented of it, and he's now seeing it pretty clearly. So I thought, maybe —"

"Jim, that's a wonderful idea! You want to redo that portrait with you, Tom, and Tommy?"

"Well, yeah. That's the idea."

"I love it. That will be so special." She couldn't help herself. She threw her arms

408

around him. "When do you want to do it?"

"I was thinking this Sunday, after church."

"Here's an idea. Why don't we invite the whole family over? Allan and Michele can probably come."

"And Doug," Jim added. "I'll make sure Doug's there."

"And we can even invite over Uncle Henry and Aunt Myra," she said.

"You sure you're up for all that?"

"I think I am. I think the family gathering together for a happy time would do my heart some good. Why don't you tell me your big thing now?"

He reached for her hand and tugged gently. "I think you'll take my big thing better if you're sitting down."

Uh-oh, she thought. This didn't sound good. She sat beside him.

"You don't need to worry," he said, taking her hand again. "It's a good thing. At least, I hope you'll think it is after you hear me out. But I guess that depends on something . . ."

"Depends? On what?"

"Whether you had your heart set on having that big ol' house all to ourselves again once Doug heads off to college."

53

Tom couldn't recall being this happy since . . . well, he didn't know when.

The whole family was back together at his parents' house, including Uncle Henry and Aunt Myra, all gathered around the long dining room table with all the leaves inserted in the middle. Way down there on the end next to Mom sat Charlotte. She seemed like part of the family now, just sitting there smiling, taking everything in.

They were just finishing up a perfect roast beef, cooked the old-fashioned way, like when they were kids. Big enough for everyone to have plenty, surrounded by tender roasted potatoes and carrots, lots of hot brown gravy, fresh bread from the bakery, and a small bowl of horseradish for the braver souls at the table.

As the meal unfolded, Tom had a hard time not thinking about something his dad had said out in the parking lot of the church, just before they got in the cars to come here: that he had two fairly big surprises for him and Jean this afternoon.

"How big?" Tom had asked.

His father just smiled and said, "You'll see." The smile had put Tom at ease. Whatever they were, at least from his dad's perspective, they were good surprises. Now that the dinner was wrapping up, Tom kept looking at his dad for some signal that it was time to unveil the surprises.

"Hey, Tom, after church Dad said you had some kind of big secret to tell me today." It was Doug, who was sitting directly across the table. Doug now knew the whole story about Tom and Jean's situation. Tom and Doug had met for breakfast yesterday morning and he filled Doug in.

Tom looked at his dad for some clue as to what he had told Doug. His dad smiled then held up his hand to block his face from view, just like Tom had done in that YouTube video the day he stopped the robbery. Tom laughed, then said, "Okay, I get it." He looked at Doug. Then Tom got an idea. "Hey, everybody, listen up a minute. Today, Dad said he's going to share some kind of secret with us. Well, I've got one of my own."

Everyone ended their conversations and turned to listen to what Tom had to say.

Tom watched as a knowing smile appeared on his dad's face. "You're not gonna believe this, but everything I'm about to tell you is totally true." Tom spent the next ten minutes telling the whole family the robbery story, ending with why he had to flee the scene before his identity could be revealed.

As he talked, their faces registered a combination of shock and surprise, but the look on Doug's face was priceless.

Once Tom finished, Doug said, "That was you? No way. No stinking way! You're like a celebrity, dude. You need to go public with this. Seriously." For the next few minutes, everyone at the table debated about whether or not Tom should reveal his secret to the world. Doug argued the loudest that he most definitely should.

Finally Tom said, "I don't think so, little brother. This one's going to have to remain an Anderson family secret."

"But I have a feeling," Jean said, "we will all be hearing that Anderson family secret fairly often for many years to come."

Everyone laughed, except for Charlotte, who seemed properly confused.

"Hey, everyone, my turn." Tom's dad stood at the head of the table.

Tom watched as he reached behind him for a box of tissues on the hutch. What in the world?

"I was trying to think of a good time to do this," he said. "Now seems as good a time as any. I'm sure we're all pretty full and need a little time before dessert. I'm going to do my best to try to get out what I have to say without totally losing it. Hence, this box of tissues."

"I have a feeling I know where you're going with this," Uncle Henry said. "Hope you're willing to share that tissue box."

"Take as many as you need. In fact, let me start with you, Uncle Henry and Aunt Myra. There really aren't words to describe the depth of gratitude I feel in my heart toward the both of you right now. The love and care, the patience and sound advice you've given my family these past several months have been like a gift from God. Marilyn and I are so grateful, and we love you both so much."

"That goes for Jean and me too," Tom said.

Marilyn reached for her napkin and dabbed her eyes.

"And now to my kids," Jim said. "I have some things I want, and need, to say to you guys. I've said some of this privately to Tom, but I want the rest of you to hear it. I am so sorry for the poor example I've been for the better part of your lives. Often I was harsh and legalistic . . . and controlling. I wasn't a good listener and far too often had far too much to say." Tears now welled up in his eyes.

In Tom's eyes too. He couldn't believe his dad was saying all these things in this setting.

"But God has gotten hold of my heart and opened my eyes to a new way to be. Uncle Henry was telling me about this teacher who totally changed his life years ago. He committed himself to be there for your uncle and was willing to do whatever it took to help him succeed. I want to be more like that teacher in your life, Tom. From now on. To both you and Jean. And the rest of you too."

Tears began rolling down Tom's cheeks. He wiped them away.

His dad continued. "Uncle Henry helped us understand how the Anderson men have been too proud to change and do the right thing for their children, for three generations now. Tom, that's the legacy you've been following these past five months. But you've put an end to it, and so have I. Like Uncle Henry did years ago." Jim looked at Marilyn and said softly, "And sweetheart, I'm so sorry you had to live through so many years of my 'Anderson ways.' Now I get to spend the rest of my years living the way God wants me to, making up for all that lost ground."

"Jim," she said, "you don't have to say —"

"I do have to say it," he said. "I want to say it. I want the kids to know how serious I am about setting a new direction." He looked up at the family. "I know this is a bit awkward for you guys, and maybe even a little corny. But these things are important. I love you all so much and I —" He started choking up.

"You're doing just fine, Dad," Tom said.

Jim whispered, "Thank you, Tom." Then said to everyone, "Well, anyway, I better get to those two surprises I told you about. Your mom and I have talked this over, and we thought of a way we could be a blessing in your life, and not just with words. You told us about the level of debt you're in now since you lost your job. And your plans to short sell the house, which will leave you guys with nothing. I also know how much you want to get that IT certification fin-ished, so you can get a better job. So here's what we'd like to do." His father's eyes looked upward, not toward heaven but the loft upstairs.

"We'd like to invite you guys to move in

with us. You can have the entire upstairs, rent free. There's more room up there than most three-bedroom apartments. You've got two baths and the whole loft area for a living room. The only thing we'd have to share is the kitchen. And you can stay here as long as it takes to get your certification and get out of debt."

Tom could not believe what he'd just heard. He looked over at Jean. Tears poured down her face.

"So . . . what do you think?" his father said. "Are you interested?"

Tom looked back at Jean. She was nodding and smiling. Tom stood up. "Dad, Mom . . . I don't know what to say."

"Say yes," his mom said, reaching for another napkin.

"Yes," Tom said. He hurried around the table toward his father and threw his arms around him. Both men were crying now, shedding tears for much more than this moment. Years of hurt and pain all being washed away.

Uncle Henry said, "I think a new generation of Anderson men is being created here today."

Just then, the doorbell rang.

"Who could that be?" Allan said.

Tom and his father released their embrace

and stood by their seats. "That's my next surprise," Jim said. "Allan, you seem to be the only one here in any shape to open the door. Could you let Nathan in?"

"Who's Nathan?" Doug asked.

"He's a young man who goes to our church," Jim said. "And he also happens to be an excellent photographer."

"Photographer?" Michele said. "Are we going to take a family portrait? I wish you'd warned us. I don't even like this dress."

"I wouldn't do that to you ladies," Jim said. "I wasn't thinking of a big family portrait. Not today anyway. But two smaller ones. The first would be of all the men in the family. Including you, Allan, and you too, Uncle Henry. Like Uncle Henry said — we're going to start forming a new legacy in this family. I think we should have a new portrait that reflects that. And second . . ." Jim turned around and opened the hutch drawer. "I snuck this from your house the other day, Tom."

Tom looked at what his father was holding and instantly knew what he had in mind.

The broken portrait.

Jim held it up for the whole family to see. "I think we need to redo this one. Because . . ." He started choking up again. "Because, as you can see, it's broken and . . .

we're not anymore."

Tom swallowed hard. "That's a great idea, Dad. Can't believe you thought of it." He looked over at Jean. "Do you want to get Tommy fixed up or do you want me to?"

Her tears started up again. "I'd love to."

"I thought we'd take this portrait in front of the fireplace," Jim said, still holding the broken one. "Make it just like the original. I'll sit in a chair with Tommy on my knee, and Tom, you stand behind me, hands on my shoulders."

"Only this time," Tom said, "all three of us will be smiling."

"And . . ." Jean said, as she stood up, "this time I get to pick out the frame."

Later that evening, after all the portraits had been taken, the food all put away, the kitchen all cleaned up (by the Anderson men, of all things), and all their good-byes said, Tom and Jean walked through the wraparound porch and down the front sidewalk toward their car parked out front on Elderberry Lane.

Jean carried Carly, who had fallen fast asleep. Tom led little Tommy by the hand. Just before opening the back car door to let him in, Tom bent down so that he was looking his son right in the eyes. "Hey, Tommy,

I want to tell you something."

"What, Daddy?"

"You know I've lived for a lot of years now."

"I know you're way older than me," Tommy said.

Tom smiled. "That's right. And I've met a whole lot of little boys in all that time. But do you know which little boy is my favorite little boy in the whole world?"

Tommy looked right at his father with a curious and somewhat concerned expression. "No, Daddy, who?"

The way he said it was so precious. Tom could tell, he really didn't know. "You are," he said, poking Tommy in the belly. "Nobody else even comes close. Come here." With that, he picked up his son and spun him around.

ACKNOWLEDGMENTS

Dan: I'd like to thank my coauthor, Gary Smalley, for being such a joy to work with and for dedicating your life to improving the quality of family relationships all over this nation for so many years.

I want to thank the love of my life, Cindi. I cherish her input and advice, reflected throughout these pages. But I'm grateful for more than her help with this book; her wisdom and discernment throughout the parenting years made it possible for me to experience real breakthroughs with my children, which is really why we now enjoy our time together as adults even more than when they were kids.

I also want to thank my editor and friend, Andrea Doering. What a blessing it has been to be able to work with the same editor for so many books. A rare privilege in this business, and one I don't take lightly. I'm grateful for the entire staff at Revell, who make all the behind-the-scenes things happen. Folks like Twila Bennett, Michele Misiak, Robin Barnett, Claudia Marsh, Kristin Kornoelje, and so many others.

On a local level, I want to thank Phill Gabriel for all his input on what it's like to be an "IT Guy." I'd also like to thank my Word Weavers critique group in Port Orange, Florida, for their input on several of these chapters. I want to thank my friend and pastor, Ray Dubois. After serving as a pastor for twenty-five years, I find it such a joy to finally experience being pastored by someone else, especially someone as kind and caring as Ray.

Lastly, to my fabulous agent and friend, Karen Solem, who takes such great care of me and helps me navigate through the ever-shifting maze of the publishing world. Her work sets me free to just write, which is what I love to do the most.

Gary: I'd like to expand on what I said in my dedication comments at the beginning, about my son and daughter-in-law, Amy. Michael just turned forty years old. I may be the dad and much, much older, but Michael has been used by God on several occasions to literally save my life and marriage. Even as a child.

When he was only a few weeks old, he had developed a serious stomach problem, and his physical problems forced me to cut down on travel. I had to actually take a different job at the company where I worked at that time. At first, I was a little irritated at him for being so sickly but, as it turned out, his serious condition caused me to remain in my home after work hours for over a year. During those days, I would watch my fellow workers driving by my house, waving at me on their way to the airport. "Wish you were with us," they would say as they drove by. But during that year, I learned a valuable lesson: it was so much better to be at home with my wife and kids than to travel to all these cities, working on these big seminars. Michael's illness saved me from becoming a workaholic and from the grind of the whole airport scene.

Then, there was one of the biggest "salvation" moments of my life, when my kidneys failed. Michael and Amy stepped up to the plate, and we discovered he was a perfect transplant match for me. Nearly ten years later, I'm doing great physically, though he still has some leftover pain from the transplant. Thank you Michael, literally, for life itself.

Finally, Michael stepped up the plate again when he saw I was stressing out too much over the amount of travel and speaking I was still doing in my early seventies. He talked to each of my doctors and discovered they also believed I was too stressed from all this traveling and all these speaking engagements. He called my wife and me and lovingly told us that he and my doctors had agreed I was actually killing myself. We listened and agreed with him, and again, he was the major factor in saving my life.

Today, I'm thrilled with the reduced pressure in my schedule, and he's even working on a plan to support me financially in my very old, senior days on earth. I'm so thrilled to have him as my son!

AUTHOR'S NOTE
FROM DAN WALSH

Gary and I are so glad you joined us for our second novel in the Restoration series. This book picks up the Anderson family's story about seven months after the conclusion of our first novel, *The Dance*. Although Jim and Marilyn are still working through some minor challenges, as you've just read, they are doing much better, as they enjoy a romantic second honeymoon in Italy.

But things aren't so rosy in Tom and Jean's relationship. In fact, they're an absolute mess. In one of the early chapters, we see Jean picking up a broken family portrait little Tommy accidentally knocked off the wall. This portrait is almost a metaphor for the condition of not only Tom and Jean's marriage relationship but also Tom's relationship with his dad.

I mentioned in my author's note at the end of *The Dance* that in the remaining books of the series a number of new storms would come, revealing the "sand founda-tion" upon which the Andersons' lives have been built. And that these storms would include some of the problems you and I face every day. That's certainly what unfolds in *The Promise.*

It seems everyone in America these days has either experienced the kinds of chal-lenges Tom and Jean are facing or knows someone who has: a sudden job loss, a dramatic drop in income, being upside down in their mortgage and possibly losing their home, credit cards that are maxed out, and all the tension and conflicts such circumstances bring to a family.

But we see even greater challenges re-vealed in *The Promise* than the obvious economic ones. Uncle Henry sees some-thing — an underlying measure of broken-ness in the Anderson family — that no one else has perceived. He's able to see this because he's experienced the heartache and pain firsthand with his own father and then witnessed this legacy being passed on from his older brother to Jim. And Jim unwit-tingly passed on the same poor example to his children. Tom, as the firstborn, bore the brunt of it.

It turns out that the problem unveiled in the book is not rare. It happens a lot, even in solid Christian families — parents who love their children but fail to recognize their great need for regular encouragement and blessing.

Both Gary and I experienced this pain in our own childhood, at the hands of our fathers. Both of us went through our entire childhood without experiencing our fathers' blessing and encouragement or even hearing the simple words, "I'm proud of you, Son." This pain continued into our adult lives, causing significant heartache and problems in our marriages and family relationships (just like we see with Tom).

Each of us has interacted with and counseled countless men and women in our ministries who have similar stories to tell. Some with their dads, others with their moms, some with both parents. In fact, this whole issue served as the theme for a major bestselling book Gary coauthored with Dr. John Trent called *The Blessing.*

The Blessing was originally published in 1986. Since then, it has sold over two million copies, gone through several reprint editions, and is still in great demand today. Which only shows how relevant this issue continues to be. I drew heavily from *The Blessing* as I shaped the story you've just read and recommend you get this book and read it from beginning to end. I'd also encourage you to look up John Trent's website at www.strong families.com. Dr. Trent continues to equip individual Christians and churches in this critical area of family life.

I also drew inspiration from another great book by Gary, called *Joy That Lasts.* You may have a hard time finding this one in stores, but it's still available many places online and worth any effort it takes to get hold of a copy. It's that good. Besides all of the great lessons you'll learn about building effective relationships, Gary includes a number of personal, behind-the-scenes stories (some that made me laugh out loud).

I hope you'll join us for Book 3 of the Restoration series. We've already begun the research and are hammering out the story lines. With each book, we'll continue to bring you up-to-date on the characters we've already met and have grown to love, but we'll also focus on one of the other members of the Anderson family in a primary way.

As always, we'd love to hear from you, especially if the stories have blessed you or helped you in some way. You can reach me through the contact page on my website, or once there, by clicking one of the buttons to connect with me on Facebook, Twitter, or Pinterest. It's danwalshbooks.com. Also check out Gary's website, which he does with his son, Michael Smalley (an amazing author and counselor in his own right). It's simply smalley.cc.

DAN'S INTERVIEW WITH GARY ABOUT *THE PROMISE*

Dan: In our first book, *The Dance,* you said you most identified with Jim's character on a personal level. Who did you identify with in *The Promise* and why?

Gary: This time it was Tom. Tom felt unblessed by his dad, and he was fearful of disappointing him. Growing up, I had never received my dad's verbal approval, and as I look back over my life with Norma, my wife, I can see that, like Tom, I made a lot of mistakes by being way too concerned over my own successes. I missed the "little areas" that meant a lot to Norma in our early married years.

Dan: In writing *The Promise,* we drew heavily from the themes in the book *The Blessing,* which you co-wrote with Dr. John Trent. Although this book originally released in 1986, it has since come out in several new editions, has been your all-time biggest seller (over two million copies sold), and continues to remain in print today. What is it about the message of this book that resonates so strongly with so many people?

Gary: Most people are not aware of the huge power of a verbal blessing from a father to his children and wife, or the actions that result when he follows through on what he says. In *The Blessing,* we outlined five steps to bless a child, but those same steps can be used to bless anyone. The book became very popular because many adults finally realized why they acted the way they did, and they finally understood that they, too, had not received their own father's blessing. The book became even more popular when people realized that anyone can give a blessing and that the results are powerfully effective in a blessed person's life. Every one of us needs encouragement and praise, and when we get it, it feels so good and satisfying.

Dan: In one part of our book, Jim is talking with Uncle Henry about his struggle to encourage or bless his children when they're still "messing up." He's afraid if he encourages them before they succeed, they'll lose their motivation to keep working hard. What's wrong with this thinking and why do parents find it hard to encourage and bless their children the way God wants them to?

Gary: No one is perfect. But most kids and adults have many qualities that are admirable. The key to blessing someone is to find those positive qualities and praise the person for them. In fact, making a lifetime list of the important, positive characteristics of a person increases our affection for them. Jesus said that our heart is always where our treasures are. Positive blessings are far more motivating than critical statements. When parents bless their children by saying things like, "I will always love you no matter what you do or say. I'll be there beside you to support you unconditionally. You will always be highly valued by me, and you can't do or say anything to lose my loyalty to you," those kinds of statements relax a child or loved one and enable them to receive more love and encourage a more loving relationship. For example, if your child or mate has an addiction, rejection or criticism actually increases their addiction. What they need is love. Our need for love is like a fuel tank. Most addictions develop when a person's tank is too low. Addicts tend to have a decreased need for their addictions when they are shown love. Why? Because that love fills their tank back up.

Dan: Parents know that part of their responsibility is to instruct, train, and even discipline their children at times. But too often, kids (especially teenagers) complain that no one ever listens to them, and all they ever get from their parents are lectures. How can a parent provide the necessary verbal instruction and correction for their children but still address this real concern children have about being heard and understood? Is there some kind of correction-to-encouragement ratio parents should follow?

Gary: With my three kids, if any of them told me that they felt misunderstood or lectured too much, I'd stop on the spot and listen immediately. I would ask them to share again what they wanted me to understand. This is simple. Teens start to become individuals by "bucking us" as their parents. They often challenge their parents' opinions. That's great. Don't resent it. Debate with them, but try to understand their point of view. Norma and I worked hard at keeping our honor high and our anger low, not just toward each other but toward each of our kids. My book *The Key to Your Child's Heart* explains in more detail how we raised our three kids. All three of them love God now, honor others, and keep their anger low toward each other. You can Google their names and see how God is using each one (Kari Gibson, Dr. Greg Smalley, and Michael Smalley).

Dan: One of the themes in *The Promise* is the challenges parents and children have once the children grow up and move out on their own. What are some of the challenges you and Norma faced (and can talk about) with your kids as adults, and what advice can you offer parents facing those same challenges now?

Gary: Life goes on and the dynamics of any relationship continue to change over time. We have had normal conflicts with each of our grown adult children and with their spouses. But in each case, we continue to do what the Andersons are now learning to do. We pray for each other, seek to understand any wrongs or hurts the other might feel, and take the appropriate actions to repair any damage. We keep our loyalty high toward each other and never give up on anyone. We tend to do our "Five Steps When We Offend Others." They are:

1. We become gentle so that we can listen fully.
2. We listen until we fully understand, and we each let each other know when we think we all understand each other.
3. When we understand fully, after we "get it," we admit our wrongs.
4. We seek forgiveness by saying something like, "I understand why you are hurting from what I said or did, would you please forgive me?"
5. We touch the offended person as soon as possible to "check" on the level of hurt or forgiveness. Unforgiving people tend to pull away and avoid touching the person who offended them.

Dan: What advice do you have for adult children? How should they treat their parents now, compared to when they lived at home? For example, is the command to "honor your father and mother" still in play, even though they are no longer required to "obey" their parents? If so, what does that look like?

Gary: This question is a delight. Honor is an act of the will; it is valuing someone and listening to his or her advice even if you disagree. A large part of honoring your parents is taking the time to maintain contact with them, to let them know you care, whether by text, email, phone call, or time spent in person. All three of our children highly honor us as parents. We text, email, and call each other from time to time just to get caught up. My son Michael is actually helping to manage my speaking and writing schedule. That's a giant help. Honoring each other is still such a huge priority to all of us. That's not something that's ever supposed to change.

Dan: Another theme we address in the book is the level of honesty that should exist between couples in marriage. Tom withholds the bad news about losing his job from Jean in an attempt to "protect" her from fear and anxiety. Clearly, he goes way too far. But are there ever times when a spouse could/should withhold something from their loved ones? Is that ever a loving thing to do, even temporarily, or is honesty always the best policy?

Gary: I tend to agree that honesty is *almost* always the best policy. But in a very few situations, we might not want to open up completely. Let's say that we are irritated at something our mate or friend is doing regularly. Can we just learn to forgive and use the irritation to work on the "logs" in our own eyes as Jesus teaches? Most people do not realize that some irritations are just that, "logs" in their own behavior. Someday (when we're old) ☺ we might want to ask if any of our actions irritate our mate or friends.

Dan: In a fiction book, it's not appropriate to go into the levels of teaching you'd find in a nonfiction book such as *The Blessing* or *Joy That Lasts*. But are there any specific points we touched on in *The Promise* you'd like to elaborate on here in a little more detail? (Of course, I'd recommend everyone get both of these books and read them cover to cover.)

Gary: Here's one. In my book *Making Love Last Forever,* I had the opportunity to expand on the major problem of holding anger within for long periods of time. Anger must be removed from our life as soon as possible. There are over thirty major negative consequences that grow within a person if they don't release the anger. One of the most damaging consequences is that we weaken our relationships with God and man. Here's something else: darkness takes over an angry person and the enemy's influence is greatly increased (1 John 2:9–11 and Eph. 4:25).

438

We need to learn to forgive quickly and seek forgiveness in a hurry to help our loved ones stay connected to both God and us.

ABOUT THE AUTHORS

Dan Walsh is the award-winning author of *The Unfinished Gift, The Homecoming, The Deepest Waters, Remembering Christmas, The Discovery, The Reunion,* and *The Dance.* A member of American Christian Fiction Writers, Dan served as a pastor for twenty-five years. He lives with his family in the Daytona Beach area, where he's busy researching and writing his next novel.

Gary Smalley is one of the country's best known authors and speakers on family relationships. He is the author or coauthor of sixteen bestselling, award-winning books, along with several popular films and videos. He has spent over thirty years learning, teaching, and counseling, speaking to over two million people in live conferences. Gary has appeared on national television programs such as *Oprah, Larry King Live, Extra,* the *Today* show, and *Sally Jessy Raphael,* as well as numerous national radio programs. Gary and his wife, Norma, have been married for forty years and live in Branson, Missouri. They have three children and six grandchildren.